DANGEROUS TOYS

BRIAN KNIGHT

Tulpa Books

CONTENTS

Acknowledgments   ix

The Final Girl   1
I Am the Coyote, I Am the Snake   19
Campbell's Pond   35
Dakota   57
A Night in the Blues   79
Number 2   93
Deathbed   109
Toys in the Attic   131
Ridgerunner   143
Night of the Dog   157
Who Killed Little Betty?   169
Hot Summer Night   181
Lucin   189
The Cask of a Thousand Dildos   207
Go Girls Rule!   221
Sister   239
Mother of Kitties   255
The Christmas Corpse   267
Dangerous Toys   279

About Brian Knight   315
Bibliography   317

ALSO BY BRIAN KNIGHT

Horror - Novels

- Feral
- Broken Angel
- Hacks

Horror - Omnibus

- They Call Us Monsters

Horror - Chapbooks

- Children of Filth
- Heart of the Monster
- Apocalypse Green
- Johnny Junk
- Death is Blind
- Midnight Blues
- The Beast Inside - The Berserkers, Part 1
- Blood Rage - The Berserkers, Part 2

Horror - Collections

- Dragonfly
- Dangerous Toys

The Phoenix Girls - Fantasy

- The Conjuring Glass (Book 1)
- The Crimson Brand (Book 2)
- The Heart of the Phoenix (Book 3)

The Misadventures of Butch Quick - Crime

- A Face Full of Ugly - A Chapbook
- Big Trouble in Little Boots - A Chapbook
- Sex, Death, and Honey (Book 1)

PRAISE FOR BRIAN KNIGHT

"Brian Knight's writing shines with a dark brilliance." Douglas Clegg, author of The Children's Hour

"Knight is a writer to watch." Ellen Datlow, Years Best Fantasy & Horror

"Say hello to horror's next big thing." Brian Keene, author of The Rising

"One of today's most exciting writers." Ed Gorman, author of The Dark Fantastic

ACKNOWLEDGMENTS

Any publishing writer has a list of people who have helped them, and when you've been publishing for nearly twenty years that list grows long. I could never include, or probably even remember, all of the people who have helped me along the way, but here are a few who have been important to me in the past couple of years.

Shawna Knight
Douglas Clegg
H Michael Casper
Lisa Lee Tone
David Wilson (both of them)
Monica J. O'Rourke
KH Koehler
Kelli Owen
Paul Goblirsch
Joe Mulak
Julie Sparkman
Judi Wutzke

For Douglas Clegg. Thanks for the kind encouragement and great advice.

THE FINAL GIRL

In the late 1970s the San Francisco Chronicle dubbed him The Headsman. In the 1980s he was known as The Turnpike John, Killjoy, and The Santa Rosa Cannibal in Oregon, Wisconsin, and New Mexico respectively.

He thought of himself simply as The Monster.

No one had connected these disparate, sensational killers, but together The Monster's victim count was just shy of Gary Ridgeway's official count of 48. The Monster never realized how much pride he'd taken in his prolificacy until 2003 when Ridgeway confessed to the Green River murders, officially surpassing him, but even then, he'd not considered resuming his old work. He'd turned 65 that year, a little long in the tooth for a predator, and the drive to kill had simply never returned after the accident that had almost killed him.

It was something he'd thought about a lot during his idle years, keeping careful track in a black hardcover sketchbook, dedicating two pages per victim, one with details of the girl and the kill, the second a drawing to remember them.

His drawings were quite good. He had always been a good artist. When he died, he hoped someone would find the old sketchbook, so he could finally take credit for his work. They would put him in the ground knowing everything he'd done, and knowing he'd gotten away with it.

For years The Monster thought his days of blood and death were long behind him.

He was wrong.

Pullman, Washington was a small town with pretensions, a farming community with a population swollen far past its comfort zone by students attending WSU, a university best known for its veterinary and agricultural programs, its football program, and drunk students falling from frat house windows. Its music and arts programs were lesser known, but also impressive.

Jenna was a junior with an art major and a minor in communications, a program director for the campus radio station, and the sole person responsible for the station's supplemental video blog. She was petite, vaguely Asian, very pretty, and politically liberal.

If The Monster could be said to have a type, Jenna was it, but he never limited himself to a type. He liked variety. The thing that made Jenna most special was her schedule, late shifts at the studio, and the long walk back to her dorm.

He had watched her before. She usually walked alone. The students felt safe on campus. It was their place.

That would end tonight.

He watched her from a tight cluster of trees where the walkway from the school of communication intersected Spokane Street. It was a quarter past nine when she stepped from the darkness on the building's south side. She had her backpack over a shoulder and a cell phone to her ear. Her voice was high and clear in the empty court-yard. She laughed, then hung up and slipped the phone into her pocket.

For the next several seconds the only sound in the night was the slap of flat-soled shoes on the cobbled path. The Monster closed his eyes, willed the jackrabbit beat of his heart to calm until it matched the slow steady slap, slap, slap ... and stop.

In the moment between beats, the monster was fully present for the first time since Rosa, in Boise, Idaho, 1996.

Rosa had not been his type, only convenient. The Monster had been in his bloodlust and she had been willing to get in his car for fifty dollars.

"Where we going?" she asked him over and over again, merely curious to start, then anxious, and finally terrified as he took her out of the city, and when she lunged across the seat to grab his steering wheel, he'd drawn first blood. He punched her in the face, swerving onto the shoulder as he pried her hand loose of the wheel, then back into his lane as he grabbed her hair and slammed her head against the dash.

A passing truck blew its air horn but never slowed. Rosa groaned and flopped unconscious back into her seat.

The Monster continued eastward away from the city, past the smaller town of Mountain Home, and finally turned off at the Bruneau Dunes State Park. He popped the glove box open, found his Idaho Parks Pass and put it on the dash, but it was past midnight and there were no park rangers at the entrance. He drove past the park headquarters, past the camping grounds and the visitor's center.

Rosa was awake again, curled into the passenger seat and sobbing quietly to herself, but she didn't try to escape. As if she was used to a little rough treatment, resigned to it.

The Monster parked in a cul-de-sac at the end of the road, within sight of southern Idaho's famous moving dunes. He pocketed his keys, shut his door, and walked to the passenger side. Rosa didn't move when he opened the door for her.

"It's okay," he said. He smiled and pulled a rolled up twenty from his watch pocket. Unrolled, the bill disclosed a joint. He offered them to Rosa, and when she reached for them, he stepped back.

Rosa stared up at him, wiped a fresh trickle of blood from her nose.

"You won't hit me again?"

The Monster shook his head.

Rosa climbed out and took the offered bill, twenty on top of the fifty he'd already paid her, and the joint.

He closed the door while she lit up and led her out to the dunes while she smoked.

The Monster took Rosa on the loose slope, pushing her deeper into the shifting sand with each thrust. She cried out again and again, biting her lips in a vain attempt at silence. The Monster was not worried. The campgrounds were too far away for her muffled cries to carry, and the dunes were deserted. He thrust again, squeezed her breasts hard enough to leave imprints of his fingers, and was excited to greater violence by the tears tracking down her cheeks.

She did not notice when his right hand released her breast and reached toward the boots he'd taken off and set beside them. She didn't see him reach inside, didn't see the gut hook blade he slid from the sheath hidden inside the boot.

His left hand released her other breast and found her throat, choking off any scream before it could begin, and he brought the hook end of his gutting knife down to the soft flesh beneath her sternum. The point of the hook made a popping sound as it punctured her, and as he finished, he dragged it down her stomach to her belly button, unzipping her in one smooth stroke. The sound of parting flesh was like old canvas tearing.

Rosa stared up at the monster, pain and horror twisting her face, clouding her eyes. She pulled and beat at his strangling hand, but her hands fell away as her strength and life ebbed.

When he thought she must be at the edge of death,

needing only one light push to send her over, he reached inside her and pulled out a fistful of her guts. He held them up for her to see.

Her eyes blinked, her lips pursed and parted. She reached up for him one last time, but her arm fell limp to the sand beside her.

The Monster spent the next hour digging a trench in the sand at the base of the dune, and when he could dig no deeper without the sand collapsing into it, dragged Rosa's eviscerated body down into it. He threw her clothes in on top of her, recovered his seventy dollars plus another eighty-five from her purse, and dropped it in beside her. He filled in the trench, burying her deeply enough to avoid immediate discovery, and covered over the bloody patches of sand he could find.

The Monster was on the road again a few hours before dawn, the Bruneau Dunes and Mountain Home behind him, when a dozing tractor-trailer driver crossed the median and jackknifed across both westbound lanes. The Monster, half-dozing himself after the night's exertions, plowed into the tipped trailer without ever touching his brakes.

Most of a year passed before he opened his eyes from a hospital bed, and a great deal more time passed before he rose from it under his own power.

Things could have been worse, he knew. Rosa remained undiscovered while he convalesced, had in fact remained hidden until after he left southern Idaho behind for good.

For all The Monster knew she was still there, her once shallow grave now much deeper as the constantly shifting sands of the Bruneau Dunes piled up on top of her.

Jenna stopped at the sidewalk only feet away from The Monster in his concealment. She searched the street in both directions and frowned. Then she saw him, and smiled, as if in happy surprise.

"Professor Smith!" After a single, surprised step away from him, she approached. "What are you doing out so late?"

The Monster returned her smile, happy that she was making it so easy for him, at least to start.

"I don't sleep well," he said. "I like to walk."

Jenna peered past him down the street, then back the other way again.

"Are you expecting someone?"

"No," she said, giving up her search. "Only hoping."

"I can give you a ride home, if you want." This was where things could get tricky. Hard or easy never used to be a concern for him, he had always been ready for a challenge, but these days he took easy wherever he could find it. He wasn't as young or fit as he used to be.

She eyed him shrewdly, tilted her head in way she no doubt thought was coquettishly cute, then winked.

"Well, I know you're not a maniac or pervert, so sure."

That's right, no threat here. Only doddering old Charlie Smith, Art History professor and everyone's favorite harmless old man.

She followed him to his car, an aging Tempo with sun-blistered paint, chattering all the while as if silence made her nervous.

"I just wrapped up the new video blog, it's about the alt-right movement on the WSU campus, but I want to do something lighter next week … maybe about the art program, if I can get an interview from my professor."

She winked at him.

"I think that could be arranged," The Monster said as he fished his keys out of his pocket. He unlocked the passenger door and opened it for Jenna.

She swept past him and tossed her backpack in the rear seat before slipping inside. He closed the door behind her, unable to suppress the predatory smile he saw reflected back at him from tinted glass of the passenger door window. Not able to slow the quickening of his heart.

He felt The Monster crouched and waiting inside him now.

Soon.

"Your door's busted," she said as he slipped behind the wheel and started the old car's engine. She pointed to the stub of broken plastic on her door, the handle that he'd snapped off that morning.

"Only on the inside. Could you get my glasses?" He motioned toward the glove box.

She popped it open and wrinkled her nose.

"Something in there stinks!" She found the clamshell case and handed it to him.

He opened it, pulled out the sopping rag folded inside, and slapped it against her nose.

Jenna squealed in surprise, slapped at his arm, but only for a few seconds. Her slaps weakened to feeble swipes, then her hands fell to her sides.

The Monster stuffed the rag back into the clamshell case, shut it back inside the glove box, and fumbled beneath his seat for a moment. He brought out his glasses, a roll of duct tape, a pair of sturdy zip ties, and a baggie with a small blue pill.

He took his pill first, he wanted to be ready when the moment came, then went to work with the tape and zip ties.

A minute later he was driving again.

Jenna sat across from him, sagging against her restraint, bound at the ankles and wrists, her mouth taped shut.

The Monster was ready to play.

He made his first kill at the age of fifteen.

It wasn't something he'd planned, just something that happened, and it was the closest he'd ever come to getting caught.

Her name was Patricia. He first saw her from his deer stand high up in the pines overlooking the Old Peck Grade. Afternoon was fading toward evening, the sun and moon peeking at each other from opposite sides of a clear sky, and it had been unusually warm for fall.

He'd been watching and waiting for most of the day, but not hopeful, and when he arrived home that night without his deer, his father was apt to whoop him again. His old man had been most of a year out of work now, and they were counting on the meat. His father had bagged three already, one legally, the other two not so much. Even his mother had done her part, shooting turkeys and quail from the back porch of their little house a few miles down the road.

He had in fact been dozing when he heard the sound

of an approaching car turning off the Cavendish Road. It
came into view, racing down the narrow gravel road, and
slid to a stop on one of the few wide spots.

The driver jumped out, scanned the roadside, then
darted into the trees.

Curious, roused out of his boredom, the boy who
would soon become a monster watched, tracking her with
the scope of his rifle.

She moved quickly at first, then more slowly and carefully through the thick underbrush. She walked toward
the tree with the deer stand, not noticing the boy
watching her from above. She lost her footing for a
moment and slid down a short incline, dusted herself off,
then looked around.

She was blonde, good looking, maybe only a few years
older than the boy, and he didn't recognize her. He knew
everyone who lived on Old Peck Grade and most of the
people who lived in and around the nearby town of
Orofino.

He swiveled the rifle to her parked car, sighted in on
the rear bumper and the Montana license plate, then
sighted in on the girl again in time to see her shimmy out
of her underpants. She slid them down her legs, stepped
out of them, then pulled up her skirt and squatted down
to pee.

Seated cross-legged in his deer stand, the boy's heart
began to hammer. He felt himself growing hard, his face
flush with a surge of hot blood, and heard the rasp of his
suddenly heavy breathing.

Later, afterward, he decided it was his excited respira-
tions that gave him away, because that was when she

looked up, saw him high up and sighted on her, and screamed.

His first crazed impulse, more a reaction to her shriek than anything, was to slip his finger over the trigger and squeeze.

Don't be stupid, he though. *She wouldn't dress out at more than fifty pounds.*

He gave a short, brief giggle as he put the rifle down. It was a little funny, but her continued screams weren't.

I have to explain to her, he thought.

What? That you were peeping on her?

That I wasn't going to shoot her.

He stood to do just that, crossing his hands over his crotch to hide the growing bulge he felt there, and she bolted. For a few frenzied moments she tried to climb up the short, steep bank she'd slid down, but when she saw him descending the rough rungs nailed to the trunk of his stand tree, she changed direction and fled away from the road.

Moments later he was chasing her.

She didn't get far.

At first, he followed the sounds of her panting cries and the noise of her crashing through the underbrush, then he found her left shoe, an open heel flat with its toe lodged in some burrowing animal's hole. He spotted her other shoe a moment before he saw her.

What had started as a panic to catch her before she got him into trouble, to make her understand he hadn't meant any harm, had turned into something else. He had his deer-gutting blade in hand before he realized he meant to use it.

He was no longer just chasing her. He was hunting her.

The road was perhaps a quarter-mile behind them when she went down and he heard the sharp crack of a breaking bone. Her high squeal of shock and pain was cut short as her contact with the hard earth drove the breath from her lungs.

He came upon her, half-swooned in a hollow between two old and broad fir trees. The skirt she'd hiked up to piss was mostly gone now, torn to ribbons by her passage through the woods, and her panties had been left behind. Her shirt was torn and open at the front, and one plump and dirt-smeared breast was out for him to see.

The Monster slowed to a walk and unbuckled his belt as he stepped into the hollow, his knife leading the way.

She was fully awake again and trying to rise on her broken leg when he fell over her.

Afterward, he dragged her deeper into the woods, almost in view of the Clearwater River in the valley below, and covered her body with that autumn's freshly fallen duff. On his way back to the road, he picked up and tossed her shoes as far into the woods as he could, and then stopped to pick up her dropped panties.

He thought about keeping them, then thought better of it.

He also thought about driving her car further down the dead-end road and pushing it off the cul-de-sac at the bottom, and again decided not to. Instead, he tossed the panties onto the back seat floor, took the small purse on the front passenger seat, and tore the license plates from the front and rear bumpers.

The car was gone by the next day, and a month passed

before he heard anything about a missing Missoula woman named Patricia Carroll.

A fisherman, ironically stepping deeper into the trees to urinate out of sight of his children, found the body, and Clearwater County Sheriff Ed Knox paid the young monster a visit later that day. The sheriff was a hard-eyed old man who held the young monster's family in low regard and knew about the deer stand overlooking the grade. It was a soft interrogation done on the young monster's own front porch, but it was only the first, and they both knew it.

An older and wiser monster understood that luck alone had saved him.

Before there was time for a second and harder interrogation, a deputy found the shell of the missing woman's car on blocks in the back yard of another Clearwater County scumbag, Jeffrey Fish. Fish's list of prior offenses, ranging from indecent exposure, drunk and disorderly, and several which the local press referred to vaguely as assaults against women, assured him a visit from the local law, the discovery of the missing woman's car on his property set the hook, but it was Patricia's panties, grimy from much handling and stuffed into his front pocket, that put him on Sheriff Knox's plate.

The Monster learned two things from his first kill.

The first was that he *would* do it again.

The second was that he must do it better, smarter.

And so, he had. He killed for the next fifty years, and was never interviewed by another sheriff, deputy, or detective.

He kept no trophies, except for the sketchbook he started in college, where his talent and love of art finally decided his direction in life, and in which he recorded every woman who had ever met The Monster.

Professor Charlie Smith, The Monster, drove Jenna to the pocket park at the corner of Grimes Way and Terre View Drive, where the Agricultural Sciences portion of the WSU campus ended and actual farmland began. The parking area was small, enough for two cars if they crowded close, but he guided his old Tempo carefully off of the gravel and onto the dirt, stopping under the cover of a grove of black hawthorn wearing their fall colors. The park consisted of a picnic table, benches, and a small square of grass. He planned on leaving her posed on the table within sight of the road. He wanted her found quickly. His doctor had ordered him to reduce his stress, and an interminable wait for the discovery of a concealed body would simply be too stressful.

"Jenna."

No response. She continued to sag against her seatbelt.

He slapped her lightly on the cheek.

Her head flopped sideways onto her right shoulder, then rolled forward again.

He'd expected her to be coming around by now, he didn't want to have to carry her, but she was a small thing. He could drag her, and he did.

Into the trees, he laid her out on a soft spot of ground covered in wild grass and the first fallen leaves of autumn. He cut the zip tie binding her ankles and stripped her, cutting her shirt away so he could leave her hands bound.

Naked, she looked younger than her true age. Short

and slim, without much in the way of hips or breasts. He felt his body responding to the sight of her, bound and naked before him. His heart began to beat harder, quicker, his penis stiffened.

He kicked her legs apart, then knelt between her knees and unbuckled his belt.

That was when her eyes opened.

There was no slow and groggy return to consciousness. Her eyes were closed one second, then opened and focused on him at the next. There was none of her usual good-humored playfulness in them, but he had not expected there would be. There was also no fear, none at all, and that gave him a moment of pause.

Her eyes flicked down to his unbuckled belt, and though he couldn't see her lips, her cheeks strained against the tape covering them in what looked like a smile. Her eyes returned to his face, and her eyebrows arched.

He could almost hear her thoughts.

Well, what are you waiting for?

She stretched beneath him, raised her bound hands over her head, arched her back invitingly.

This isn't right, he thought, and his body responded to his sudden sense of unease. He broke out in a sudden, clammy sweat, and his prick began to shrivel.

"Bitch," he whispered, and produced the gut hook blade. He brought it down close to her face and waited for a more appropriate look of fear to widen her eyes. He needed her fear to continue, could not be a man without it.

There was no fear, only a single, sly wink.

Her knees suddenly tightened at his waist, almost

painfully, and her bound hands shot up and closed over his wrist as he brought the blade down.

The struggle that followed was short.

Jenna was stronger than he had imagined, and as she turned his blade to the side, she rolled him off of her. A knee found his groin, smashed into it again and again. He felt a pop in his wrist and the blade flew from his hand. He swung at her blindly with the other hand, felt his old bunched knuckles smash into her cheek, but she held on. He swung again, and she ducked under his fist, falling flat over him.

Her bound hands found his throat this time and squeezed.

He scrabbled at her clenched hands, reached for her throat, clutched at it, but couldn't hold on.

This isn't happening, he thought. *This cannot be ...*

The Monster slipped into darkness.

"I'm disappointed in you, Professor Smith."

The Monster awoke in pain, his throat swollen, his broken wrist a nest of needles, his back aching, his skin naked and cold with a cooling sheen of sweat. He tried to rise but couldn't. The only part of himself he could move was his head, and he lifted it to find Jenna, dressed again, bent down in his car and wiping down the glove box and dash with the rags of her ruined shirt.

"You seemed like such a nice old guy, you even opened the door for me." She stood, pushed the door closed with her elbow, and wiped down the handle. "I guess you didn't want me leaving my fingerprints everywhere in your car."

She approached him, and he saw she was wearing his shirt now, an old paisley thing far too large for her. Her backpack swung from her right hand and his blade was clutched in her left.

He tried to rise again, but couldn't. Tried to move his legs, lift his arms.

He was caught. Stripped naked and taped around his chest, thighs, and ankles to the picnic table. She must have used the entire roll on him, saving back just enough for a double wrap around his head, sealing off his mouth.

"I thought you were one of the nice guys, but you weren't." She shrugged, set down her backpack, unzipped it and reached inside. "Look what I found in your trunk while you were sleeping."

She held up his sketchbook, opened it and flipped through the pages until she reached his last entry. Her entry.

"I guess you were a maniac and pervert after all." She set his sketchbook on the table at his feet and reached into her backpack again. She pulled out a red and white football jersey, a WSU Cougar jersey, and held it up for him to see. "He wasn't very nice either. He was a rapist, but not anymore."

She reached in again, pulled out a pair of bent and cracked glasses.

"He was a stalker." She set the glasses down and pulled out an absurdly large gold and silver belt buckle. "This guy hit me in a bar last year when I wouldn't go home with him. He called me a whore, then he hit me. I had to wait a while to get him, wanted everyone to forget about it before I took care of him."

She dropped the buckle onto the growing pile by his feet.

Next, she pulled out a small tin and shook it at him playfully.

"This is for you," she said, and smiled. She set it down, then placed a lighter next to it and began repacking her bag of trophies. "I've met a lot of shitty guys, professor, but I think you might be the worst of them."

She held up his sketchbook again, seeming almost to admire it, then packed it away.

"I thought about leaving this behind for someone to find, so everyone can know what a shitty person you are, but I think I'm going to keep it."

When her bag was repacked she set it aside, then picked up his blade again. She grabbed his flaccid penis with a grimace of distaste and stretched it out until he started to howl with pain behind his gag of tape.

The gut hook blade removed it quite efficiently, with a single swipe.

He'd always kept it sharp.

"Someone should have taken this away from you a long time ago," Jenna said, shaking it in his face. She slapped him across the cheek with it, then dropped it on his chest.

The Monster screeched silently behind his gag, strained against his bindings. His heart hammered, seemed about to explode in his chest.

"Well shit, I guess we're about finished here," Jenna said, then popped the cap off her tin of lighter fluid and sprayed him down with it. "I don't believe in hell, I think it's all bullshit, so you'll just have to burn here."

Jenna picked up her lighter and let The Monster burn.

I AM THE COYOTE, I AM THE SNAKE

I don't remember my real name, but I remember his.
He took me when I was thirteen ....

Her last good memory, the last day of her childhood, was walking home from school on a day bright with the promise of the summer vacation yet to come. It was too fine of a day for riding the school bus, so she'd missed it intentionally. She liked the walk home, the bustle of the square, the apple orchard at the edge of town, the wooded path to her home.

But before home, there was the highway. Rush hour was still on the horizon, but the four-lane was lousy with over the road trucks, and the approaching thunder of motorbikes.

Instead of waiting for an opening she left the main road and walked along the highway to the parched bed of

Dry Creek. It wasn't far, she could hear the town clock chime the hour as she slid down the bank on the flats of her shoes. She scanned the dry channel that crossed beneath the busy blacktop to the other side of the highway. It was empty.

Thinking only of home, some ten minutes away from the other side of the channel, she entered.

She noted the growing rumble of motorbikes overhead but wasn't worried. She was thinking of finishing her homework as quick as she could, then drinking cold soda and watching TV while she waited for her friend, Laura, to arrive for their overnighter.

The sound of a single motorbike, amplified by the concrete walls of the tunnel, slammed her from behind. She turned in time to see the rider bearing down on her, then the bike's headlight flashed on, bright in the subterranean gloom, blinding her.

She screamed and jumped out of the rider's path. He blew past and a heavy fist hit her chest like a sledgehammer, blasting the air from her, knocking her to the cold concrete.

She lay there, wanting to get up and run, but unable to. She struggled for breath and couldn't find it.

The thunder of the bike's engine died, was replaced by the sound of heavy-booted feet and the lazy rasp of a zipper being drawn down.

Again, she tried to get up, away, but could not. She had no air.

Then he stood before her, dropped down onto her, straddling her legs between his massive thighs. She couldn't see his face, its features were shrouded in shadow and thick beard. His penis sprang from his open fly, huge and stiff, pointing at her. Large hands yanked her skirt up past her waist and ripped at her panties.

Finally, she found her breath. She filled her lungs and screamed.

"Let me go!"

He reared up and hit her. Just once.

Thankfully, she remembered nothing more.

They kept me drugged most of the time. They didn't need to, they never let me out of their sight, but the drugs made me easier.

They liked me easy....

Her life after that day was a blur of strange landscapes viewed from the backs of motorcycles. North to south, east to west and back again with the outlaw bikers, The Outriders. She was their youngest *Old Lady*, their party girl, their prostitute, their slave.

His name was Dot, the man who took her. He liked to pretend she was his daughter during the day and his wife at night. He called her Sweetness. The name didn't stick. He traded her a few months later to one of his brother Outriders for a new saddlebag and a pair of chaps.

In the next few years they traded her five times. Each had a different name for her. She remembered all of these names, but not the one she was born with. That name was gone, left to rot beneath the blacktop of Wisconsin Highway 10.

When I was fourteen I had a baby. I named it Freedom. We left it in Idaho, highway 12, between mile marker 27 and 28....

It was time. She'd felt it coming on since she'd awakened that morning at the campground outside Orofino. After a little more than a half-hour on the road her water broke, drenching the seat of her old man, Wolfie's, bike. They pulled off at the next rest area, restrooms, a park, and angler's access to the Clearwater River.

"C'mon now. Push that little bastard out."

She lay curled up on the piss-puddled floor of the men's room, Wolfie standing over her. There was pain, more pain than she would have believed. It felt as if all the hurt they had forced into her had gathered itself up into a ball, and was now forcing its way back out.

Then the baby came. It had felt very large coming out, but looked very small, lying where it had landed between her legs. It moved, but just a little. Wrenching, jerky movements. It didn't cry.

Something looked wrong about it.

"You poor little bastard," Wolfie said. At first, she thought he meant her, but he was looking at the baby. He'd made a little bed of paper hand towels, and after cutting its cord, laid the baby on it.

"You named him yet?"

A boy. It was a boy.

"Yes," she said, but Wolfie interrupted before she could say it.

"Keep it to yourself." He picked up the baby, looked down at it, his expression cold. He knew it wasn't his. "You've got ten minutes. Clean up."

"I can't," she said. "It hurts too bad." She was beyond crying now. Only wanted to find a corner to die in.

"Suppose it does," he said. "I'll take care of it." He cradled her baby in one arm and brought a pill bottle out of the inside pocket of his jacket.

For a moment she thought he was going for his gun, and she would not have cared. That would have taken care of the pain.

He thumbed the cap loose and shook two pills onto the floor next to her. "Take 'em. Hurry your ass up."

The pills worked. It was hard to stand, harder to walk, but she cleaned up and was comfortably stoned when she walked back outside.

Wolfie was not at his bike. Neither was her baby.

She waited.

He came back a few minutes later, climbing the riverbank. His arms were empty.

For the first time in her time with The Outriders, her anger dwarfed her fear.

"Where's my baby?"

He smiled but said nothing, as if he was returning from taking a leak.

"Where's my …."

His fist cut her off.

Darkness blossomed behind her eyes, a new pain cut the numbness of the drugs. She tasted blood and felt gravel against her cheek.

"What baby?" he said, and laughed again. The others laughed too, but not the women. The women were silent. "I don't see any babies."

He pulled a rag, damp with river water, from his back pocket, and tossed it to her.

"Get up and clean my bike. We ride in five."

———

Then Samus, the desert trader, found me ....

———

The Outriders spent winters at their southern nest, an abandoned ranch at the edge of the New Mexico Bad Lands. There was no power, but they didn't need it. There was no water, after decades of disuse the desert had reclaimed the well. There was no road between the ranch and highway, just a half mile of hardpan, what might have been good grazing land when Billy The Kid still rode it.

The closest town was a trucker's oasis on the Nevada border. The Outriders would take their women there and pimp them out to the drivers.

Sometimes Samus came to their camp from the deep desert to trade peyote and his macabre scrimshaw, knife handles, belt buckles, and pendants. The Outriders prized his scrimshaw, death art carved from human bone.

The Outriders feared him too. The desert trader seemed as much animal as man to them. His face, what was visible beneath his pelt of hair and beard, was deep tanned and rough as leather. He wore a jacket of coyote that fit like a second skin. His pants and boots were sand colored sidewinder, ornamented with a garnish of rattles. Sometimes the rattles sounded his approach. Sometimes they did not.

His race was uncertain, but Dallas, The Outriders club president, said he was a tribeless Indian Shaman.

One day she caught his eye.

"I want her," Samus said.

She sat beside Slick, her current keeper, on an ancient sofa in the old stable where they parked their bikes, and gasped as his hand, resting on her leg, clenched.

Heads turned toward them. Ears tuned in.

"Well," Slick said, "Brittany ain't for sale." Brittany was Slick's name for her. He'd named her after the singer, had even bleached her hair blond to complete the fantasy.

She tried to get up, she wanted nothing more than to disappear until the desert trader was gone. Slick's fingers tightened even harder on her leg and pulled her back down.

"She's pretty," Samus said. He didn't look at Slick when he spoke. His eyes, bottomless black things, never left her. He didn't blink.

"Yeah, she's pretty, but she ain't on the table." Fear was plain in Slick's voice, but he spoke firmly. The others were watching the trade. She'd seen how these things played out before, if Slick let Samus bully him into trading his *Old Lady*, he'd never be able to keep another one. He'd be weak in their eyes, and The Outriders did not barter with weaklings, they *took* from weaklings.

No response from Samus. He stared at her, rose from his chair and approached them.

"Hey, desert man," Slick said, and now he was angry as well as scared. The trade was sacred, and Samus was shitting on it. "You said you needed gasoline and food."

He tapped the base of a fifty-gallon drum between them with the tip of a boot.

"I'm here for business, but Brittany ain't part of the goddamn deal!"

Samus seemed not to hear. He extended a slow arm toward her.

"No," she said, then turned to Slick. Whether she liked him or not, he was her man, her protection.

"Shut up," Slick said to her, his face flushed with mingled shame and rage. His right hand twitched toward the butt of the revolver on his hip.

All other conversation in the stable died, The Outriders waited for the showdown. The women had left, gone into hiding.

"I want her, too," the desert man said, and touched her cheek with a single callused finger.

Slick drew his gun. He was fast. His aim was good. He put a bullet through Samus's chest, almost point blank. The smell of singed coyote fur filled her nose.

The slug smashed splinters from the stable wall behind where the desert man had stood.

Slick screamed. A wave of alarm passed through the watching crowd.

As swift as Slick's draw was, Samus was swifter, and before the revolver's report was dead, he stood before Slick. In a lightning movement he lifted the biker from his seat. His other hand passed before Slick's face like a mirage, and blood rained down on her.

She screamed and ran from him, into the crowd at the other end of the stable, but they would not let her pass.

"No!" This was her clearest memory of her time with The Outriders. Fear had sobered her. "Please, don't let him take me!"

Dallas caught her and held her close as Samus approached.

The crowd parted for him. She and Dallas stood alone.

"Hush," Dallas said, his tone soothing. He let go of her, reached inside his jacket. Instead of his gun, he produced a syringe.

"No!" She pushed away from him, and the others grabbed her, held her.

There was the sting of the needle, then the numbness.

"Take her," Dallas said.

She slept the familiar poison sleep.

I awoke in chains, in the dark ....

"You are my girl." The voice of the desert man came to her from all around, wrapped around her in the cool still air of ... wherever she was. It touched her through the cold stone of her prison floor.

She sat up, still faint from the drug, felt rough stone against her arm, and pressed her back against it. A fuzz of light shone in the distance, the mouth of the cave. It was the moon.

"I am the coyote," Samus said. "I am the snake." He came to her from the darkness beyond, from deeper in the cavern. She felt the grit and grime of his body against her before she even knew he was there. "You are mine."

His fingers traced the contours of her face, her chin, her throat. They stopped above her breasts, hesitated, trembled, then withdrew. Before they had been callused skin, now they were claws – long and jagged.

The curls of mustache and beard tickled her cheek. His lips touched her, they felt like strips of wet leather, then parted to show his teeth.

She didn't try to stop him. After her time with The Outriders she knew better than to fight it. But she pleaded, that she could not help.

"Please, let me go. I just want to go."

"No," a growl in her ear. "You'll leave me. You won't come back."

He pressed into her, but not with the rough urgency she was accustomed to. In his own animal way, he was gentle.

He is the coyote, he is the snake ....

"Samus," she called into the darkness.

For some time, there was no response. She almost

didn't expect one. The snake didn't like to talk. The snake liked silence.

Finally, it came from deeper in the darkness, where he lived. "I'm here."

"I'm hungry."

He brought her food, dried meat, from what she did not know. Beast or man, it didn't matter. She thanked him and ate.

He sat, crouched against the cavern wall across from her, watching.

When her stomach was content she set the rest of the meat aside. She was aware of his eyes on her, even though she couldn't see them in the shadow of his form. "Do you want me now?"

He didn't answer, and after a time rose to his feet and started back into the darkness.

"I've been your girl for a long time," she called after him, and he stopped. "If you want to be my man, take these chains off and let me go with you."

"The snake will try to hurt you," he said. "The snake needs silence."

"What about the coyote."

"I am both."

"Does the coyote love me?"

"Yes," he said, then left her.

He returned an hour later with a key. He removed her chains and took her with him.

She heard the hum of a generator and saw the phantom glow of electric lights long before they reached his den. He lived in an old silver streamline trailer. Parked in front of it was the little Land Rover he used to travel for trading and his raids on the fringes of the civilized world.

A wall-mounted floodlight illuminated all.

There were fuel drums lined up against the cavern wall, some full, most empty. Some of the empties overflowed with trash. Stacked in rows beside the camper, his silver cave within a cave, were crates of dried and canned food.

The smell of death, rotting meat, hung in the air. It took only a few seconds to spot the source. A pile of meat and sinew-laden bones lay in a tall mound before a dead fire pit. Flies swarmed the bones as beetles and insects feasted on their rotting bounty. Most were indistinct, could have been from any kind of animal, but the grinning countenance of a dozen or more human skulls, some large, some small, left no doubt.

I don't know how long I was there ....

Time blurs in a lightless world: time as a measurable thing. They rarely used the generator, only when the deep winter nights below were too cold, or when Samus needed the light for his scrimshaw. Her only calendar was the daily cycle of hunger, and her monthly curse of blood.

He stayed away when the blood came. It roused the snake, and the snake still did not like her.

The coyote was kind, kinder than any of the others

had been, and she grew to love it in return. But she knew one day the snake would return.

And then that day came.

———

The snake needs silence.
  It was time for me to leave ....

———

She was pregnant again. She knew it when the curse of blood did not come. She didn't tell Samus, but somehow the snake sensed it. He'd been gone for a long time, but she didn't leave. There was nowhere to go but the desert.

He would come back. He always did. The coyote loved her.

She kept the fire burning for him and waited. It was all she could do.

"Samus." She spoke his name, hoping he would answer, knowing he would not.

So she waited, and slept, and in her dreams, the snake came.

She was in chains again, in the dark. She heard his rattle, a soft sandpaper sound, and felt the snake as it slid between her pressed thighs.

"No, Samus!" She cried and struggled against the chains, squeezed her legs together until the muscles cramped, but the snake found its way in.

It was dry inside of her, and cold.

She screamed in pain and loss as it found her child and devoured it.

Then the chains were gone.

She was awake.

The fire had burned to coals, and she moved closer to them to drive the cold of her dream away.

In far distance she heard the warning rattle. The snake was coming home. It was coming for her child.

"I'm sorry, Samus." She went to the Land Rover and found its key in the ignition. She'd never driven it before, but she'd watched Samus drive it and knew what to do. She turned the key and let out a scream of shock when the engine started and backfired.

As she shifted it into drive, Samus appeared. He came for her, arms outstretched, mouth open in a silent scream, teeth bared. Coming for her. Coming for her baby.

Thinking about her last child, Freedom, she stepped on the accelerator and drove straight toward him.

Samus never slowed. Neither did she. They met with a bang of metal and the crunch of bone. The impact jolted her forward in her seat sent him spinning through the air. He landed in a loose-jointed roll next to the dying fire.

He was still, but she did not trust that. The snake was tricky.

"I'm sorry, Samus," she said again. She began to weep as she charged the line of gasoline barrels against the wall. The Land Rover struck the first in line and folded it into itself. The lid tore loose, gasoline gushed over the side and ran in rainbow streams toward Samus and the fire.

She drove as fast as she dared, headlights blasting the darkness before her, toward the outside world. She heard the hungry sound as the fire tasted gas, and liked it. Soon the other fuel barrels would go up in the heat and tear Samus's cave down.

She found the moon before that happened.

Then Samus began to scream.

The sound of his pain followed her into the cool desert night.

The night is cool, but the sand is warm.

I am tired. So fucking tired.

Somewhere behind me, the viper rattles and the coyote sings his sad, sad song ....

CAMPBELL'S POND

Lester was a fat, pale, pimply boy. Sixteen years old, and he had made only a few friends in his life.

Girlfriends? None.

As bad as things were for him at his old home in Missoula, city living had its advantages. He could always trade the hostile faces at his school or neighborhood for the merely indifferent ones a few blocks away where no one knew him.

Then came Uncle Frank.

Uncle, right.

Uncle Frank claimed to be an Indian, but Lester couldn't see it. He looked more Italian than anything else. He fancied himself a medicine man, but his only medicine was meth, and after Lester's mom was thoroughly hooked on the shit Frank cooked, their house had become *his* house.

The arrangement had started with Frank crashing and eating there in exchange for free product. But in no time at all Frank was living there full time, cooking his product and treating Lester's mom like a fuck doll.

Then the bust, which was good because it meant no more Uncle Frank, but bad because it meant no more mom.

Now Lester lived with his real uncle in Pierce, and his already troubled social life had taken a definite turn from bad to worse.

Pierce was a speck of a town in the mountains of north Idaho, and had nothing to interest him. No arcades, no music stores, no bookstores. The closest Wal-Mart was almost a hundred miles away.

What Pierce *did* have was a small grocery store, a bar, a single convenience store, another bar, a lodge with two dozen new cabins built in anticipation of Lewis & Clark Centennial tourists who never came, a sports shop that consisted solely of hunting and fishing supplies next to a third bar, and a small, rickety hotel, with a bar in the lobby.

Pierce also had approximately five-hundred residents, almost half of them unemployed since the local mill closed down, all of whom spent the bulk of their time drinking and getting into each other's business.

His real uncle, not a Frank but a Larry, didn't have cable TV, so Lester spent most of his time in his room reading and re-reading the same dog-eared books he'd brought with him.

Lester had no friends in Pierce, which was nothing new, but in a small town there was no place to hide from the locals who had taken an instant dislike to him. The local boys favorite new sport was pounding Lester whenever they caught him outside, so he only went out at night if he couldn't avoid it. His uncle was usually gone at night, his preferred haunt was the The Flame Bar and Grill, and he slept through most of the day, so Lester didn't have to spend much time with him.

Sunday nights were the exception. By state law the bars stayed closed on Sunday, so after waking sometime in the early afternoon, Lester's uncle spent the rest of the day sulking around the small house, yelling at anyone who called on the telephone, yelling at the evening news, and yelling at Lester to walk to the Mini-Mart and pick up his beer.

Uncle Larry had a special relationship with the woman at the Mini-Mart, one that prohibited him from going within a hundred yards of her, so she was happy to break the no beer to minors rule to keep Uncle Larry safely at home.

These trips usually happened at twilight, so Lester would take a long route through cluttered, dusty alleys to avoid the town boys, and once at the little store he hurried to get out before one of them happened to stop by. This approach had been largely successful. He didn't want to know how Uncle Larry would react if someone stole his beer on the return trip.

It was on one of these Sunday trips that Lester got the surprise of his life in the form of the girlfriend of one of Lester's most enthusiastic tormentors.

"Having a party?" She stepped from behind the chip rack as Lester heaved a cube of Keystone from the cooler.

Lester closed his eyes and prepared for the worst. He

knew that voice, everyone knew it. Every penis equipped person in Pierce wondered what it would be like to hear it moan into their ear or shout their name in the height of ecstasy. It belonged to the hottest girl in town. The girl, Samantha Zenner, belonged to Rick Durham, the person Lester least liked to hear saying his name.

Might as well get it over with, Lester thought, and turned.

Rick was not there. Samantha was alone.

Lester blinked, scanned the aisles on either side of her, but Rick's grimly grinning face remained absent. Finally remembering to breathe, Lester hitched in a deep one.

She stood in front of him, arms crossed under her plump and perky breasts, her bright blue eyes moving from his face to the case hanging from his hand, then back again.

"Is it a private party or do I get an invite?" Her impatient foot tapping caused her already short denim skirt to ride up a few inches.

"It's for my uncle." He searched the mostly empty store again. "Where's Rick?"

Her narrow smile vanished. She raised an eyebrow. "You that anxious to run into him?"

"No," he said quickly. Too quickly. He felt his cheeks glowing with embarrassment. "I just thought …"

She stepped closer to him, and words failed. He couldn't honestly verbalize what he was thinking.

"If I know Rick he's off at The Log Yard fucking some hillbilly skank."

The Log Yard was an actual log yard. Durham Logging, owned by Rick's dad, put to use most nights by Rick and his friends as a place to get drunk and fuck girls.

Samantha took another step toward him, and Lester had to fight an urge to retreat. She poked him in the chest with a long, pink fingernail.

"Do you want to party with me or do I need to go find someone else." She gripped his arm high up and pulled him close to her, her breasts pushing against him, and whispered in his ear. "This could be your lucky night. I want to get drunk and I want to fuck. If you want some of this, then make a move or I'll find someone else to party with."

She's only doing this to get even with Rick, he thought.

Rick will kick my ass, he thought.

Uncle Larry will kick my ass worse, he thought.

It's fucking worth it, he thought.

"Where do you want to go?"

Samantha drove her father's pickup out of town and down the narrow, twisted highway as twilight sank into night. Lester couldn't help but notice the way she stroked the gear shifter's knob absentmindedly with her right hand.

"You ever fuck before?" She gave him a quick, speculative glance before facing forward again to negotiate a sharp twist in the road. She shifted down, and Lester watched her skirt ride up her thighs as she worked the pedals. She did not attempt to pull it back down. "Lester?"

Answer her, dumb ass.

It was his big brother, Charlie's voice. Charlie always came to him at awkward moments to coach or berate him.

Lester thought he should lie and say yes. Tonight appeared to be a sure thing, but he didn't want to look like a total loser.

"No," he said.

Shit.

Samantha giggled, and drove on.

"Where are we going?" Lester had never been this way before. The road had taken a decisive downward slant, and Lester wondered if she was taking him to the bottom of the mountain. He knew there was a river in the valley below. Maybe they were going skinny-dipping first.

Lester imagined a look of disgust on Samantha's face at seeing him naked and felt sick to his stomach.

Good thing you brought a whole case, little bro. You'd better get her shit-faced before you show her your man-tits.

"Have you heard of Campbell's Pond?"

"Uh, no," Lester said, though the name did sound familiar to him. He liked the sound of her voice, and if he could keep her talking, there would be fewer uncomfortable questions about him.

"It's an old campground down the highway a little ways." A car passed coming the other way and honked. Samantha waved out the window and honked twice in return. "It has about twenty camping spots with fire pits, tables, bathrooms, and it's all around a big pond. It used to be popular, but a few years ago a boy from town got lost there. He never turned up, and when a reporter came to do a story about it she disappeared too."

"Sounds creepy," Lester said, then wished he hadn't.

God, you sound like a wimp.

"A little," Samantha said, and winked at him. "Not too creepy, I hope."

Lester laughed nervously and shook his head.

"After the reporter disappeared, another boy fell in the pond and drowned. They never found him either."

A long straight stretch opened up before them, and Samantha shifted up again, putting on speed. Her skirt rode a little higher. Lester could see the color of her panties.

Pink!

His dick, which had spent the last half hour in a state of semi-hard anticipation, pushed at the crotch of his pants. He crossed his hands over his lap.

"So no one goes there anymore," she continued. "Someone blocked the road that goes there with trees. The Forest Service won't even go there to maintain it. I mean, why bother? No one uses it."

"Oh," Lester said. He tried to think of something better to say. "Have you ever been there?"

"Only once, during the day. There it is," Samantha said, slowing and pointing to a faded sign in the truck's headlights.

Campbell's Pond – 5 miles.

A newer neon orange sign below it said, *Closed To The Public.*

A narrow dirt road forked off the main road, swallowed by the trees and the dark.

"Wow," Lester said. "It's a long way in there."

"Uh-huh," Samantha said. "And since no one comes here, we can do anything we want without getting caught."

Lester suddenly found it hard to breathe. He tried to say something witty but only managed a weak croak.

Samantha leaned close to him as they slowed and

turned onto the dirt road. "You've got almost five miles to think about how you want to do me," she said, and placed a hand on his thigh.

"Oh Jesus," he said, panting, almost hyperventilating.

This was just too good to be real.

As if reading that thought, Samantha slid her hand along Lester's leg and squeezed, reminding him that she was real.

Lester watched the odometer turn and almost groaned when Samantha stopped the truck still a half-mile shy of their destination. The road was still blocked. Two old logs lay crisscrossed in their path. A sign fixed at the crux of the decomposing logs read *God Damned This Place*.

"I guess we're going back now," he said, not able to keep the pouting tone from his voice.

"Uh ... no," Samantha said, and giggled. "You can walk, can't you?"

She tore open his uncle's case of beer and opened one, tipping it back and guzzling the whole can. After an unladylike belch, she tossed the can out of her open window and grabbed another as she stepped from the cab.

Lester grabbed the case and followed. When he tried to pull a beer out for himself, she slapped his hand.

"Not for you, big boy. I want you focused."

She straddled the logs briefly as she climbed over them, pausing to throw a sly glance back at Lester. Then she slid her leg over, showing more panty, and waited for Lester.

He set the beer down and worked his first leg carefully

over the logs. He was much heavier than Samantha, and not near as limber. It took a few moments, and he almost fell over the other side.

When he was on the other side he found Samantha holding the case of beer in the crook of her left arm. Her pink panties hung from the index finger of her tilted right hand. She flipped them at him, and his clumsy swipe was too slow. They hit his face, hanging for a moment from his nose before he snatched them off.

She ran down the road ahead of him, looking back once to smile as she flipped the backside of her skirt up, exposing herself. He saw her ass for just a moment. It was perfect, shining pale pink in the moonlight.

"Come and get some, Lester."

Then the dark swallowed her, and Lester ran to catch up.

When Lester found the lake minutes later he was out of breath. He stumbled to a stop and fell to his knees next to a castoff sign that read *Closed For The Season* in faded letters. For a moment he thought he was going to puke, and he fought his gorge. He couldn't see Samantha, but he knew she was there somewhere, watching, waiting for him to find her.

He thought his chance of actually getting laid would suffer if she saw him puking his guts up in the dirt.

When his trembling legs would support him again, he rose and scanned the area. There was the pond, its water dark and still, and a few nearby camp spaces, littered with what might have been years old trash.

No Samantha.

He walked the remaining distance to the lake.

Closer, Lester could make out a dock poking into the dark water from the shore of a pond-side camping spot. Tied to a post at the end of the dock, a dilapidated raft rocked lazily. He spotted his beer at the foot of the dock and smiled.

He jogged the remaining distance and paused before the dock. The case of beer was a few cans emptier. A discarded T-shirt, bra, and denim miniskirt lay in the dust next to it.

A hand slid by his cheek, coming from behind, and Lester screeched as it closed over his eyes, blinding him.

"You're excitable, aren't you?" Samantha said, and her other hand slapped the back of his head as he tried to face her.

"Hey," he said, reaching up to rub at his smarting head.

"No you don't," Samantha said, and did her giggle again, a sound Lester now associated with lust and the perfumed smell of her panties. "We're going to do this my way, to start."

"Okay," Lester said, and trembled.

"Keep your eyes closed," she said, and he felt her hand slide away. "Now take your clothes off."

This was the moment Lester dreaded. He'd hoped it would be too dark for her to see him when it came to this part, but he knew she could see him perfectly well in the moonlight cast against the lake. He did it with only the slightest hesitation though, dropping her panties and starting with his shirt. He shook so badly he almost tripped stepping out of his pants.

"Wow! Nice package," Samantha said from behind

him, and he felt himself blush, his face burning with embarrassment, and a little pride.

He kicked off his underwear, hoping she didn't notice the skid marks that inevitably decorated every pare he ever owned, and waited.

"Keep your eyes closed," she said, grabbing his arms from behind and guiding him onto the dock. It rocked beneath him, water splashing up between the worn and slimly boards to drench his feet. For just the barest moment he felt flesh press against his back, and thought, *it's a nipple*!

Hold your wad, little bro, the voice of his brother spoke in his head. *You don't want to blow it over a nipple, do you?*

Finally, she stopped, and he stopped with her, ready to take whatever direction she gave. "Just one last step," she said. "You don't want to miss the raft, so make it a big one."

But they did not take the last step. She held him in place. He felt her press against his back again, and her breath tickled the hair on the back of his neck.

"Have you ever been fucked in a cemetery?"

"Uh …," he said, but she cut him off with another giggle.

"Of course you haven't. You've never been fucked at all. You're going to be fucked in a cemetery tonight."

"What?" Unease stabbed at his excitement.

"We're standing over one right now," she said. "Beneath the water. Some crazy preacher dammed up a creek and flooded it, but it's still down there. They found headstones when they were looking for that boy."

She urged Lester forward, and he took the last step reluctantly.

A cemetery under the pond?

"Lay down, I'll be right there."

Lester laid down, his lust cooling a little when water lapped at his backside from between damp, warped boards.

The raft rocked and whispered through the dark water.

He waited, the night air blowing cool kisses on his naked skin.

The giggle came again, this time from farther away.

Lester opened his eyes and groaned when he saw her standing on the dock. Her skirt hung crooked on her hips as she tugged her shirt back into place.

Standing behind her, what remained of Lester's beer hanging from his meat-hook hand, was Rick Dunham. Lester's clothes were bundled under his other arm. His laughter boomed across the pond. He raised an open can in mock salute.

"Now you've been fucked in a cemetery, Lester," Samantha said, and her giggle dissolved into shrieking laughter.

She's got a point, bro. You certainly are fucked.

Samantha waved goodbye before following Rick onto the dark path that led away from Campbell's Pond.

Lester just lay there for a while, gazing into the sky at a fat, pale moon, trying not to cry. A fat, pale slug of a boy, stranded and naked on a wet old raft. Pondweed and water washed up between the warped boards and slapped his backside. His arms spread wide, his fingers brushed the dark water.

"Ouch!"

He jerked his right arm up, shaking his hand. Something had bitten him. He pulled his other hand from the water and sat up, examining the stinging middle finger of his right hand.

A spot of blood welled from a tiny cut on the tip, just below the fingernail.

Even the fish had it in for him tonight.

You plan to stick around here forever, bro?

Lester sighed and scanned the shore. He didn't see Samantha or Rick, not that he'd thought they would stick around, but he wanted to make sure before going back to shore. His long trip back to town would be embarrassing enough without an audience, especially those two.

He would have to face them again though. In a place as small as Pierce there was no getting around it.

He rolled onto his belly and slid closer to the edge of the raft so he could paddle back to the dock. His *package* had flopped into a crack between two boards, and he felt water splash up against it. He arched his back and slid to the side. He could imagine the fish down there, gazing up at what might look like a fat pink worm, trying to take a bite out of it as they had his finger.

Samantha had complimented him on his package earlier, but he imagined her driving back to town, or wherever they were headed with his Uncle's beer, laughing to Rick about it.

The story would be all over town within hours. Everyone would know.

Lester cursed his mother for what might have been the

millionth time. The selfish old junky cunt. It was her fault he was stuck in this redneck infested shithole.

His mom had assured him the move was not permanent, a few months, a year at most, and she'd be out of jail with her shit all together again, but he had a feeling when she did get out, she'd pull a quick fade and resume her life as a junkie whore in a new place.

Lester had thought about trying to reach Charles, he had the number for the institution he stayed in, but Uncle Larry wouldn't allow it.

Someone who puts themselves in the boobie-hatch is even crazier than the ones that get put there, Larry said, then told Lester to shut up so he could watch Nascar.

Fuck 'em, Charles spoke in Lester's head. *Fuck 'em all. Just because everyone else in our family is screwed up doesn't mean you have to suffer.*

"Fuck 'em," Lester said, dipping his hands into the water and paddling, beginning his humiliating trip out of Campbell's Pond. "I'm out of here."

It would be a long walk back to Pierce, but if he didn't stop to rest he might make it back before daylight, so he might not be seen waddling naked into town. There were clotheslines aplenty, so he'd pick out some clothes, maybe sneak into his uncle's house for a bite to eat, then he was out of there. He'd hitchhike back to Missoula or walk the whole way if he couldn't find a ride. Even if he didn't have any friends willing to take him in, Charles was there. Charles could leave the institution anytime he wanted to. He would help him.

Lester let anger fuel him as he paddled back, but his throbbing finger reminded him not to let his hands linger. He didn't want another bite.

As he drew nearer the shore, he felt something like the pounding of a drum vibrating his belly through the water. He looked around thinking there must be a motorboat on the pond somewhere, but he was alone. The thumping smoothed to a steady thrum. The water seemed to vibrate.

A fish jumped in front of him, and another one to his left.

Lester paddled faster. He was nearly to the dock.

Only feet away, Lester pulled his hands in and let the raft coast, steadying himself to grab it.

A cry from shore shattered the nervous silence and made Lester jump.

Samantha?

She ran toward the lake, from the direction she and Rick had gone. Her shirt was off, her breasts bouncing with each stride.

He got drunk and raped her, Lester thought. A savage voice in his head, not his brother's this time, said, *she deserved it*!

He waited for Rick to come from the darkness behind her, but Rick didn't follow her. A sleek tan figure flew from the narrow, tree-lined road and landed on the moonlit ground. It chased her, and before she made another dozen steps, launched itself onto her back and took her down.

The mountain lion swiped at her back, and Samantha twisted under it, shrieking her pain. The giant cat shrieked in return, a strangely unnatural sound, and lunged, fixing its jaws over the back of her head.

Lester heard the crunch of bone, and Samantha's struggle ended.

The mountain lion gave her a shake for good measure,

then released her. It did not feed. It abandoned her body and turned its head Lester's way.

Lester found his voice and screamed as his raft bumped the dock.

The cat let loose another strange cry and streaked toward the pond.

Lester screamed again and pushed himself away from the dock, paddling at the water furiously. The water around him boiled with jumping fish, but he ignored them. Fish bites seemed much less intimidating now.

The giant cat leapt onto the dock but skidded to a stop before reaching the end. It growled, watching Lester as he put more distance between them. It didn't follow him out, as though its fear of water outweighed its desire to kill, and as it paced at the end of the dock, Lester saw the big cat was in bad shape. One glowing feline eye watched him as he moved farther away from shore, but the other was gone.

The mountain lion stopped pacing and settled at the end of the dock, still watching him. There was a great bloody hole in its chest, and its ribs showed through its fur, as if it hadn't eaten in a very long time.

At last, Lester quit paddling and rolled onto his back, panting. His arms ached, his chest hurt, and he was more frightened than he had ever been. Despite what Samantha had done to him ... he felt horrible about how she'd died. He glanced over to where she lay, the mountain lion's final, brutal shake had flipped her onto her back. Her skirt was bunched up at her waist, and her front was dirty from her tumble in the dirt, but untouched by the mountain lion's claws. Even dead, she was hot.

He felt the breeze against his prick again and felt a twist of shame that didn't quite kill his lust.

He forced himself to look away and found a fish flopping on the raft's warped wood inches away.

The smell of the thing hit him as he faced it, making his gut clench. Its mouth gulped air, its gills hung in loose flaps. Pondweed hung from the empty sockets where its little fishy eyes should have been. Most of its flesh was gone, and Lester saw a knot of blackened, slimy guts behind exposed ribs.

It flopped again, landing a few inches closer to him.

Lester slapped it back into the water with a cry of disgust.

His bitten finger throbbed with fresh pain, and he brought it up to his face, resisting the urge to stick it in his mouth and suck away the pain.

The finger had gone a light shade of blue to the first knuckle, and it was swelling. The skin around the bite was black, and puss trickled from it like yellow tears.

"Oh god, oh god, oh god," he said, holding the finger close to his face. "Oh god, oh god …"

Lester fainted.

———

He awoke with a jerk as something jabbed him in the side, and screamed when he saw what it was. He'd drifted close to the shore at the other side of Campbell's Pond, coming to rest against a tangle of exposed tree roots. They poked out of the water, scraping against the side of the raft. Collapsed against them was the half-exposed body of a long dead moose. Mostly bones, with scraps of hide draped over it in spots, the snout of its skull was wedged between two thick roots. Its wide antlers stuck out over the edge of the raft. A gentle wave pushed him closer, and they jabbed him again.

A single glowing green eye stared at him from the brush up the bank, and a growl made the hair on his neck stand.

He grabbed the protruding antlers and pushed himself back into the open water.

The green eye disappeared, and Lester heard the brush rustling as the mountain lion moved from its spot, prowling the shore of the pond.

Waiting for him.

Lester wondered how patient a mountain lion could be.

It looked half dead already, maybe more than half dead. Maybe he could wait it out. He certainly had enough meat on his bones to sustain him, and when he got thirsty enough, he was surrounded by water.

He looked around at the weed-choked, muddy water.

The fish had given up trying to board his raft. They'd quit jumping around him too.

He paddled farther out, stopping only when his bitten hand began to throb with greater pain. He brought it to his face, the blue hue had spread past his wrist, and the swelling had moved to his other fingers. The black spot had also grown, and the fingernail on his middle finger had fallen off. He grimaced and lowered it.

The night air had grown very hot, very humid. Lester wiped sweat from his brow with his good hand and stared at the water. It was cool, inviting. He stuck his feet in the water and sighed with relief. He thought of letting himself slip into the water, just for a moment, just to cool himself off before the fish came back, but Samantha's words came back to him.

They found headstones when they were looking for that boy, she'd said, and though that might have been bullshit, he didn't quite dare to go in and chance finding the head-stones for himself.

He had a clear image of an old leaning stone surrounded by clinging vine-like strands of weed.

Here I lay all broken hearted –

Although I'm dead, life's only started.

Lester brought his legs back onto the raft in a near panic and brought his knees to his chest, hugging them.

Thinking about Samantha again, remembering her body, stunning even in death, he couldn't help taking another look. When he looked though, she was gone.

The mountain lion had finally dragged her off. Maybe it was eating her now.

Maybe now was his chance to get away. There wouldn't be another one after the mountain lion finished eating her and came back.

Another image, clear in his mind as the strange snatch of epitaph on the underwater gravestone, arose in his mind. He saw Samantha's dead body, face in the dirt, perfect ass pointed up in the air, while the emaciated one-eyed cat humped it.

You are a fucking pervert, Charles informed him.

Lester blushed.

It was now or never, he decided. If it turned out he was wrong, well, he wouldn't have much time to regret his decision. He wasn't going to last long if he didn't get out. The blue had moved down past his wrist, and his swelling hand was going numb. The middle finger had split, but he couldn't feel that at all anymore.

Some kind of weird infection, maybe blood poisoning.

It would kill him long before he had a chance to starve.

He scanned the shore again as far as he could see, and he could see much better now that dawn was coming. The mountain lion did not show itself.

Steeling himself, Lester paddled toward shore.

He heard it before he saw it. A loud purring sound announced the return of the mountain lion. It stalked lazily down the dock and settled itself at the end. It growled once, but the growl sounded more like a spoken word. Not English, but something older. Something forgotten.

"No!" Lester shouted. Somewhere close by a bird squawked and exploded into flight.

"Yes," the giant cat growled, and its cleft upper lip curved into an eerie caricature of a human smile.

"Lester," Samantha said, coming from the trees behind the mountain lion. "Have you ever been fucked in a cemetery?"

She stepped onto the dock, giggling, and patted the mountain lion's head as she paused before the water. She unbuttoned her torn miniskirt and pushed it down her hips, letting it fall over her feet, then dove into the water.

Conflicting emotions sped Lester's heart as she surfaced and swam toward him: fear, revulsion, and lust. Her breasts bobbed above the water for a moment, and she slid beneath the surface again.

He fell back onto his elbows, panting, on the verge of passing out again, and saw her hands break the water.

They grasped the edge of the raft, and she lifted herself out.

Lust won out as she slid onto the raft, crawling toward him. He sighed as her cold, wet flesh glided over his, shuddered as she pressed into him.

The mountain lion purred, lapped at a bloody paw.

The fish went into a frenzy around the raft, breaking the water and splashing them.

"Have you ever been fucked by the dead?" Her cold hand found his penis, guided it, and with a hungry groan, she impaled herself on him.

Awake again, watchful, Lester hid under cover of pondweed and muddy water. The open grave was like a bed, partially filled over the years by silt, it was still deep enough to admit his bulk.

He watched the surface of Campbell's Pond.

People had quit coming to this place, but they always forgot. They always came back eventually.

Lester, Samantha, and the others would wait until then, and if their bodies rotted away before other people came, the thing that had resurrected them would find another way.

It always had.

DAKOTA

90 days.

"Momma, can I see my grave today?"

June flinched at the question, but recovered her composure quickly, setting Dakota's breakfast tray across her lap and turning away. She felt the familiar burn of tears pushing behind her eyes, felt the halted breathing that would disintegrate into sobs if she didn't stop it quickly. Taking bracing, measured breaths, she fussed with Dakota's bedspread, smoothing it until she could distinguish her daughter's thin legs from the folds and wrinkles.

Her girl was withering away, and June could not squash the persistent fear that she would soon begin to vanish, one piece at a time.

When the burning behind her eyes eased, she turned to face Dakota.

"I don't know what you're talking about." She helped

Dakota sit up and propped pillows behind her. "What kind of juice do you want?"

Dakota pushed scrambled eggs across her plate with her fork, frowning. "I'm not hungry. I heard you talking to Grandma last night. You guys got me a spot at Grove Cemetery."

Since her terminal diagnosis, Dakota had grown increasingly morbid, curious about her illness, but somehow indifferent at the same time, as if her approaching death was a new television show that she was still making up her mind about, to see if it was worth staying up late for. On the subject of death in its generalities, she seemed enthusiastic, collecting macabre anecdotes and stories the way she'd once collected dolls.

Dakota gave the eggs an unenthusiastic jab and lifted the fork to her mouth. Her pale skin beaded with sweat, and her whole body seemed to tremble as she brought the fork up and took the tiniest lump of egg into her mouth. Chewing the egg seemed a great task, swallowing it pure torture.

"I'm not hungry," she said again, dropping the fork to her plate.

"I didn't mean for you to hear that. I thought you were sleeping."

"I'm sorry, Momma. I didn't mean to eavesdrop." She stared through her bedside window for a moment, and June saw the weakest of smiles touch her lips. "Can I go? I want to see it."

"Why?" June's frustration broke through her delicate facade, and she cursed herself silently for letting it happen. She suspected, not for the first time, that Dakota enjoyed breaking her down. "Why would you want to see that?"

Dakota faced her again, her smile wider, mischievous, dimpling her hollow cheeks. Then it was gone. The morning light played across her pale scalp, making it look almost like bone.

"I just want to go out," Dakota said. "I'm feeling better today, really."

June almost said no, but could not force the word out. "Not today," she said finally.

"I'm not hungry," Dakota said, pushing the tray away and turning back to the window.

Damnit, June thought. *I don't know why I play this game with her. She always wins.*

"All right, if I say yes, will you eat?"

Dakota frowned at the eggs again, but said, "Yes."

"Juice?"

"Apple."

Dakota took another bite, and struggled to get it down. For a moment June was sure her daughter would lose the fight, but her stomach seemed to have accepted the food, if only grudgingly.

When June returned with her juice, Dakota's fork lay on the plate again. "I can't finish them, Momma."

"It's okay, baby." June hid her disappointment behind a false smile as she swapped a glass for the half-eaten breakfast. "You did good."

Dakota seemed more interested in the juice than she had food, taking two long swallows before coming up for air.

"Do you need your pills this morning?"

Dakota shook her head. "It doesn't hurt today."

She showed no obvious signs of discomfort, but June knew she could be bluffing. Dakota had lived with pain for long enough to learn to hide it when she wanted too. If it wasn't too bad.

The pills made her sleepy, and she didn't want to sleep today. She wanted to go out. Dakota was on another of her morbid quests. She wanted to see her gravesite.

Dakota's therapist said her morbid fascinations and quests were a coping method, her way of coming to terms with death, and perfectly normal. June didn't know if it was normal or not but decided to trust the professional. She indulged Dakota's new fancies, within reason, even if her gruesome stories and horror movies gave June nightmares.

"Do you need help dressing?"

Dakota didn't answer at once. She handed the glass to June and pushed the bed tray down past her knees. Slowly, carefully, she drew her knees up and pulled her bed spread off. Her legs were sad shapes under her gown, large lumpy kneecaps, her legs like sticks. She seemed stronger than usual though. She swung her legs over the side of the bed and put her feet on the floor.

"No," she said at last. "I can do it."

June walked downstairs and waited, listening for the sound of the bell that would mean her daughter needed her, but not really expecting it. Dakota didn't like to ask for help if she could do things on her own.

The bell didn't sound, and a half hour later Dakota came down the steps, grasping the handrail with one hand, carrying her ever-present black notebook in the other. June had asked Dakota several times what it was she wrote in the book, but Dakota never answered, and she never let the book out of her sight.

They had to pull over once on the way to Grove Cemetery, Dakota shoving the door open at the curb and throwing her breakfast up into the gutter.

The morning's brief battle was over, the small bit of sustenance Dakota had taken was lost.

Dakota seemed untroubled, but June fought tears again as they continued to the cemetery. She watched her daughter wither day by day, growing weaker while the thing inside her grew stronger, larger, and continued to eat her alive.

They arrived at the cemetery, and June saw a canopy erected over an open grave. There was no crowd, no somber procession of cars winding through Grove's central thoroughfare.

June parked along the street and led Dakota to the spot.

The headstone next to Dakota's plot read: *Joseph Miller – dedicated father – loving husband.* June scanned the dates and saw he'd lived well into his seventies. She had no pity for him.

For a while Dakota only stood, staring at the perfect grass at her feet. Then she knelt, slowly, and June could tell the pain had returned. Dakota sat in the grass, smoothed her dress out over her legs, and lay down, crossing her arms over her thin chest.

That was more than June could stand. The tears that had threatened to come all morning finally did. She cried silently, her grief was always silent when Dakota was near, and turned away.

"It's okay, Momma," Dakota said. "This isn't so bad. I think I'll like it here."

---

80 days.

June slept alone. Michael had not come home that night, and she'd wondered as she began to drift if this was the time he wouldn't come home at all. She knew the time was coming, she knew he would leave them. The only question was when.

Her husband wasn't a bad man. He still loved Dakota, might even still love June. He wasn't the man June thought she had married though. He was weak, and as Dakota's health worsened, he became weaker still. Some nights he couldn't handle it at all.

A soft keening woke June from her half-sleep, a sound she had first taken for the whining of a neighborhood dog. It came from upstairs, from Dakota's room.

June threw her robe on and navigated the dark halls and staircase, stopping behind Dakota's closed door to steady herself. Seeing her daughter in pain was nothing new, but it wasn't something she thought she'd ever get used to.

She pushed the door open and saw Dakota's face in the glow of her nightlight, pale, crinkled in pain, eyes closed. Still sleeping despite the pain. The girl whimpered.

June slid Dakota's top dresser drawer open and found the right bottle by feel. There were a half dozen bottles in the drawer, and June knew them each by touch, by their width, height, and placement. She scanned the label to be sure, then twisted the cap off and shook a pill into her palm.

Dakota kept a bottle of water on her bedside dresser. June set the pain pill next to it, and smoothed the bedspread to sit down.

She pressed her hands to her mouth to stifle an involuntary scream.

She couldn't find Dakota's legs.

"Mom?" Dakota rolled over, her thin arms scrambling free of the twisted sheets, and her legs stretched out from her body, where she'd been holding them. "What's wrong?" She groaned again as a fresh wave of pain hit, and rolled back onto her side, clutching her knees to her chest again.

"Nothing," June said. "Here, sit up." June helped her up and cradled her while she took her pain medication.

She held Dakota until the girl slept again. Held her until the medication went to work, Dakota's crying stopped and her contracted limbs relaxed.

June went back to bed but did not sleep.

Dakota woke once again later in the day, crying in frustration and anger. She'd slept too long, too deep, and wet her bed. That was another thing she didn't like about her pain pills.

June bathed her, changed her sheets, and made a light lunch that went uneaten.

Dakota went to sleep again early that afternoon, and did not wake until the next morning.

70 days.

It was a good day. Dakota had been having them more often the past few weeks. She slept well the night before and woke up cheerful. If there was any pain, she hid it well. Best of all, Dakota had developed a taste for yogurt. Her typical meal of yogurt and juice hardly seemed like a meal at all to June, but she *was* eating, and gaining weight again.

She was able to spend time with friends too, they had come earlier that day, then gone home for lunch, but as June carried Dakota's lunch up to her room, she heard her daughter talking, and wondered if one of her friends had come back unnoticed.

June pressed her ear to the door and listened for a moment.

"You're a bitch, and I hate you." Dakota spoke in a neutral, almost conversational voice. "I wish you would just go away and die."

"Dakota!" June pushed the door open and stopped in the doorway. Dakota sat at her vanity, facing the mirror. Her eyes flicked up to June's reflection, and she blushed.

"What on Earth are you doing?"

Dakota looked at her hands, folded in her lap. "I was talking to Lumpy."

She tapped her stomach.

"I had an idea I wanted to try," she said, sounding nervous, but also hopeful. "I gave it a name, and I talk to it. Like talking nice to plants to make them grow, you know? But the other way around."

Dakota smiled. "I think it's working."

"Don't," June shouted. She didn't mean to shout, but it happened anyway. Hating herself for the sunken look on Dakota's face, but unable to stop herself, she continued. "It doesn't work that way, Dakota, and you know it. I don't ever want to hear you talk that way again."

She strode into the room and set Dakota's juice box and yogurt in front of her.

"I'm not hungry."

"Don't start that again. You're going to eat."

Dakota looked up at June, her eyes wide, shocked. "I'm sorry, Momma."

June couldn't take that look. She turned and walked from the room, down the stairs, into her own room, shutting the door and taking a seat on the edge of her bed. For a while she just sat there, hands clenched into fists in her lap.

What did I just do?

She did her breathing exercise, watching her clock while she did so, and when five minutes passed, she was calm again.

She needed to apologize.

Halfway up the stairs, she heard Dakota choking, and broke into a run.

She found Dakota on the floor by her bed, on her hands and knees, her back arched as she convulsed. Her face was a startling violet shade. Then she vomited, spraying her unwanted lunch across her carpet.

Her breath came again in a great gasp as June dropped down beside her.

"Oh god, baby, I'm so sorry!" She lifted Dakota from the floor and rocked her thin, trembling body. "You're okay now. Just breathe."

"I'm sorry, Momma," Dakota said, and burst into tears. "I tried, I really did."

"I know, baby. I know."

That was Dakota's last good day.

---

60 days.

Michael was gone now. He never actually left them, but the weekend trip he'd taken was now going on a full week, and he had not called to say when he would be back home.

His supervisor had called on Monday to ask where he was, and when he'd be back, to which she could not give an answer. His manager had called on Tuesday to warn that if he didn't show up Wednesday, not to bother coming on Thursday. On Wednesday, there was no call.

"I don't know what I'm going to do, Mom." She kept her voice low, her hand cupped over the phone's speaker. "There's no insurance now. I can't afford her treatments."

"I don't want them anymore."

June spun in her chair, startled. The phone dropped from her hand.

Dakota stood at the kitchen entrance, leaning against the wall. Painfully thin and pale. The thing in her belly had grown so large its shape now showed through her shirt.

June heard her mother's voice calling from the floor, shouting in concern, but ignored it.

"I don't care about the money, baby. We'll figure something out. I promise!"

"But I *don't want* them. They won't help, Momma, they just make me feel sicker. I don't want them anymore."

Dakota turned and walked toward the stairs to her room, and June found herself frozen, wanting to go to her, wanting to pick up the phone and quiet her mother.

"I'm going to die, Momma. Just let me die."

50 days.

They had flown to Seattle that morning for another round of tests, and by five that evening, facing Dr. Wilson over his too-tidy desk, June was ready to put the day to rest, ready for Dakota's last flight home.

Dakota was with the staff therapist, a young woman fresh out of her residency. Dakota was very fond of her, and June suspected Dr. Wilson had sent Dakota to her after his tests to keep her occupied so they could speak alone.

"Are you sure that is a decision you trust your eleven-year-old to make?" Doctor Wilson sounded neither stern nor surprised. He sounded resigned.

June waited for his suggestion that they give the treatments another chance, but he remained silent, paused over markings he'd been making on his clipboard.

"Yes," she said. "She's the only one who has the right to make it."

June expected him to give her that condescending doctor's look, a flick of the eyes as sharp as twin razors, over the top of his reading glasses and down his long, narrow nose, a thin-lipped frown for emphasis. She expected him to call her response to his question rank and dangerous sentimentality, to call her a horrible mother for letting her daughter give up.

He did not give her the look, did not question her decision, merely closed his eyes for the briefest moment, and nodded.

"I understand."

He set his clipboard aside and opened Dakota's folder, shuffling through papers, reading words he undoubtedly already had memorized. Taking too long.

"What is it?"

"Dakota's treatments weren't as effective as I'd hoped they would be." He closed the folder and startled June by slapping it down on his desk. He pulled his glasses off and wiped at his eyes with the back of a hand as he folded them. "The growth in her original tumor has not slowed, and the cancer is spreading. It's moved into her chest, neck, and her brain."

June gripped the armrests of her chair until her fingers hurt, keeping a determinately straight face. "How long?"

"A few months," he said. "The spread won't change anything at this point. The mass in her brain is surprisingly large, but the original tumor ..."

Lumpy, June thought, and shivered.

"... will kill her first." his voice broke, and he covered it with a forced cough. He picked up the clipboard again, holding it in front of his face as though scanning it. "Pardon me. The original tumor will kill her first. We could buy more time, most likely, if we continued the treatments."

"No more treatments," June said.

Dr. Wilson coughed again, and without lowering the clipboard, said, "I am very sorry."

June found Dakota waiting for her three doors down, playing Candyland with the therapist. They were beyond the need for therapy now, they all knew there was nothing left to say. Dakota was as well-adjusted as she would ever be. They were just killing time.

"It's time to go, baby."

"Momma, I don't want you to call me that anymore. Call me Dakota."

"Okay, Dakota," June said. "We have to go now. We'll miss our flight."

The therapist sighed.

"Well, I guess Dakota wins," she said, removing the game pieces and folding the board to put away. "Skunked again."

Dakota giggled and reached across the desk. They hugged, and the woman kissed the top of Dakota's pink headscarf.

"Thanks for playing. It was fun, even though you beat the pants off me."

"Goodbye," Dakota said. She paused at the door, as if to say something else, then stepped into the hallway without looking back.

As June stepped out, closing the door behind her, she heard a sob from inside the office.

The ride to the airport was bleak, rainy. When they reached the terminal, Dakota was soaked and shivering.

Flying over Seattle for the last time, Dakota stared out the window. "Seattle's pretty from up here."

June said nothing. She didn't know what to say.

Two hours later they were home, Dakota tucked in and sleeping. June lay in a recliner next to her bed, warm and comfortable under her own blanket, but sleepless.

She had known for a long time, but there had always been some hope of remission or reprieve. Hope had died that night in Dr. Wilson's office. Soon Dakota would die too.

For June, that moment had truly been the beginning of the end.

With Dakota snoring slightly in her chemical induced sleep, June gave in to her despair and let herself grieve.

---

40 days.

They were at the graveyard again, Dakota lying over the place where she would one day rest forever. But she was smiling, peaceful, happy, so June was happy too.

A butterfly roamed low over the grass, then danced across her face, tickling her cheeks.

Dakota laughed and rolled in the grass, like she'd done on trips to the park when she was younger and healthier.

More butterflies came, dancing across her face, and she laughed harder, whipping her head from side to side.

Her headscarf came loose, slid to the grass beside her, and waves of baby fine blonde hair fell onto her face, shoulders, and the ground.

Dakota's hair had never been blonde. Before her treatments had taken it away, her hair had been a thick, rich brown.

A cloud drifted across the sun, throwing Dakota into shadow, stripping the illusion away.

There were no butterflies, but a swarm of fat, black hornets, piercing her over and over again while she thrashed in the graveyard grass. The glowing illusion of health the sun had given her was gone, her body was withered, her face sunken and gaunt, her skin gray.

The blonde hair had turned gray too, and moved through the grass like a million fine tentacles, seeking the soil below, and burrowing into it.

Pulling Dakota down, into her grave.

June woke with a gasp, and found Dakota rolling beneath her sheets, clutching her head.

The graveyard had been a dream, but her daughter's pain was real.

"It hurts, Momma! Oh, God, it hurts!" Tears streamed from clenched eyes, and June saw bruises already forming where Dakota's thin fingers pressed the flesh of her scalp and temples.

June scrambled through the top drawer, found the pain pills, and struggled the cap off. She tipped the bottle over her shaking palm, and they spilled out.

For a moment everything else fell away, Dakota's screams of pain, the throbbing of her back, which hurt worse every time she slept in the chair next to her daughter's bed. There were only the pills, sitting benign in her cupped palm.

I could end her pain now, June thought. *I could end our pain and let her sleep forever.*

Without realizing she'd even moved, June found herself standing over Dakota, lowering her fistful of pills over her daughter's mouth.

Her stolen senses returned, washing over her in a film of icy sweat. The reality of what she was on the brink of doing slammed her back to her seat like something physical. She forced her fist open, and the pills spilled across her lap.

"Momma, please!"

"I'm coming, Dakota."

She plucked a single pill from her lap, leaned forward, and pressed it between Dakota's lips.

Enough to ease her daughter's pain, if not to end it.

---

30 days.

The constant headaches had relented over the past few days, and as her level of pain decreased, Dakota became more her old self. June couldn't call it a good day, but it was better, at least. It would have to be good enough, she supposed.

"Good afternoon, sunshine." She was happy to find Dakota awake, writing in her notebook.

Dakota looked up, smiled. "Hi, Momma." She made a final scribble, then closed the notebook and stuffed it beneath her pillow.

"You ever going to show me what you're writing in that?"

Dakota shrugged. "Sure, someday."

"Let's go out back for a while. I have your hammock and umbrella set up, and I'm brewing sun tea. You need some fresh air."

Dakota grinned and nodded. "Okay."

June carried her downstairs, careful not to bump her into the walls. She bruised so easily now.

June scanned the kitchen as they passed through it, hoping she had not left anything behind that might give the surprise away. Everything was tidy, everything as it should be.

The sliding glass door to the back patio was open, a breeze teased the curtain. June nudged it aside and stepped out with Dakota in her arms.

"Surprise!"

For a few seconds Dakota scanned the back yard, shocked. All of her friends were there, their neighbors, her mom's friends, standing around the trees that supported her hammock. The limbs were decorated with a hundred paper chains, and a banner hung between them.

We Love You Dakota!

Their television sat on the picnic table, its screen a frozen image of her favorite actors face.

June pulled the VCR remote from her pocket and hit play.

"I'm sorry I couldn't make it kiddo, but your mom told me this is a very special day, so I wanted to be there for you in spirit …" The view panned away from his face, and Dakota saw other faces she knew from television, all smiling, cheering, shouting her name.

"You forgot, didn't you," June whispered in her ear.

"Yeah," Dakota whispered back. "But you didn't. Thanks, Momma."

"Happy birthday, kiddo."

20 days.

June brought Dakota her morning juice. There was no yogurt now, she could no longer stomach it. She set the cup on her nightstand next to the ever-present bottle of water.

"Dakota, darling."

No response. Dakota did not stir.

She bent lower, whispered in Dakota's ear. "Dakota?"

Nothing.

"Baby!" She shook the bed. She didn't dare put hands on her to shake her awake, she bruised so easily.

Dakota's head rolled on the pillow, but her eyes did not open.

June sat down in the bedside recliner, put her hands over her face, sighed. She didn't have the strength to cry yet. That would come later.

It's over. Her pain is over.

She sat like that for a few minutes, then looking between her fingers at Dakota's still, expressionless face, saw a corner of her black notebook peeking out from under the pillow. She reached for it with a shaking hand.

"No, Momma." A whisper, soft as a baby's breath. "Not yet."

June cried then. She cried in guilt for the relief she'd felt a moment earlier, guilt for the spark of selfish joy that Dakota's whispered voice had brought.

She cried for Dakota, whose pain lingered on.

10 days.

Sometimes June had good dreams, dreams of what might have been. Dreams of a future where Dakota had never been sick.

All of her hopes for Dakota's life that had not quite died.

Rushing down a hospital corridor, filled with an unfamiliar kind of anxiety. Not fear, but excitement.

There had been good news, fantastic news, not just a second chance for the little girl who was supposed to have died, but a second chance for a child who should have never been born at all.

June turned onto the Maternity Ward, passed a dozen familiar faces, smiling from pressed white uniforms at the nurse's station.

She didn't ask which room was her daughter's. She knew.

She found Doctor Wilson blocking the door, Dakota's black notebook in hand, looking grim. "I have to tell you, I don't believe a word of it. I want a second opinion."

June shoved him aside and rushed into Dakota's room.

Dakota's room.

She lay on her own bed, her emaciated body lost under the sheets, propped on pillows. Clearly dead.

Smiling.

A nurse, Dakota's Seattle therapist, fussed with something bundled in ash-covered rags, made cooing sounds at it, then bent and laid it in Dakota's withered arms.

"Grandma's here," Dakota said, her wide, dusty eyes turning to the thing in rags. "Come on, grandma, come see my baby. Come meet Lumpy."

Her dead hand brushed the rags away from its face.

Another of June's un-surrendered hopes died.

The last day.

June brought Dakota's morning juice, and paused beside her empty bed. A moment of confusion turned to dread as she spotted a bony foot resting on the carpet in front of her chair, and dread turned to cold acceptance as she turned and found her daughter slumped in the recliner, her pink headscarf crooked, her hollow cheek resting on June's pillow.

Her crossed arms held her black notebook against her still chest.

Gently, June lifted her, cradled her, and sat down. Silent tears streaked her face as she rocked Dakota, opened the notebook, and read her last words.

Dakota's last words.

As Dakota's flame had burnt, flickered, and died, so had the summer. The spring had seemed too short, a blur of mindless, grim activity. June kept busy, first with Dakota's funeral arrangements, then accepting the endless condolences of family and friends.

As fall arrived, June finally found the time to grieve properly. She visited Dakota alone for the first time since the burial.

She stood before Dakota's headstone, the tattered black notebook in her hand, reading and re-reading the poem, Dakota's last words, on the clean marble slab.

Momma, don't cry for me – I was never afraid.
  We walked through the dark hand in hand.
  I am not gone – we have just moved along.
  Different forks in the path.

June cleared leaves off the grass and sat down. A wild *Felicia* had grown near the headstone since her last visit, a tense hour spent in the company of her mother-in-law and soon to be ex-husband, and the flower's bold pink blooms brought to mind Dakota's favorite headscarf.

June picked one of those blooms, placed it between the pages of Dakota's notebook, and sat, silent and still until dusk. Sharing a quiet moment with her daughter, reading from the notebook. Dakota's thoughts and lessons.

It was time for her to live again, or to try, anyway. Time to move on and focus on the future instead of the past, but she would never forget.

Never.

Before she moved on though, she would build one last memory, spend one last peaceful evening alone with Dakota.

A NIGHT IN THE BLUES

Lost in the woods is bad, even a ten-year-old city girl like Taylor knew that. She had a cousin who was lost once on a field trip to Dworshak reservoir in Idaho, and only for a few hours. They found him lying behind a rotting deadfall a stone's throw from the main trail, curled up and crying. He'd even wet his pants. Taylor's mom had gone on about it during the flight from El Paso, Texas, to Washington. It was her mother's well-meant attempt to frighten Taylor into caution.

Lost in the woods was bad.

Lost in The Blues was worse.

She knew people got lost in The Blues sometimes, and sometimes they stayed lost forever. From her window seat in the sky above them, the Blue Mountains stretched from horizon to horizon.

Taylor had visited her Uncle Niko's cabin in The Blues during the last three summer vacations and had never dared to let it out of sight when she was outside alone. She'd never been lost before.

She was lost now.

A brief daydream while wandering the trail by the pond, a moment's inattention, and she was lost, big time. The trail was gone, swallowed by encroaching trees and underbrush, and the sky vanished in a canopy of green.

Taylor knew she should stay put and wait. Uncle Niko and Mom would come looking for her soon if she didn't go back. Her feet were impatient though, bent to spend their nervous energy, and she hadn't walked *that far*.

I can find the trail back, she thought.

She tried to backtrack, searching for her own footprints on the mossy ground and through the crushed undergrowth, found what she thought was her trail, and followed it.

Taylor walked until the setting sun broke through the boughs above. The muscles in her legs ached, on the verge of cramping, her back hurt, sweat stung brush scratches on her face, neck, and arms. The mountain air had grown chilly.

Instead of finding the trail back to the cabin she found herself in a stony clearing, facing the edge of a great gray and green abyss. The gray of mountain stone, the green of the Blue Mountain's varied flora.

She crept to the edge in small, cautious steps, and looked down. It was a near straight drop, maybe thirty feet to a stone ledge below, a narrow one, and beyond that a distance so great the bottom was nothing but an indistinct blur. The strength seemed sapped from her, her legs felt weak as twigs. A sudden gust of cold wind nudged her, almost pushed her over.

Taylor let loose a small scream, tried to run backward, away from the abyss, then tripped, falling on her ass, scraping her legs and the palms of her hands. She backed to the edge of the forest that way, an awkward crab crawl, pushing with her feet and hands. When she felt the rough bark of a dead-fallen pine against her back she stopped, lay down on the spongy carpet of moss, and cried.

Are they looking for me yet?

It was near dark. She supposed they were.

"Mommy!"

Her shout echoed back to her from the canyon at the edge of the clearing, but she thought the forest would muffle it in the other direction, the direction that counted. Unless they were close, they probably wouldn't hear her.

"Uncle Niko!"

No reply but the expected echo. It taunted Taylor, told her she was as alone as a little girl could be. Just her and The Blues, and she was so small.

Then her shout echoed again, and Taylor realized the echoed voice was not hers that time. It was a boy's voice, the words not quite right, the vowels a little too rounded. A bad mimic.

"Hello," she said, and was still, silent, awaiting reply.

"Elohoa," not quite the word she'd said, but the same plaintive tone. Not from the woods around or behind her, this time, but from that wide canyon in the mountains before her.

"Who are you?"

"Ho-r-u?" Not just a disembodied voice drifting out of

the canyon. It was closer now. Whoever it was, was just over the edge, coming up.

"Who are you?" She tried to shout it, but her voice was too weak.

No response, just a grunt of effort and the sound of shifting and falling stones.

Then the top of a head crested, an explosion of black hair. A twisted hand followed, digging at the stony soil.

Then she saw his face. It was without shape or definition. A mouth with no lips, black teeth gnashing at the air.

Taylor screamed, found her feet and ran into the woods. She ran until the sound of the boy's mimicked scream was as lost as she was, then sat on the needle-covered ground, back against the rough skin of one of a million pines, panting. She rubbed at a cramp in her calf. A deep stitch pulled at her side.

She waited for the sound of a voice, any voice, hoping the voice would be her mom's, or Uncle Niko's, afraid it would not be. She wanted to call out but didn't quite dare.

She was afraid of the twisted mimic she might hear if she did.

Terror is exhausting, and the adrenaline in her blood spent far too quickly. Taylor waited for a long time, still and listening for any sound beyond the nocturnal soundtrack of The Blues. There was nothing but fear and fancy, and as she slipped into sleep it was the fancy that followed her down.

Taylor found herself sitting in her favorite easy chair, the one in the cabin's main room facing the dead fireplace. It was summer, for her The Blues were all about summer, and a comfortable mountain night chill brushed her cheeks. She held a piece of cinnamon toast in one hand, dipped it into the mug of hot cocoa in her other. Her favorite late hour snack.

Uncle Niko sat across from her, a chair to the right of the fireplace. He was telling her his favorite Blues horror story. She realized it was the summer before, a quiet summer, a good summer. It was Niko's story about the family from Seattle who came to The Blues for a week of hiking and huckleberry picking years before, and had never been seen again.

"A whole family?" She nibbled at the cocoa dripping toast, sipped from the hot mug. "How does a whole family get lost?"

Uncle Niko tapped pipe ash into the cold fireplace, adding to the remains of warm autumn nights long gone.

"In The Blues," he said, his light Finnish accent spicing his words, "it is very easy."

A cold wind wafted through an open window, coaxing a shiver. Uncle Niko seemed not to care. He puffed at his old pipe, his words coming through smoke that looked like small clouds.

"I came to this country when I was a little boy. I know this place very well, but I rarely leave the trails, and then only if I have a good reason. The Blues are beautiful, but dangerous. They cloud your good senses," he elaborated. "They draw you in if you let 'em. Draw you in and swallow you whole."

"But a whole family," she challenged. "A whole family can't get lost on a trail."

She didn't exactly doubt him, only wanted to keep him

talking, keep the story moving. Taylor liked his stories, and the sound of his voice when he told them.

"Ooo-ah-ooo," he said. He leaned toward her, his face breaking through the hanging smoke like an apparition. He grimaced at her, teeth black and rotting. His eyes looked funny, buggy and discolored.

Taylor dropped her half-eaten toast. The cocoa mug shook in her tiny fist.

"What?"

"*Waah!*" A twist of tongue poked from his mouth-hole, tasted the air. Then he lunged for her, reaching with fingers like bent and broken twigs.

Taylor awoke in a blur of panic and pain, expecting the boy to be there, biting and choking, the cause of her sudden pain, but he was not. It was a cat, a big cat, its tufted ears tilted back like horns while it nipped at her ankle. Not a cougar, she would already be dead if it were, but a bobcat.

She screamed in pain and fright, kicking at it. The cat flinched away from her, ears flattened, hackles raised, and made a sound that was half hiss, half moan. Its muzzle was a rich liquid red. It was deathly scrawny, hungry.

"Go away!" Taylor cradled her torn leg and sobbed in terror.

It didn't go away, but didn't pounce. It crouched, watching her with glowing green eyes the size of half-dollars.

Taylor knew something of The Blues wildlife from her Uncle Niko's countless stories. It was strange for a bobcat to attack a human, even if it was half starved. Strange, but not unheard of. It must have seen her sleeping and thought she was dead already. Now it had tasted her blood and seemed to like it. She was a very small human after all.

Taylor felt around with her free hand, found a stone half buried in the needle-littered dirt and pulled it free. "Go away," she shouted, and threw it.

The stone flew high and wide. The bobcat cringed away, making itself smaller, and swiped at it as it flew by. Then it turned back to her, pounced forward and clawed at her foot. She kicked at it and it backed off again, giving another low growl.

It backed off again but did not leave.

Taylor moved the hand that cradled her wounded leg. It wasn't as bad as she feared. The flesh was torn and bloody, but she couldn't see bone. She tried to stand, had to push herself up with her hands, and the bleeding leg held. Taylor considered the low boughs of the nearest tree. She could reach them and pull herself up. The cat would climb faster and better than she could though. She took a tentative step away from the tree. Her ripped ankle hurt badly. She took another slow step, looking around for something, anything she could use to defend herself. There was nothing.

Taylor caught the cat's movement in the periphery of her vision, it moved low to the ground, ears laid back against its thick neck, bloody mouth open in a low buzzing growl.

"Get back! Go away." It was only feet away now, and when it lunged the final distance Taylor kicked at it. She missed, over balanced, and cried out as her good ankle twisted underneath her. There as a pop, like the sound of a pine knot exploding in a fire. She hit the dirt hard, eyes already closed, bracing herself for the coming attack.

It didn't happen.

She looked at where it had been. The frightening green eye shine was gone. The bobcat was gone.

Taylor followed the sound of movement through underbrush and saw a boy-shape vanish deeper into the evergreen darkness, the dead bobcat flopping from the crook of one arm.

Even summer nights in The Blues were chilly.

Taylor sat, cold and shivering on a dew-drenched bed of moss for a long time before deciding to walk again. She was tired, but walked anyway, picking her way over the rough ground with the help of a branch she'd broken from one of the smaller pines. It was thin and flimsy, but it worked. She could barely see. The never-ending ceiling of evergreens killed most of her starlight.

She had still not found the trail.

Her ankle, only sprained and not broken she hoped, was in agony. Each step was a new exploration in pain.

The darkness endured, the night would not end.

Though Taylor never saw him, she knew the boy followed. She could hear him occasionally, and she felt him close, always close.

What felt like hours passed, and at last she found something that seemed to be a trail. She followed it to starlight. At the end Taylor found the clearing, and the canyon.

Too tired to cry, she sat down and rested her ankle, then drew a straight line in her mind from where she was to where she thought the cabin was, and followed it.

It'll be morning soon, she thought. Finding her way would be easier in the light.

As she stepped back into the trail, the distant shriek of a cougar sounded, and Taylor wondered if she would be alive when morning came.

She walked, her pace slower than before. The sprained ankle was fat inside the high top of her canvas shoe. Only the pain kept her awake. She rested twice, and each time it took more of her dwindling resolve to rise and walk again. At some point what passed for a trail disappeared.

Taylor continued in as straight of line as was possible through this high mountain jungle, and after another cycle of walking and rest, she found another trail.

This is it, she thought. *The trail to Uncle Niko's cabin.*

Encouraged, Taylor quickened her pace as much as the pain in her ankles, one bitten and one sprained, would allow.

The sun did not rise. The night seemed as never-ending as The Blues. The starlight was better than no light though, and when Taylor stepped into a break in the boughs, into the moonlight again, she let out a little cry of joy. A light fog obscured the path beyond the pines and settled over the pond. A morning fog. She turned her head to the sky and saw the stars were paler, the sky a little lighter. The night was almost over.

Taylor ran to the pond, toward the trail that would take her home, and when she was only feet away her ankle let go. The stick flew from her hand as she went down, disappeared into the layer of fog covering what she'd thought was the pond. But there was no splash, just the faraway sound of wood striking stone as it bounced away.

Not the pond.

"No!" she cried out, pounded the ground like a baby throwing a tantrum, then cried out again as her fist struck stone. She plucked it from the dirt and threw it into the fog as far as she could. No splash.

Not the pond at all. She lay at the edge of the canyon again, the great and hungry mouth of The Blues.

"It's not fair!" she screamed into the canyon, but there was no echo this time. "I just want to go home!"

The cougar's cry, much closer this time, startled another shriek from her. Taylor rolled onto her back, eyes darting everywhere at once, and saw the big cat strut into the clearing. Its head was low to the ground, its eyes locked on hers. It slinked forward slowly, in no hurry, then stopped.

She sensed him before she heard him. The boy.

"Waah," the boy said, though to her or the cougar she could not tell. One crooked claw hand came to rest on her shoulder. The other held a crude spear, like the one she'd used for a walking stick but with the bark peeled off and one end sharpened. The sharp end slanted up toward the sky, the other end was braced against the ground between them.

"Help me," Taylor said.

"Ep," the boy said, his mutilated face pointed to her with its lipless black grin.

The cougar cried out again, and the boy mimicked it with a cry of his own.

The cougar crouched, then leapt, and its sleek blond figure blotted out the sky.

Taylor saw the point of the boy's spear come up.

It pierced the cougar's chest and drove deep before snapping in half.

Taylor screamed as the cougar landed on her, then its weight drove the air from her lungs. For a moment everything went dark. She felt the earth move beneath them as the dead cat's momentum pushed them toward the edge, then over it.

She felt the earth again a few seconds later but could not see it inside the fog. It came hard, tore at her with sharp edges like teeth. She clawed at the dirt to slow her descent. Stones pulled loose as she gripped them, rolled over her, past her, hit something solid below her. She came to a slow rest with them on the narrow ledge.

The pain in her ankle was nuclear, a white agony that stole her other senses, but she could not voice it. She struggled to regain the breath knocked from her. Then the white pain faded to black.

It was hunger that woke Taylor, must have been hunger, because she entered consciousness doubled over, clutching at her empty belly. The pain of her sprained ankle was down to a low throb now, calm embers needing only movement to stoke them again. She waited, grimacing, for the cramps to subside, and when they did Taylor remembered where she was.

She sat up, her back against cold rough stone, and took it in.

She was inside a cave, looking out toward the stone ledge she'd spied from the edge of the cliff before the boy had scared her away.

The boy!

"Hey," she croaked. Her throat was dry. Taylor swallowed and tried again. "Hey! Are you here?"

There was no answer, no imperfect mimic. After a moment she saw why.

The boy, almost a young man and naked but for a scrap of filthy cloth tied around his waist, lay against the cavern wall cross from her. His skin was weathered and leathery brown, every inch of it scarred. His scrawny arms and legs were knotted and bent, as if they'd all been broken and healed badly. His claw hands held one side of his bald and misshapen head, as if trying to hold his brains in. One eye, dusty and drying, watched her. The other was fixed in another direction, a spot on the cavern's ceiling. His head was misshapen, crushed in the long fall. Most of his black teeth were gone.

The cougar was nowhere to be seen, probably dead or dying at the bottom of the canyon.

Taylor cried for the dead boy, a silent thank you. Then she followed the light. She could not stand, so dragged herself to the cave's mouth. She stared up for a moment, knowing there was no way she could climb back up, then crawled back inside.

Taylor knew she should stay put and wait. There was still a chance Uncle Niko and Mom would find her. But in her heart Taylor knew inaction would be death, so she took the only path left to her, deeper into the cave.

She found bones just past the dead boy. Human bones,

adult bones. The boy's family, maybe. They had no power to shock her.

Taylor went on, and soon the light behind her was small. She dragged herself ever deeper into the belly of The Blues, praying it would not lead her into a final, ever-lasting night.

NUMBER 2

I'm a' tell you all a story 'bout a man named Ed,
A simple civil servant trying to earn his daily bread.
One day he was a' workin' at the city cess-lagoon,
And up from the sewage came a' bubbling poo.
Stinky-poo – Icky-poo,
A steamin' heap of Number 2.

This is it, the place I told you about, right over there. That is where it all happened. You see those four ponds at the end of that little dirt road? Those sewage lagoons have been here since I was a kid, went up about the same time the Army Corps of Engineers put Dwarshack Dam in at the mouth of the river's north fork.

My Pa worked for the city of Orofino maintaining these ponds and all the hardware that keeps 'em gurgling and spewing: pumps, the back-up generator and the likes.

He worked that job up until about ten years ago. Then I replaced him, so he could retire.

Now, do you see the one on the far right, the one with the big fountain blowing foam and gray-water into the air? That's the one, Lagoon Number 2, solid waste removal. That fountain is fed from a turbine at the bottom, it cycles gray-water twenty-four hours a day and passes the *clean* water through ducts to the other ponds for purification.

Now most around here would call me loony if they heard me say this, so I'll thank you not to repeat it, but these lagoons, Number 2 in particular, have as much history in them as the courthouse or the fair grounds. Everyone who lives in Orofino leaves a bit of themselves here, anyone who has lived here in the past half century. You take a dump anywhere in Orofino and it ends up right here.

This is where flushed goldfish and turtles go.

This is where old tampons and toilet paper go.

I've seen things in there that would make a dog puke.

This is where a little boy named Johnny Butts drowned when I was a kid. He disappeared in Number 2 and never came up again.

The lagoons are a mile or so out of town, where Riverside Avenue turns into Highway 12, and right next to them is Hidden Village. Hidden Village is where I grew up, where I still live. A nice, tidy little trailer park with a population of about two hundred.

I lived in Hidden Village with my Pa. Ma had been

gone since before I was old enough to remember, Pa told me she just up and left one night. I had a handful of friends there, none of them lifelong friends, just kids I used to chum with. One of them was a native boy named Johnny Butts.

Yeah, that was his real name.

Me and the others used to tease him something awful about that name. The teasing didn't last long though, it never seemed to bother him, so it stopped being fun real quick. Besides, he was a hell of a nice kid.

Me and that gang of trailer trash rug rats had some interesting times out here in the sticks. I'll tell you about 'em some time, if I make it through tonight that is. Yeah, Johnny Butts was a nice kid, good natured and fun to play with. Don't think I ever saw him pick a fight or say a mean word to another person. Good kid, but dumb as shit.

What I'm about to tell you now I've never shared with another living soul, my Pa included. Me and the other kids in Hidden Village used to give Johnny pennies to dive down to the bottom of Number 2 and bring up handfuls of the muck. We all knew damned well what we were doing was wrong, my Pa must have told me a hundred times not to be playing around those old shit ponds. You know a kid understands he's doing wrong when he works as hard as we did not to get caught.

Hell, we weren't *bad* kids, in fact we were mostly pretty good, but even the best kids'll get up to evil if you give them a long enough leash.

Anyhow, one day, a nice late spring Saturday it was, we were all hanging out in the wilds without much to do. You see over there, the church, the parking lot, and that gas station? That used to all be wild; trees and marsh from where the river backed up each spring thaw. Well, we were all out there, feeling good and dangerous. Spring weekends are good for that. We hadn't seen Johnny dive since late the last summer and we figured it was past due.

We sent Johnny into Number 2 that day, a five-cent purse waiting for him, but he never did come back up.

Watch your step now, that edge is damn slick. Don't want you falling in there. When I was too young to look after myself during summer vacation and such, my Pa would bring me out here with him to work. There's a game I used to play out here on those days.

I spy.

I played it sitting in the cab of Pa's work truck, straining to see over the dashboard or out the passenger side window, or following him around from chore to chore. I played it when I got older too, and spent my free days helping him with those chores.

I would scan the shore of #2 for anything man made, anything that didn't naturally belong out there in your run of the mill pond, and every item I found was one point, two points if I happened to know what it was, not that I usually did. Mostly I just made up my own names for those bizarre bits of human flotsam.

I spy a Red-Striped Stingray, I would say to myself, seeing a woman's panty liner beached on the muddy Shore. Or, *I spy a big rubber tadpole.* No need to explain that one I guess.

I measure my growing up by the times when I was

finally able to understand what those odd floaters really were.

One day Pa and I came out to check the fuel for the backup generator and found some boys floating in rubber tubes on Number 2. Their mother was close by, stretched out in a lawn chair and reading what Pa used to call a *Crotch Novel*.

He turned three different shades of red in about two seconds, drove the rest of the distance to Number 2 with his foot to the floor and skidded to a stop a few yards from the lounging mother.

"What in the holy hell do you think you're doing?"

I never heard my father speak to another person that way. It wasn't like him at all.

She lowered the book and pushed her sunglasses up.

"Excuse me?" Her voice was cool, barely interested. She was a pretty lady, I could see that my pa thought so too even though he was pissed at her. But there was an aura of trashiness about her. Nothing that you could label, but it hung on her like flies on you know what.

"There's no swimming here!" Pa shouted, waving a wild hand in the direction of Number 2.

Her boys watched the exchange with great interest. The youngest even paddled closer to shore. I knew her boys a little. I'd talked to them once or twice after they moved to Hidden Village. I never played with them though. None of us did.

They were strange, those boys. Like their mother it was nothing you could put your finger on, but it was there. Something about them was just off. I think kids, most kids anyway, have a kind of mental radar that detects strangeness. Yes sir, they are good at pointing out the stranger. If the world ever was invaded by a race of aliens, evil clones, or pod-people, it will be the kids who sniff them out first.

"I didn't see any *No Swimming* signs," she said, then pushed her glasses back down and resumed her reading.

Pa just stood there for a few awkward moments, blinking, then shook his head. He turned to me, a grin on his face.

"Ma'am," he said, this time in a calmer voice, "did you know those are sewage lagoons?"

Those words hit her like a slap on the ass. She jerked forward in her chair, dropped the book in her lap. She tried to push her shades up but knocked them off. Her eyes turned up and rolled over us like big bloodshot marbles. When I saw those eyes, I thought maybe she was hung over. As it turned out she was stoned.

"They're what?"

"Sewage lagoons," Pa repeated.

She stared at him for a few seconds, apparently not comprehending.

"Shit ponds," he elaborated.

I thought she would freak then, but she didn't.

"Get out a here," she said with a crooked smile, a smile that said she could appreciate an off-color joke as much as any of the guys.

"I'm not kidding," Pa said.

"You're fooling," she said, and actually laughed.

"Ma'am," he said with a little more emphasis, "I *ain't* fooling."

Just then one of her boys walked up, the youngest of the two. "Hey Momma, lookit what I found." He held out a plastic tampon applicator, discolored and still dripping with raw sewage. "A whistle," he said, then put the open end of it between his lips and blew.

She screamed.

She jumped up and slapped the applicator from his mouth, and he screamed.

"That's so fucking gross," she groaned, then leaned over and puked on her bare feet.

"Yuck Momma!"

"Jess, get out of . . .," but that's as far as she got. She stopped, stared at the empty tube floating on Number 2's murky water, mouth quivering.

Jess, that was the older boy's name, was gone. Just the empty tube and menacing ripples of disturbed water.

"*Jess!*"

The next few moments were a blur. Jess's mom ran to the edge of Number 2, but couldn't quite bring herself to go in after him. Pa dropped his clipboard and ran the remaining distance to the lagoon. He dove in and vanished into the murky water. He was gone for the better part of a minute. I remember my mild horror for Jess turning into outright terror that my Pa wouldn't come back up, just like Johnny Butts. I was about to go in after him when he finally broke the surface with a great splash, sucking air and screaming.

The expression on his face was pure terror, and not necessarily for the boy he dragged ashore behind him. Pa swam like the Devil himself was down there, swimming up after him.

———

Pa brought Jess up alive, but only barely so. The boy was a

mess of torn clothes, blood, and raw meat. He wasn't breathing. Pa gave him mouth-to-mouth. His mother had fainted, and his younger brother held onto her like bloody death, screaming his little head off.

I ran to Hidden Village's office and called for the paramedics, and when I returned Jess was breathing again, but still unconscious. Pa sat in the dirt next to him, dripping wet and stinking of shit, staring at Number 2 with wide, haunted eyes.

"There's something in there, boy," was all he said.

I looked down at Jess. Pa grabbed my shoulder and turned me away.

"No, you don't need to see that."

The paramedics showed up a short time later and took Jess and his family away. Then the sheriff came. He looked around for a few minutes, scribbling in his little notepad and saying *uh-huh* or *right* to himself every couple of seconds. He spoke to Pa for a few minutes, then left. I overheard some of their conversation.

He had concluded that the turbine had caused Jess's injuries. The boy swam in too close and got sucked in. It was a reasonable assumption, but it was wrong.

"Wasn't no piece of machinery chewed that boy up." Pa raised a hand to my face and opened it. There was a tooth in it. The tooth was old and half rotted. It was big too, two inches from the tip to where it had broken off. Sharp and pointed like a spearhead.

"What was it?"

"I don't know," he repeated. "It was damn big though. I found that boy stuck in the mud at the bottom, like it was swallowing him. When I pulled him out that thing came up after us.

"I couldn't hardly see it under there, that water is nasty thick. It looked like a big glob of mud, or maybe shit. It had arms, it kept trying to grab me, but its hands were slick. It couldn't hold me. It had a face too, a mouth big enough to swallow a kid, and it had pennies for eyes." He shook his head, closed his eyes and began to massage his temples. "I'd never have believed it if I hadn't seen it with my own eyes, boy."

I said nothing. I didn't know what to say.

He stopped rubbing his temples and fixed his eyes square on mine. He scared me. I'd never seen him look that way.

"I didn't imagine it boy. If that's what you're thinking you can quit it now." He slammed his fist down on his knee. "God and the whole wide world knows I ain't bright enough to imagine something like that."

"I wasn't thinking that, Pa."

His eyes softened then; he looked ashamed of himself. "I know you weren't. I'm sorry." He put a hand on my shoulder and gave it a comforting squeeze. "This has been a mighty ugly day."

He stood then, brushed at the seat of his pants and grimaced when the muck caked to them only smeared his hands. We left the truck where it was and walked back home. Later that day, after a shower and change, he left me at home and went back to put up a new *No Swimming* sign. Later the next week he started work on a fence that would surround the whole area. By then Jess was dead, having human shit packed into his open wounds had caused an unstoppable sepsis. He never did wake up, never had the chance to tell his story. Only Pa and I knew what happened at the bottom of Number 2 that day.

I snuck out that night and walked back to Number 2. There was something heavy on my mind. It was something that Pa said – *it had pennies for eyes* – keeping me awake.

I found the tooth where he had dropped it earlier, pocketed it, and dug in the same pocket for the five shiny new pennies I'd robbed from my piggy bank.

I watched the dark surface of Number 2 for a while.

Nothing.

I tossed the pennies in, one by one. As far to the middle as I could. Me and the other kids had never been able to settle up that last bet with Johnny Butts.

"What you doing here, boy?"

I barely had time to flinch before I felt his hand on my shoulder. I didn't answer him. I didn't know what to say. He didn't push it. We stood there for a time, just watching the water.

"Do you know anything about what happened here today?" The question put ice in my blood. I teetered on the edge of confessing it all to him then, telling him what me and my friends did. How Johnny, who everyone thought had run off or been kidnapped by a sex pervert or something, dove down into Number 2 and never came back out. "Have you seen anything … strange around here?"

"No, Pa," I lied.

"It's an ugly thing happened here today. Maybe me and you's gonna have to put a stop to it." He looked down at me, a hard, bitter smile breaking his lined face. "What you think, Ed?"

That was something new, him calling me by my name instead of just *boy*. I mark that as another part of my growing up, the part of it where Pa finally realized I *was* growing up.

"Don't know what to think," I said.

"Me neither." He took my arm and we turned to leave.

Something splashed at the surface of the lagoon just then, and there was a light, metallic ring as something landed close to my feet. It was the pennies I had thrown in.

Pa didn't know what to think of it. He just stared at the pennies for a second and turned away.

I thought I knew what those rejected coins meant.

———

Pa said we should go back there and do something about the horror in Number 2, but we didn't. Not right away anyhow. For years nothing else happened, no more trespassers or dead kids. Our population of corn-fed ducks dwindled, sometimes I would see them cruising the surface of Number 2, doing whatever it is that ducks do, and then one would go under with a startled squawk. All that was left would be a few bloodied feathers. Eventually the ducks abandoned Number 2 for the more hospitable lagoons.

That was when Johnny Butts stopped skulking at the bottom of Number 2 and came up to hunt.

———

There were these two local kids, a young man and his

younger cousin, a girl. Kissing cousins you could call them, except they'd been caught doing more than kissing. There was a lot of screaming about who was the porker and who was the porkee, and a dirty family feud started. Those two kids decided they'd had enough of it and ran away together.

It was big news around here. Not much else going on at the time so everybody made it their business.

Well, a few weeks after those kids ran off Pa and I found the young lady's purse in the woods behind the sewage lagoons, about the same spot where the church stands now, and a trail of dried blood leading from it to Number 2. I guess that's when we knew we'd waited too long, and we decided to finally do something.

Pa reported our find to the sheriff, leaving out the part about the shit monster and why those ponds didn't support as many ducks as they used to. After some convincing he gave the okay to shut down sewer service to Orofino and drain Number 2. He was there through the whole thing, and when we reached bottom he was the first one, hip waders and all, who went down into the muck to search for the bodies, if there were any bodies to find.

We found those kids, what was left of them, and we found more. There was another runaway kid down there, a local woman whose husband had spent the past few years in prison for her disappearance, and an old drifter. These bodies, except for the drifter, were identified later by dental records, there wasn't enough left of them for accurate visual identification.

There was no trace of Johnny Butts, nothing at all.

By nightfall it was over. The bodies had been taken

away, the rubberneckers had left, and after the sheriff left we began the chore of starting the whole thing up again. But before we did, Pa tapped into the drum of SX-PRO that he'd brought along. It was a fifty-gallon drum, a chemical cleaner like Draino, but more powerful. It's full of little shit eating enzymes, little living organisms that serve no other purpose but to clean up the messes we make. We used the stuff in diluted form to clean the water in the other lagoons.

This time we did not dilute it. Pa hooked it up to his power sprayer and shot it full strength down into the empty pit of Number 2.

The spray hit the bottom and the ground started to shake. There was a low moaning sound from the bottom of the pit. The headlights of Pa's truck were trained on the empty lagoon and I could see what was making that sound. All the muck at the bottom of the lagoon was shaking, moving, gathering. It smoked, as if burning up from exposure to the SX-PRO, shit's natural enemy. It gathered into a giant lump at the bottom, and where all that muck had been was nothing but clean, dry soil.

The thing seemed to swell, to shape itself, to grow into something recognizable.

We were both scared shitless. Pa's eyes were so big I thought they might fall out of his head. His mouth made funny little twitching movements, but he held his ground, and he kept on spraying. He kept the stream full on that thing, even as it grew arms and a head with pennies the size of dinner plates for eyes, and drug itself up toward us. Its teeth were the same as the one I had kept hidden away all those years, but much bigger.

Johnny Butts had grown up too.

The thing kept on coming, reaching hand over hand, dragging a pulsing body of shit behind it. It left a trail where it had been, like a big brown slug.

And Pa just stood there, spraying it all over its body, its arms, and its face. He was pissing it off, even hurting it a little, but it didn't stop coming.

"*Pa*," I shouted. "*We got'a pop the top! Where's the crowbar?*"

He didn't hear me, or he didn't understand what I was saying. He just stood there as the thing reared up at him. Butts stood before us then, arms raised like a grizzly getting ready to swat. It opened a mouth large enough to swallow a man whole and roared at us.

A storm of shit, tampons, and chunks of undigested food hit us, the force of it knocking Pa from his feet. It reached down for him, and before he could get away it grabbed him. It held him up with one huge hand and lifted him toward its mouth.

I can't claim any bravery for what I did next. I wasn't thinking straight enough to be brave. I was moving on pure impulse. I ran to Pa's truck. It was only a few feet away, and we'd left it idling to keep the battery charged while the lights were on. I put it in gear and just stepped on the gas. I rammed that barrel of SX-PRO hard enough to pop the lid and knock it over.

Fifty gallons of undiluted shit killer washed down on the monster from Number 2 like a tidal wave.

It screamed, the sound of it echoed between the mountains that hold our little town, and it dropped Pa.

I watched from the cab as it turned tail and slunk back into the pit.

Pa stood, dripping shit as he walked to the truck, and

we watched as the monster smoked and gurgled its way back to the bottom. It shrunk as it moved, and by the time it reached the bottom, little was left but a small burping blob. We watched as that small blob finally flattened out and sank into the clean dirt with a flatulent whimper. Then it was gone.

"Ed, that is the nastiest thing I've ever seen."

After that, we filled the lagoon and put Number 2 back into service.

We thought the monster was dead, but we were wrong.

Last week I saw him take down a duck swimming across Number 2. Last night my little neighbor boy went out to play and never came home.

You best get going. It's getting late, be dark pretty soon, and it's past time I cleaned up this mess I made. If I make it back, I'll be sure to tell you how it went.

If I don't come back, you take this story and tell the world. Tell them about Johnny Butts, and tell them to stay the hell away from Number 2.

There was a big messy battle at the pond that night,
Lasted from the eve of dark until the crack of light.
Our poor hero Ed was never seen or heard again,
And that, faithful reader, is how his story ends.
Pointless – asinine, an extra chunky waste of time.
Y'all stay back now, ya' hear?

DEATHBED

"Were you and Jessica close?"

"Not really. We used to be but … you know." Donny Leonard looked away from the social worker, taking in the campy charm of his office. Moodily lit, yards of polished wooden surfaces, many books, and a picture of an old man on the wall between two shelves that might have been the therapist's father.

"I understand. Siblings grow apart, especially at your age." He consulted an open folder on his cluttered desk. "She was a year younger than you, but the difference between sixteen and seventeen can feel like a big one."

"Yeah," Donny agreed. "Mostly it was just *us*. We were different."

"You say the … the thing under your sister's bed went away when you gave her the nightlight?"

"Yes," Donny said. Then, remembering what his stepmother had said about using good manners added, "Mr. Friend."

"Call me Rudy." Rudy smiled at Donny from across his

cluttered desk, a smile that seemed mechanical rather than organic. It didn't touch the rest of his somehow unnaturally expressionless face. Pale gray eyes bulged and blinked at Donny from behind the thickest glasses he had ever seen.

Rudolph "Rudy" Friend came off like a nice enough guy, even his damn name was friendly, but Donny thought he was a little frightening. Fine gray hair ringed his bald scalp, clinging and floating like cobwebs on old furniture. His eyes were overlarge, owlish, staring from behind the thick round lenses of his glasses like some wild 3D special effect. His face was plump and lineless, expressionless and somehow lifeless, like the hard plastic skin of one of Jessica's old baby dolls. Donny thought he looked like the kind of guy who ate babies and danced around poorly lit rooms in robes made out of dead hooker skins.

"Okay. Rudy."

Rudy Friend glanced back down at his notebook, maybe notes from their previous sessions, maybe pornographic doodles of the receptionist. "But it came back when ..."

"When my dad took the nightlight away," Donny said. This was all ground they had covered thoroughly in their last session. Donny was trying to stay on good terms with his stepmother, who he thought didn't like him much anyway, and that included these little visits to their friendly neighborhood social worker, Mr. Friend, but the guy was starting to piss him off again. Donny was one more redundant question away from letting good manners take a flying fuck.

"Your dad removed the nightlight?"

Donny nodded. "He said she needed to *stop acting like a baby and toughen up*. His exact words."

Rudy Friend nodded. "He wanted her to face the dark without crutches, but when he removed her crutch the night terrors came back?"

"Not night terrors," Donny shouted, once again forgetting good manners in his frustration. "I don't know what it was, but it was not in her head. It was real enough ..."

Donny could not make himself finish the thought.

"To kill her," Rudy Friend said.

Donny said nothing.

"Why did it stay away for the few weeks Jessica had the nightlight?" Rudy's eyebrows lifted, a burlesque movement that none the less failed to touch the rest of his face. Donny thought it made him look like a poorly executed portrait.

Botox, Donny thought. *Has to be. No one is that expressionless.*

Rudy leaned forward across an avalanche of paperwork and books spread across the surface of his desk, clasping his hands under a chin so weak it almost wasn't there. A standard Rudy Friend gesture, one clearly calculated to express exasperation held at bay by endless reserves of patience.

You're going to answer my question, that gesture said. *I can wait all day if I need to.*

A worthless gesture. Their session ended in another fifteen minutes.

Donny settled more comfortably into his own chair, not realizing until that moment how tense the exchange had left him.

Rudy Friend sighed and sat back again.

"Was the, uh," he seemed to struggle with his own tongue for a moment, clearly uncomfortable with what he was about to say, "thing under her bed afraid of the light, perhaps?"

Their last session ended with that same question, phrased only slightly differently, still unanswered.

Donny decided to give a little this time, though he had an idea he might regret it later. The poor guy was trying so hard.

"Nope."

He spoke with such certainty, such authority, that Rudy was shocked into an extended moment of silence. He blinked his huge 3D eyes.

"It's not afraid of anything," Donny said.

"Then why ..."

"Because *she* was afraid. She was afraid of the dark."

"I don't believe that," Rudy said, clearly deciding the time for indulgence in Donny's dark fantasy had ended. "And I don't think you do either."

Donny shrugged, swiped tangles of his long black hair out of his eyes. "Whatever, man."

Rudy stretched out a hand, pointing out the rows of cuts on Donny's arms. Some were fine white lines of scar tissue, some still red and scabbed over, the latest fresh and oozing under wraps of gauze.

"What I believe is that you're lying to yourself about what your father did. What you *saw* him do. Those cuts are your way of dealing with the guilt and stress of that knowledge."

"He didn't do anything to her!" He was shouting again, good manners forgotten. It was more of the same, and Donny was tired of it.

"Your father confessed to it," Rudy said, employing his ultimately Zen tone, his *your anger has no power over me* tone. Donny wished that once, just once, Rudy Friend would stop trying to be his new best friend and yell back.

"The marks on her wrists and ankles, the marks on her throat, the ligature marks, corroborated his confession."

There were other marks, other wounds Donny knew, but Rudy was tactful enough not to mention them.

Donny leaned forward, eyebrows raised and hands clasped under his chin, his best Mr. Friend impression. "Tell me, Mr. Friend, how long have you been receiving Botox treatments?"

"*What?*" Pure shock. His gray eyes grew impossibly wide behind his thick round lenses. A most wicked 3D effect.

"Quid pro quo, Rudolph. You tell me what I want to know, and I'll tell you what you want to know."

Rudy Friend's mouth dropped open. There was a moment of dead silence. The tight, lineless face wanted to express his shock, but seemed unable. Clearly he was not a fan of Hannibal Lector.

Donny pressed on, smiling for the first time in a long time. "Are you afraid that if you look too old you won't be able to win the confidence of your young clients?"

Rudy spluttered for a moment before regaining the power of speech. "Mr. Leonard, this is hardly productive."

Donny agreed, but at least he was having a little fun now.

Rudy Friend was wrong about the cuts on Donny's arms. They weren't his way of dealing with stress or guilt. They were his way of dealing with fear.

The pain pushed fear away, if only temporarily,

covered it in a tide of endorphins, and Donny thought that it was fear, first his sister's, then his, that brought the monster.

———

Donny's Sissy, he didn't call her Jessica unless he was pissed at her, was three months in the dirt when he ran away from home.

Things had not been good, how could they have been, but Tamara, Jessica's mom, his stepmother, had tried to maintain some illusion of family, and he had felt obligated to try for her sake. He knew it was hard for her, he was not her son. Her child was dead, worse than dead, and Donny's father was locked away for her murder. She'd found him sitting on the edge of her daughter's bed, naked but for his undershorts, had seen the marks on her little girl, the final moments of terror and pain frozen on the dead flesh of her face, and had lost her mind. Every day she faced Donny sapped a little more of her tolerance, and whatever love (not like, he was pretty sure she had never really liked him) she still held for her stepson.

By slow degrees, prejudice replaced tolerance, and though she never said it out loud, Donny knew she hated him.

Even at the end Tamara maintained some illusion of family, she fed him and allowed him to sleep in the house that was now hers instead of theirs. His regular visits with Rudy Friend continued, but she wouldn't talk to him. The nights when she was sober enough to acknowledge his presence in her home were rare and growing rarer, and some nights she didn't come home at all. He assumed she went straight from whatever bar she graced after her workday to a friend's house. Maybe a new boyfriend, maybe more than one.

He didn't know for sure, and never found out.

Cutting didn't work anymore.

Donny had tried drowning fear with booze next, dipping into Tamara's formidable supply at night, hoping to find an end to fear at the bottom of one of her bottles, but that didn't work. He spent nights at his friend Travis's house when he could, putting up with his sister Erika's shameless flirting in exchange for the rare nights of peace he found there.

When he left home, the thing under his Sissy's bed lost his scent, when he returned, the monster found him again.

Home wasn't safe anymore.

Rudolph "Rudy" Friend would have his own professional opinion, a panic reaction triggered by his favorite scapegoats, guilt and stress. Who knew what Tamara thought, or even if she did think about him.

His father would simply think he fled out of fear, fear of discovery, fear of punishment.

Donny had tried to tell them all what he thought, what he knew, but none of them had believed him.

What have you done, Donny? What have you done to her?

Out of them all, his father was closest to the truth. It *was* fear that drove Donny to run. Fear of the thing, the monster. Every night he'd spent at home the thing was a little more there, a little closer to finding him.

For three months, Donny slept with his light on, but he had never been afraid of the dark, so when the grief for his Sissy, who he had not always been nice to but always loved, receded and fear of the thing that killed her grew stronger, the light didn't help. So, he cut, then he drank, but the thing came back anyway.

It had tasted his fear the night it killed his Sissy, and his fear drew it back.

When Donny awoke from dreams of slithering and sucking sounds in the dark under his bed to the lunatic tempo of his own beating heart in his ears and the stink of something rank and rotten in the air, the light seemed like a childish defiance.

On his last night in his old room, sleeping in his old bed, Donny awoke to all those things, and something more, a thought in his head, spoken in his sister's voice.

It's here with you now, just not here enough.

But it would be soon.

So, he ran.

Most of Donny's first week on his own passed in a haze of exhaustion and relief. He found shelter in the basement of a condemned house just outside the port district. Rumors of the places eventual demolition had circulated for years, but the house remained standing. Local kids used the once notorious party house for years, until the local police had made a habit of busting up the Friday and Saturday night parties.

Travis and Erika brought food once or twice a day, but by the end of that first week he began to miss the everyday luxuries he'd never appreciated before: electricity, running water, clean clothes and a well-stocked fridge. He even grew to enjoy Erika's endless flirting.

Erika had had a crush on him for as long as he'd know them, and in the past couple of years he'd taken a lot of shit from Travis over it. Relentless but mostly good-natured teasing that didn't quite hide Travis's deeper feelings on the matter.

You two can flirt if it breaks up the monotony. I'm gonna give you shit, but it's okay. Touch her though, and we're going to have a problem.

Erika was cute, red haired, athletic, and her breasts, which he had really noticed for the first time at her fifteenth birthday party, pushing nicely at the old khaki tank top she'd worn to rags, now drew the appreciative eyes of every hetero male between the ages of ten and one-hundred. She was only a year younger than him, so if she hadn't been his best friend's little sister he would have hooked up with her by now, though he thought she wouldn't have been half as interested in him if he didn't keep turning her down.

By the end of that week in the old house, he began to suspect hiding was no longer necessary, or *as* necessary as it was at the start. He was only a few months from his eighteenth birthday, and the only family he had left was probably happy to have him out of the house.

That Saturday night when Travis told him his parents were out of town and invited him to stay over, Donny was happy for the change in scenery.

There was music, but Travis kept the volume down to stay out of trouble with the neighbors. For a while it was Travis's selection, a mix of old metal, punk, and slightly more modern screamo, all of which Donny liked. Then Travis's girlfriend Shelly arrived with three of her friends, two guys and a girl that he knew by face rather than name. Pantera and The Cramps made way for Adele and Macklemore.

Erika made herself scarce when Shelly and her friends, those *preppy assholes* she called them, arrived, and after only a few minutes Travis tipped Donny a wink and took Shelly by the arm.

"Be good while I'm away."

Shelly giggled as Travis led her to the cellar door. They vanished through it, and the new arrivals watched after them a little irritably. Donny had the impression they didn't want to be there. Then the girl took one of the boys by the hand and dragged him to the couch, leaving the odd man out to glare after Travis and Shelly alone. The boy's eyes turned from the closed cellar door to Donny, and a glimmer of recognition animated his face.

"Hey, I know you."

"Do you?" Despite the pleasant buzz he'd cultivated over the past few hours Donny had no desire to spend time with this asshole.

The couple on the couch considered what was left of the beverage supply, half a case of beer and a couple bottles of hard lemonade, frowning.

"Weak," the boy said. "Told you we should have brought our own."

His girlfriend rolled her eyes and twisted the top off of a bottle of hard lemonade.

"You're that kid whose Dad ..." The kid seemed to rethink his words. "Sorry about your sister, dude. That sucks."

Donny didn't think the kid sounded sorry, didn't think he looked that sorry either. He looked almost excited, like a man who has discovered a moderately interesting silver lining on a boring, gray-cloud day.

Not getting laid tonight, but at least I'll have something interesting to talk about at school Monday morning.

The couple on the couch were giving Donny an entirely different kind of look, a look he'd gotten used to in the past few months, half speculative, half disgusted.

I bet you knew what your dad was doing to her. I bet you even helped.

Not a pleasant look.

Donny felt a familiar anger begin to pulse from the pit of his stomach, up into his chest, as if he would vomit out pure rage. His face felt hot. He could hear his pulse beating faster, could feel the veins throbbing in his neck. He wanted to punch, pummel, and stomp those staring faces until a more satisfying expression bloomed from their burst and bloody flesh. Fear and pain.

Some of this must have gotten through to them. As one the three turned and found safer objects to scrutinize.

Donny moved away from them and sat on the bottom steps of the narrow stairwell leading upstairs, happily cocooned in the passage's darkness.

Then he heard steps behind him, startling him, and before he could turn or move a hand settled on the back of his head, fingers sliding downward to caress the nape of his neck.

For one heart-stopping and terrified second, Donny's mind and imagination shrieked at him – *It found me oh fucking shit it found me!* – then Erika whispered in his ear. Afterward, he couldn't remember her words, only the skunky-sweet scent of marijuana on her breath and the shiver of pleasure that crackled down his spine like a shock of electricity.

She took him by the arm and led him upstairs.

The last time Donny saw Rudy Friend his long, hanging all over the place hair was shaved down close to his scalp and he was dressed in a style he thought of as neo-institutional: an orange jumpsuit, shackles on his wrists and ankles, and a pair of armed guards standing sentinel outside the door.

Donny missed the moody darkness and amiable clutter of Rudy Friend's office. He missed the comfortable, overstuffed chairs even more. The new arrangement was much less casual and much less comfortable, a small room with bright fluorescents, blank cinderblock walls, and no personality. A room that was very much like his new cell. It smelled like a stale stew of sweat, piss, and fear.

There was a small desk, the kind Donny had seen at church rummage sales piled high with twenty-year-old junk electronics that probably didn't work, sitting between them. This desk was clear except for a single open file folder.

Donny's file.

Donny and Rudy sat in hard wooden chairs, facing each other over the contents of the open folder.

"What would you like to talk about today, Donny?"

Donny had a single, short moment of doubt, if he told Rudy Friend everything this time, the whole fucked-up story, things were going to end badly for a lot of people. Then he thought about where he was, about the certainty of his own unhappy ending.

No one gets a happy ending this time, Donny thought. *Good*.

Not a nice thing to think, not a nice way to feel, but it was the only thing he had left. The only thing he could look forward to with any degree of satisfaction.

"I would like to tell you about how Jessica and Erika died."

Rudy squirmed in his chair. "Donny, I have to advise you against that. This isn't an interrogation and you don't have a lawyer present."

"I don't care. You asked me what I wanted to talk about."

Rudy regarded Donny, his magnified mad doctor eyes not blinking for several seconds. "Do you understand this is not one of our sessions? This is an evaluation." He pointed over Donny's shoulder, to the camera mounted above the closed door.

Donny didn't bother to follow the pointing finger. He'd seen the camera on his way in.

"We're being recorded, I know. Anything I say may be used against me in a court of law." He chuckled, a small, sardonic sound. "Or to send me to a place with rubber walls."

Rudy Friend nodded, his Botoxed face expressionless as ever, his huge eyes once again unblinking. "Yes."

"Good. I want people to see it."

Rudy sighed. "Okay, tell me about how they died."

Donny knew Jessica was having a tough time sleeping. In the span of a few weeks his happy and energetic little sister had turned morose, irritable. Her old bouncing off the walls energy seemed drained. She was always exhausted, always close to either tears or tantrums.

For a while Donny tried to ignore this new emo version of his Sissy, he knew when he was feeling down the last thing he wanted was his family's well-intentioned but irritating concern.

Tamara, even his dad, had tried talking to Jessica, tried to get her out of the alarming funk. They reasoned with her, yelled at her, even tested her for drugs, but nothing had helped.

One late night on his way back from the bathroom, Donny passed her room and heard her crying.

They'd been close once, but in the past couple of years they'd drifted apart, each asserting their own independence from the other, falling in with separate cliques, forming radically different styles and tastes. Their interaction was minimal and usually tense, but Donny couldn't ignore her tears.

He opened her door and stepped inside, expecting her to yell at him to get the hell out, but she didn't yell. Her sobs grew stronger and she began to whimper.

She wasn't depressed, she wasn't sad. She was terrified.

Donny flicked her light on. "Sissy, it's me. What's wrong?"

She didn't answer with words, she leapt from her bed and rushed across the room to him, almost knocking him over with the force of her embrace. Her tears continued, and she shuddered in his arms. She clung to him as he pushed her door closed behind them, then led her back to her bed. Her grip on him tightened when he tried to pry her loose.

"No no no please no ..." Her words trailed off into renewed weeping.

Donny held her like that for a while, suddenly very aware that he had not held her like that for years, uncomfortably conscious of the shape of her body beneath the long nightshirt she wore. When had his Sissy developed all these new curves? When had she grown breasts?

She pressed her face hard into his neck, her tears falling against his bare shoulders, cutting cool trails down his back.

"Shh, it's okay, Sissy." He soothed her as best he could, thinking in a detached way that this whole scene would be laughable, if a little creepy, if it wasn't so fucking weird.

Finally, she let him go, turning away to wipe her eyes.

"What's wrong, Sissy?"

When she turned back to him she seemed calmer, but her eyes were large, frightened, still leaking tears. She looked half mad. Maybe by then she *had* been half mad.

"Something was in here with me."

"I didn't believe it at first, but I know she believed it. Sissy wasn't a good liar. I would have known if she was faking." Donny shifted in his chair. The hard metal seat was an ass buster. Rudy twitched nervously in response. "She was terrified that it would come back again."

"And did it?" Rudy's face held an expression Donny had never seen on it before.

He considered the tight, lineless features for a moment, then realized the expression seemed alien because it was the first time he'd seen *any* expression on the man's face.

Simple, strong curiosity.

"Did it come back?"

"Of course it did. It came back every night, just not all the way."

"I'm afraid I don't get you." Rudy's eyes seemed wider than ever as he regarded Donny between furious bursts of scribbling in his notebook.

"It was always with her, but never all the way. Never real enough to hurt her until the end."

"Nightlight?"

"Yeah, that helped, but I stayed with her in her room whenever I could. Until Dad found out and freaked on us. He thought we were doing ... things we shouldn't."

"What kinds of *things*?" Curiosity had receded once again into blandness.

"Fucking." Donny hoped to shock some expression back onto Rudy's plastic baby doll face but was disappointed. Probably that was exactly what he was expecting to hear.

"And were you?" No eye contact now. Scribbling.

"No."

After a few silent moments Rudy regarded him again, eyebrows raised, perhaps hoping for some elaboration, some qualification. Maybe an admission to a little under-the-shirt action. Something to liven the story up.

Donny didn't elaborate. There was nothing else to say on that particular subject. He and his Sissy had played and fought, teased and defended each other, loved and hated each other, but they had never fucked.

"How did your father keep you separated at night?"

"He put a fucking alarm on my bedroom door. Tiny little thing that runs on a watch battery and squeals like a smoke detector. Couldn't open my door at night. Couldn't even take a piss without waking everyone in the house."

"But the nightlight you gave her helped? Kept her monster away?"

"Yeah. He'd scream at her if she tried to leave her light on at night, but he didn't know about the nightlight."

"And then?"

Donny could hear renewed excitement in Rudy's voice. They were finally getting to the good part.

"One night I woke up and heard him yelling at her. He decided to check on her and found the nightlight. He'd gotten a little nuts about us by then. He took everything we did as an act of defiance, including Sissy's nightlight. *Stop acting like a baby and toughen up*, he said." Donny squirmed in his chair again, setting his chains to rattle.

"He took it away?"

"Yes."

"And then?" Rudy prompted.

Donny had stayed awake for as long as he could after his father left her room, listening for the sounds of weeping, screaming. Anything. But it was late, and he was tired. He drifted off after an uneventful hour passed.

Then the screams came.

He was on his feet before he even knew he was awake,

pulling his door open and sprinting down the hallway to Sissy's room. The alarm hadn't gone off, either his father had forgotten to set it or the battery was dead. He had not bothered to ask his dad which it was, it just hadn't seemed important at the time, but all those months later the question seemed strangely important. It haunted him in his many sleepless hours.

The short run couldn't have taken more than a few seconds, though it seemed to last much longer in his dreams and memories, but by the time he reached her, Sissy's screams had ended.

He shoved her door open, striking her light switch as he entered her room, then stopped. He tried to scream, but could only manage a weak, horrified grunt.

She was dying, and the thing that was killing her, the monster that Donny hadn't really believed in, but had still tried to protect her from, was still there.

What was it? Rudy Friend would ask months later during their final meeting, but Donny couldn't tell him. He didn't know what it was.

Tentacles that seemed to have been woven from strands of wet red and black hair waved and slithered across her bed and body. There were hundreds of them.

One yanked the torn remains of her nightshirt off and flung it across the room at Donny's feet. Others bound her wrists and ankles, stretching her naked body across the bed. One continued to squeeze her swollen and bruised throat, while others explored her body in quick, slithering movements. One sought the crevice between her parted legs and pushed itself inside of her.

Those tentacles. Donny would later think they looked

like living dreadlocks, the creeping, exploring appendages of some Rastafarian demon.

Her face was a pale shade of blue, her mouth opened and closed fruitlessly, unable to voice her terror and pain, unable to draw breath. Her eyes bulged, rolled in their sockets, then found his and locked onto them. What her mouth could not say, her eyes did.

Help me.

At that moment he could not think, there were no comparisons, no metaphors. His brain had ceased to work as a thinking machine. It could only continue to receive and store the night's horrible stimuli. He could not move, his body was locked in its posture of surprise just inside her door.

They swarmed her, binding, exploring, caressing, raping. They came from some unseen source under her bed, something that breathed, sighed, and squelched in the darkness.

Donny's locked vocal chords finally let go. He screamed and jumped at the monster. He reached for the tentacle around her throat, but before he reached it, Sissy's eyes rolled up to the whites, her body shuddering once, quickly, weakly.

There was no life in the body he landed on, and no monster. The swarm of tentacles faded as he passed through them, grew opaque, then blew away like smoke.

When his father came running to the sound of Donny's screams, he saw only his son, dressed in his underwear, laying on top of Jessica's naked corpse. Shouting, crying, shaking her. Trying to make her not dead.

Rudy scribbled his notes long after Donny's narrative ended, and now Donny was the one uncomfortable in the silence.

"Have they let him out yet?"

"Your father?" Rudy looked up only briefly from his notes to acknowledge Donny. "Gosh no. They overturned his murder conviction but he's facing other charges now. Obstruction, a few more serious ones."

"They're keeping him in prison." Not a question, a conclusion.

"Everyone understands trying to protect your children, but now there are two dead girls instead of one, and the consensus is that your father is largely responsible for the second." Rudy underlined, double underlined, something in his notebook, then faced Donny again. "So, this monster came for you next?"

"Yeah."

"And finally found you."

"Yeah."

"In your girlfriend's bed."

"She wasn't my girlfriend, but yeah."

Rudy considered him before responding. "If she wasn't your girlfriend then young ladies are much more giving than they were when I was your age."

Donny shrugged. "Welcome to the sexual revolution. Everybody's fucking now."

Rudy cleared his throat, giving Donny a quick, disapproving glance. "And it got her instead of you?"

"You could say that."

"Any idea why it let you go?"

"Because it already knows me. It'll find me again no

matter where I go. She was something new. A surprise I guess."

"Everybody loves surprises," Rudy said, then scribbled a bit. "Maybe your monster has a thing for pretty young girls."

"Now you're just being a smart ass."

Rudy smiled, showing lots of perfectly capped, startlingly white teeth. Looked like he'd had them bleached since their last meeting.

"You've made a strong case for the room with the rubber walls," Rudy said. "But juries can be unpredictable. Even odds I'd say."

"Doesn't really matter where I go," Donny said. The meeting was almost over now, and he was glad. He wanted out of that cramped and smelly room, away from the creepy doll faced little man sitting across from him. Judging him! "I'll be dead before you're able to make any kind of recommendation to the court."

"I've already made one recommendation," Rudy said. "I've recommended they keep you on a suicide watch. You will make it to trial."

"When they find me, you're going to remember saying that. You'll know it wasn't a suicide."

"That so?" Rudy had closed his notebook and laid it on top of Donny's case file. He gestured at the camera.

"Yes," Donny said, rising to his feet and drawing Rudy's full attention back to him. "You'll begin to wonder, and then you'll begin to believe."

Rudy fell back a step and gestured wildly at the camera again. "Hurry up! Get me out of here!"

"You and everyone else who hears this," Donny said,

walking to the edge of the desk, then leaning over it toward the social worker. "You'll all start to believe."

The door behind him burst open and slammed against the cinderblock wall. Strong hands seized him from behind and began to pull him away.

"And once you start to believe, you'll start to be afraid. Then it'll come for you!"

Donny began to laugh as the guards dragged him down the hallway toward his holding cell.

Toward his deathbed.

TOYS IN THE ATTIC

Four things about the attic stood out above all others: the creaking of old warped boards, decades of dust, powder fine and covering everything, the smell of mothballs, and the dark.

In the dark there was no play, only the long silence and stillness where they would lean against each other, backs to the big toy chest that had been their mother's when she was a child. In the dark they pretended they were dolls, just two more toys in the attic. Beth and Jamie: Raggedy Ann and Andy.

Sometimes the long darkness was broken by sleep, dreams of the daylight, the outside. Often there was no sleep. Sometimes the silent scratching of little claws broke the silence. Rats, or perhaps monsters.

If they were lucky, the sound of a springing trap would mean food the next day. They had run out of food a week ago, and now the rats were scarce. Mom had never been gone this long before.

I wonder how monsters taste, Jamie thought at Beth.

Kids don't eat monsters, Beth thought back at him. *It's the other way around.*

Sometimes when they became toys they could do that, talk to each other with their minds. Only in the dark though, only if they were touching, and only if they were as still as the dead. Sometimes they even dreamt together.

When the light came they became kids again.

It came from the attic vent, filtering through the slats in fat slices that fell first on Beth and Jamie and their toys in the morning, then moving across the room until it touched the edge of *The Place We Dare Not Go* before finally fading to nothing.

The Place We Dare Not Go was a maze of boxes, two generations of McFarland castoffs stacked to the ceiling in rows that ended in impenetrable darkness, from the familiar world of their attic to a world of nothing. Long abandoned clothing hung from the rafters, a black duster faded almost to gray, a raincoat, and a comic robin's egg blue tuxedo. In the light they were just relics, but at night they became sentinels to that world beyond the maze. The place where rats hid from the light, and monsters slept.

Snap!

The sound of death, and of life.

The toys in the old chest gave no notice, nor did Beth or Jamie. They didn't move, didn't blink, remained still as the dead. But inside they cheered.

They watched the subtle movements of the sentinels, and if they hadn't known better they would have blamed it on a draft. They did know better, and so they did not move. They let the monsters think they were just two more toys, because they left the toys alone. They didn't carry the toys away kicking and screaming to *The Place We Dare Not Go*. They did not eat the toys.

Then Beth and Jamie slept, and dreamt of the sun on their faces and grass underfoot.

The light came again. Jamie and Beth opened their eyes and stretched.

"I'm hungry," Jamie said.

"How hungry?" Beth asked. She'd worked out a 1 to 4 system for eating, a way of saving the food for as long as they could. When they still had real food, and some hope that Mom would come home soon, they waited until they were at 2 - very hungry - before they ate. Beth had since modified the system. They didn't eat until they were at 1 and crying with pain.

"My stomach thinks my throat's been cut," Jamie said.

"Let's play," she said. She was only at 2, and he wasn't crying yet. They could wait.

"Marbles?"

"Go Fish."

Jamie frowned. "Go Fish is boring."

"Yeah, well the marbles stink." Beth wrinkled her nose.

"Please." Jamie scrunched his face into a grimace, narrowed his eyes and bounced with frustration. "I hate Go Fish."

"Okay," Beth said. "We can play marbles."

Truth was, she was bored with Go Fish too.

"Yeah!" Jamie pumped a fist in the air, then dropped to his knees and opened the toy chest's heavy lid. He kept the marbles in an old tobacco pouch pilfered from the duster a few weeks before, when the light had been particularly radiant, and he'd been feeling brave.

Beth searched the traps while Jamie dug through the toys. There were six traps, two sprung. Two rats, a large and a small. The attic had been generous that night.

"Found 'em," Jamie said. "Hurry up!"

"In a minute." Her back was to him. He never did like this part. She pulled a barrette from her hair, the silver finish dulled by weeks of built-up grime and hair grease. She poked the narrow end into a rat's eye and dug until it came out. She pried the other eye out, baited the trap with them and reset it. She put the first rat in her dress's pocket and started on the second.

"Ready," she said when it was over.

He drew a circle in the dust with a finger and emptied the leather pouch into it.

Mothballs colored with crayons from the toy chest. Solids, stripes, multi-colored swirls. Her shooter was red with a black stripe.

"Yuck," Beth said. "They really do stink."

There was only one real marble in the circle, Jamie's shooter. He loved it, kept it in his pocket and would not let her touch it.

The game ended when Jamie's special marble missed its mark and skipped out of the ring, rolling toward the shadows of *The Place We Dare Not Go*.

"No!' Jamie screamed and jumped awkwardly to his feet. He ran only three steps before falling. He was much thinner than a few weeks ago and getting weaker all the time. "No!"

His shooter rolled into the shadow of the hanging raincoat, into the darkness of the row beyond. She heard it roll across the wood for a few seconds, and then it was gone.

Jamie lay there and cried for a while.

Beth bagged up the mothball marbles and put the pouch back into the toy chest. She had tried to teach him blackjack once but he hadn't got it. She would try again when he was done crying.

The first cramp gripped her gut and she cried out as much in surprise as in pain.

"Jamie."

He sniffed. "Yeah?"

"You still hungry?"

"Uh huh."

She gave him his rat and went off to the far eave near the locked attic door to eat hers.

It had been so long since Beth had heard anything but the native sounds of the attic that she almost didn't recognize the sound of the car engine outside. The vent was beyond her reach, so she could not see out. If she slid the toy chest beneath it she might be able to reach the wooden slats, but not look through them.

"Jamie, come here. Hurry up." She shoved the chest toward the wall, her sneakers barely able to get traction on the worn boards. She lifted the lid and let it fall open, then hauled toys out by the armload.

"What are you doing?" Jamie stepped next to her and gathered the scattered toys into his arms, trying to put them back in. "If you make a mess..." he didn't have to finish the thought. She knew what their mom would do if she saw the mess.

Beth slapped his arms open and let the toys piled in them scatter at their feet. "We can pick 'em up later. Just help me."

For a moment she thought he might cry. She knew if he started she wouldn't be able to calm him down in time to help. He didn't cry, just looked at her a little shocked.

"Okay," he said, and helped her empty the heavy chest.

When it was empty she slammed the lid back down. "Help me slide it over."

He did, and when it was against the wall, under the vent, she climbed on it and pulled him up.

"Can you lift me up?" She was doubtful, but it was worth a try. She could lift him up, let him look outside to see who was there, but she trusted her own eyes more than his. Sometimes when they spent too much time up here his imagination got away from him and he became overly fanciful. No telling what he might *think* he sees down there.

"I can't lift you," he said. "You're too big."

"Okay, I'll lift you then. Step up, hurry!" Beth laced her fingers together, hands joined in a stirrup, and when he stepped into them she lifted him to the vent. She could still hear the faint hum of a car engine outside, but fainter than before. Whoever was out there was leaving. Not her mom then, probably a lost driver using the private drive to their house to turn around.

"Can you see?" Beth's voice was strained. Jamie was much thinner than he had been a few weeks before, but he seemed heavier than ever. She was getting weaker too, Beth realized.

"Yeah, it looks like a cop car. It say's *serif* on the side."

"You mean sheriff?"

"I guess," he said, and shrugged.

"Help us," Beth shrieked. "Please help us!" She sagged against the wall. She was getting tired, the muscles in her arm hurt from Jamie's weight, and yelling made her head pound. She felt like she might pass out. "Yell at him, Jamie! Make him stop!"

"He's going the other way," Jamie said, but screamed with her anyway.

"*Help us, we're up here! Please stop!*" Jamie drummed his small fists against the slats while they screamed. Even after the sound of the sheriff's cruiser engine had faded to nothing, they continued to shout, and Jamie to pound at the vent.

When the first drops of blood fell on her trembling arms Beth gave up, and only after she lowered Jamie back down to the chest did he stop. His fists were bleeding, swollen, the skin worn down to meat where they had drummed their desperate message, and riddled with large slivers.

Beth gathered her dress up to her knees and ripped at the hem. The cloth was old and thin, it ripped easily. When she was finished her old dress was three inches shorter.

She went to her little brother. He sat against the wall, not crying, only staring into an unreachable distance somewhere within his own mind. She lifted his bloody hands from his lap, and when she released them, they did not fall back. They hovered like a pair of charmed snakes. She'd seen him like this before. It scared her when he was like this, but she knew he would get better. He always did.

She pulled the slivers from his hands, the ones that were not too far under the skin to grab with her finger-nails, then bandaged them with the strips of cloth torn from her dress.

She didn't put the toys back. She sat cross-legged in the center of the mess and gathered them around her: toy trucks, teddy bears, a few porcelain dolls, matchbox cars, a large plush puppy dog.

One of the Barbie's reminded her with the force of a revelation, of her mom. Hair in a plait, burgundy evening dress with black pumps, waiting with a painted smile for her next drugstore Ken. She slammed it into the floor again and again, until its limbs were bent and twisted, and the head came off. Then she threw it as hard as she could into the shadows of *The Place We Dare Not Go*. She had always feared and loved her mom, a confused sort of love, but at that moment she hated her worse than monsters or death. Giving her mom to the monsters in the shadows, in effigy if not in fact, felt good.

She pulled the toys around her in a mound until only her head and arms were uncovered.

Beth went away for a while in search of whatever happier place her brother had found.

———

She did not find him in her sleep, but when she awoke the toys were cast off of her, and Jamie lay asleep with his head in her lap. The slanted bars of light, weak and dusty, fell upon the threshold of the monster's place. She scooted backward, pulling her brother along with her, until her back was against the comforting solidity of the toy chest.

She watched the place where light and shadow met, that black whispering place.

The light fell slowly until it touched the broken Barbie doll. There was a scratching sound in the darkness of the box maze, monsters or rats, then the mom-Barbie was gone.

Jamie was sick. Very sick. Very sick and very weak. He hadn't played in four days, hadn't moved from his quiet place in two. He was lost in himself again, and this time Beth didn't think he would come back.

All of the rats were gone, and she hadn't realized until then how much they had depended not on just their meat, but their juice. She was very thirsty.

Beth played solitaire and waited in vain for the sound of the sheriff's cruiser, or her mom's old Saab. She feared she would hear neither. She should have known when her mom left them this time it would be the last. The sleepless nights stomping down the halls of the old family home, cursing her bad luck at being saddled with worthless property, a broken-down house, no money to pay the taxes, and two thankless brats who would never be able to pull their own weight.

Then the new boyfriend had come unexpectedly.

Beth tried again to pry open the door that sealed them in and cut herself on the nails driven up from below that held it shut. She crawled back to the toy chest through a sea of cheerless faces, frowning teddy bears, sneering dolls, and the pot metal grills of toy trucks that looked like the grins of demons. She kept a fearful eye on the toy dog, which had once given her so much comfort, but now watched her with its own hateful button eyes.

Beth settled next to her absent brother, there but not there, and slept.

———

She awoke with the last of the afternoon light.

It was cold.

Jamie was awake, walking toward *The Place We Dare Not Go*, his steps slow but purposeful.

"No," she said, or tried to say. It came out in a dry croak. "Jamie."

He stopped.

"I'm going to get my shooter," he said. "They can't have it. I won't let them, it's mine."

"No, come back." She found the energy to sit up, but could not find the strength to follow him.

He turned, and if she had the strength she would have screamed. Her brother had truly become just another toy in the attic, not Raggedy Andy, but Raggedy James. His skin was pale cloth, his clothes stitched to him, his sneakers black cloth sewn over toeless feet. His hair was wild, matted yarn, his mouth an unmoving stitch-line, and his eyes as black and spiteful as the once loved dog that now watched her from its own shadows.

"It's my shooter," he said. Then he stepped into the maze of boxes and was gone.

Beth shivered. She felt a clammy hand in hers and realized it had been there all along. Jamie's hand was limp in hers. She let it drop to the floor.

He did not stir.

"Jamie." She tried to shake him awake. He would not wake, and he was cold.

She moved away from him, then lifted the heavy lid of the toy chest and crawled inside.

Mom had told them time and again not to get into the rows of boxes that occupied the one side of the attic. She told them the things in those boxes were old family business, not theirs.

Beth and Jamie had their own reason to stay away from them.

The Place We Dare Not Go was the forest of their attic kingdom. To them it was as real as anything else in their small world, a world limited by size but not imagination. And as the days shortened and the coldness grew, the outlines of the attic shadows grew less distinct.

Beth half-slept, shaking away the last of her strength while she waited for the scraping of claws against the surface of her toy chest sanctuary to stop.

RIDGERUNNER

Call me Hunter. That's what I am.

It was just after midnight and I was only beginning to drift off. I'd been up late reading a book, saw the time, made myself put it down.

That's when Lea called out.

I had just enough time to consider going to her when she came to us instead. I heard the slap-slap-slap of her bare feet on the hardwood floor, then she was in my room, cannonballing into the bed between Dana and me.

This was almost a nightly occurrence lately, Lea unable to last a full night in her own bed. When questioned she always offered the same explanation, she was afraid of the ghost outside her window. I thought she'd probably picked that up from the opening scene of that new Scooby-Doo movie. She hadn't made it past that scene, wouldn't quit screaming until we turned the tape off.

Hell, at her age it could have been anything.

Lea wrestled herself beneath the sheets, whining in tired frustration. Dana was still asleep, so I helped Lea get comfortable and slipped her one of my pillows.

"You have to quit doing this, baby," I said while I tucked her in.

"I know," Lea said, but it came out sounding like *I'm sorry*. Lea's only four years old, she'll be five in a few weeks. I love, no, adore, the sound of her voice. So sweet and expressive.

She turned away from me and cuddled into her mother.

I drifted again…

And woke to the sound of something thumping against the south side of the house where the sun porch is.

The glowing red numbers of the digital clock read a quarter till one in the morning.

There was another thump, the rattle of the sun porch's large plate window in its frame. Then snarling.

I got out of bed and went to the back door in my slippers and thermal underwear, hair standing on end like a countrified version of Einstein. I grabbed my coat off its hook by the door, pulled it on, and went out onto the sun porch.

I expected to see my mutt, Bronson, scratching against the glass, wanting to be let in. Didn't much blame him. October in the high country is cold. Dana would skin me alive if I let him in though. Bronson is not an indoors kind of dog, too big and too full of bounce. Lea thinks he's a Tigger, like on Winnie the Poo.

It was not Bronson I found on the other side of the sun porch glass, I didn't find *him* until much later that morning, and by then I pretty much knew he wouldn't be scratching at the back door anymore.

I saw a tall, naked man, dark skinned and hairy as an animal, pissing against the glass. He'd shit all over the driveway, the thumping I'd heard was him smearing handfuls of it over the window.

He saw me and just stood there, pecker in hand, staring at me. Remembering me, I think.

Then he crouched, hands to the ground, and hopped away like a monkey into the dark. I heard his passage through the brush past my shop, and then the trees that mark our property line a few hundred feet away.

He was gone.

I hadn't seen the Ridgerunner in twenty years, sure as hell didn't think he could still be alive, but I knew it was him the moment I saw him there, pissing against the side of my house.

Marking it.

Ridgerunner has a history around here. Most of it is pretty unbelievable, but I think even some of the more outrageous stories about him have a seed of truth. It's the kind of stuff you'd have expected to see in *The Enquirer* during its glory days, before it tried to clean up and look like a respectable celebrity gossip publication. I'm surprised no one around here ever clued them onto it. They would have paid good money for this kind of shit.

From the years of local gossip, and my own experiences with him, I've separated everything I've heard about Ridgerunner into two camps, pure fiction and tentative fact.

I'll start with the facts.

His name is Donald Davis.

He's been running loose in the area since my grandpa Will was a young man. In fact, grandpa Will, my father's father, went to grammar school with him for a few years before he dropped out. Some years later a man killed Donald's mom in a barroom knife fight.

This is the part where my story, like many small-town stories I suppose, gets incestuous. The man who killed Arline Davis was my other grandfather, on my mother's side. I never knew him, but from what I hear I didn't miss much.

Jacob Decker was a failed prospector turned gambler. A man, as rumor has it, who would steal the pennies out of a dead man's pockets, then rape his wife and daughters before moving along.

Story is she'd accused him of dealing from the bottom of the deck, and he had opened her up like a grain sack, from belly to throat, and let her guts out onto her feet. Grandpa Decker was never arrested for the crime. There was no trial, no justice. He walked away and that was that.

Donald vanished after that, not that anybody tried too hard to find him. His mom was something of a black sheep, and the small-town wisdom that the apple doesn't fall far from the tree kept the mostly good Christian folk around here from caring. I suppose I'm as guilty of this kind of lazy and ignorant thinking as anybody else who ever lived here. When there's some distance between you and the situation it's easy to see their prejudice for what it was.

Not long after the murder, a stable boy found my grandpa Decker dead in the town stable where he kept his horse. His horse was dead too, all cut up and the meat taken from its fleshier parts.

The locals assumed it was Donald come back to take revenge for his mother, and I think they were probably right. If it was Donald who killed Jacob Decker, then he did my family one hell of a favor. My mother hadn't been born yet, so she was spared living with a father who beat his wife as a matter of routine and had raped his oldest daughter by the time she was five.

Regardless, I don't think doing my family a favor was what he had in mind.

That is all the stuff I know is true. What follows is speculation, the subjective history of Ridgerunner.

The stuff of rural legend.

Ridgerunner origin theory #1: Ridgerunner is the son of the devil, and his *real* mother was a local Indian witch. He was puked up from the throat of Hell to avenge the white man's crimes against the Nez Perce Tribe.

This story is popular with the religious folk. Not the average Sunday morning churchgoers, but the folks who speak in tongues and would have happily employed inquisition style persuasion to bring the Nez Perce Indians to The Lord, had they been allowed.

Ridgerunner origin theory #2: He is the half-breed son of Arline Davis and a Sasquatch, or Bigfoot if you like that handle better, that was said to haunt this part of the Clearwater River Valley and harass local farmers and hunters.

I don't think anybody really believed this theory, but *I* liked it better than the Son of Satan theory. I've seen Ridgerunner up close three times in my life, and I have to admit he looks the part.

The name Ridgerunner was given by farmers and hunters whose property and hunting grounds stretch the fifteen-mile distance from Huckleberry Ridge, west of my hometown of Orofino, and Crow's Nest Ridge to the east. That fifteen-mile stretch, including Orofino, was Ridgerunner's stomping ground. Every week or two there would be another sighting and another story about him. A lot of them were probably even true.

Dick Steiner, he owned a small farm by the Clearwater River's North Fork, swore that Ridgerunner kept breaking into his coops and pens, stealing chickens, pigs, or anything else fit to eat. His son, Daniel, had the same problem after he inherited the farm. Daniel didn't keep the place for long, he sold out to the Army Corps of engineers so they could build Dworshak Dam. The old Steiner place is under a thousand or so feet of water now.

Mabel Wilson, who babysat my sister, Michele and me when we were children, told me once that she saw him streaking, *naked as a jaybird and hairy as an ape*, down our lane in Hidden Village, a large trailer park outside of town where we lived.

I believed her story about as much as I believed in Santa and his evil doppelganger, Black Peter, but a few days after Mabel's story, my dad found shit smeared across the door of our woodshed in the back yard. He was mad as hell that day. My sister and I spent most of that day avoiding him. When my dad was in one of his moods it didn't matter whose fault it was, he was likely to explode at anyone who looked at him wrong. Mabel, not the sharpest pencil in the drawer, told him that it was, without a doubt, that hairy son-of-a-bitch she'd seen running around just the other night.

Michele and I stayed awake that night, and when everyone else was asleep we snuck outside and hid in the woodshed. Partly, we wanted to disprove Mabel, but mostly we wanted to catch the shed-shitter in the act and make Dad happy with us.

Michele fell asleep almost immediately, and I kept watch. Nature called at some point in the night, and I reluctantly gave up my watch to answer it.

The last time I saw my sister was on my way back to the shed. She hung limp from the arms of that hairy bogeyman neither of us had believed in.

There was blood in her hair, on her face.

Ridgerunner saw me, flashed a yellow, rotting grin, and swatted me aside as he fled with her.

A few weeks after that, before the local search and rescue team gave up looking for her, but after we'd given up hope of them finding her, I overheard a new Ridgerunner story, one that I had not heard before. Mom and Dad thought I was asleep. I could not sleep. I sat with my ear pressed to the thin wall of the room I had shared with Michele and listened.

Years earlier the same thing had happened to my mother and her sister - their shared room broken into while they slept. Grandma was working the nightshift at the newly constructed State Hospital North when it happened.

They never found her, my mother's sister. It's hard to think of her as an aunt. I never knew her.

The night before my mom lost her sister, someone had marked their front door. The way Ridgewalker had marked my dad's woodshed.

The way he had just marked my house.

I locked all the doors and windows in the house, watched my baby and my wife while they slept, oblivious. Then I cleaned up Ridgerunner's mess.

I found what was left of Bronson and buried him.

Dana rose with the sun. I brought her coffee and told her everything. By noon she and Lea were packed. By afternoon they were gone.

I didn't know if Ridgerunner would come back to my home or if he would somehow sense that Lea had gone, perhaps bide his time until she was home again, or perhaps track her down. I thought he would come, find her gone and try to take me instead.

I hoped he would.

I fixed a late lunch, eggs and toast. I wasn't hungry, but I knew I'd need strength for the coming night. I forced the food down, but it came back up an hour or so later. I was cleaning my rifle, my dad's old browning .30-30, when it happened. There was no warning, no telltale taste of acidic bile to give me a head start to the bathroom or kitchen basin. It came up in an orange-yellow gush that splattered my boots and the floor between my feet. For a while I just sat and shook. Then I mopped up the aborted meal and finished cleaning and loading my weapons.

Besides my rifle, I carried my .45 semi-auto. I don't much like magazine-loaded weapons, I prefer my revolver, but the semi-auto held twice the rounds, and when it comes down to it I prefer overkill to moderation. I also had my hunting knife for any close work. I hoped I wouldn't have to get close enough to use it.

A shot of Hover Denison's home brewed huckleberry brandy took the edge off while I waited for dark.

When the dark came, it brought the cold with it. I dressed warm, thermal underpants and shirt, wool socks, my hunting cap. I warmed my insides with cup after cup of hot coffee.

He came just after midnight.

He didn't come from outside, as I'd expected, but through the house, from Lea's bedroom. He'd smashed the window, and before the sound of falling glass died he was coming for me. He must have passed right by the sun porch without me seeing him, and when he found Lea gone I became the next target. He smashed everything in his path, stomped the floor hard enough that I felt the vibrations from outside, screamed a path through the house.

I left the rifle where it was, hanging from the strap over my shoulder, and drew the .45 from its holster. I thumbed the safety off, pointed it at the back door, and waited.

His path didn't take him to the back door though, but through the kitchen wall to my left. He smashed through, snapping the wall's skeleton of 2x4s, ripping down sheetrock, snapping electrical wiring like rubber bands.

Sparks lit his exit. Something popped in the fuse box and the lights went out.

I had a fix on him though. I emptied the 12-round magazine into him as he charged. Most of them hit him, I think, but they didn't slow his charge. He had too much momentum. I turned to dodge him but not quick enough. He rammed me, and on the other side of the blank spot in my memory I found myself lying in the grass, pieces of glass and wall falling around me.

I'd lost the .45, but the rifle lay under me.

I was surprised to still be alive.

I heard animal whimpering, grunts of pain, snapping twigs from the pines at the edge of my back yard. He was hurt, perhaps dying, but still alive. Getting away. The coward in me would have been happy to let him go but I knew Lea and Dana couldn't come home unless I finished it, until I *knew* he was dead.

I inspected my rifle, saw it was clean, the barrel clear of debris. I ran inside and fetched a flashlight from the closet.

I tracked Ridgerunner into the woods.

I went hunting.

I think it's true that there are still places that no man has ever laid eyes upon even in moderately populated places like Clearwater County, Idaho. Most doubt it with all the hunters and outdoorsmen who live around here, and until that night I would have doubted it too. I followed Ridgerunner to such a place that night. When I tried to find it again days later I could not.

Tracking him was easy. He remained far enough ahead

that I couldn't see him, but the pain I'd inflicted on him and the trail of blood he left killed his stealth.

The chase lasted for hours. I followed him until my flashlight went dead and the pains of my age and strain were almost too much to endure.

Then the sun rose.

I saw him again for just a moment. There were a half-dozen exit wounds in his back from shoulder to ass. No animal I'd hunted before then had taken that kind of damage and kept running. My respect and fear for Ridgerunner went up several notches. He was one strong son of a bitch.

He dropped out of sight on the other side of a small rise. When I topped the same rise, he was gone.

It only took me a few seconds to find the door to his den.

Hole in the ground, halfway down the slope next to a thick deadfall. It had a door of sorts, the end of an old cable spool, round, wood, about three feet in diameter. It reminded me of Bilbo Baggins's home from The Hobbit, or maybe Bilbo's poor country cousin.

I slid it from the hole and peered inside.

The tunnel was narrow and deep, flickering light, fire-light, from somewhere at the other end casting his shadow back at me. I could hear him in there too, not quite crying, but making a mewling noise like a wounded kitten.

I tied a handkerchief around the barrel of my rifle to protect it from the dirt, then crawled in after him.

My Bilbo Baggins analogy wasn't far from the mark. Ridgerunner's den was like a hillbilly Hobbit's bachelor pad. He'd collected, or stolen, enough pieces of castoff furniture to give the place a semblance of humanity. There was a round throw rug in the center of the earthen floor, tattered along the edge and falling apart. A torn beanbag spilled its hoard of foam pellets around the legs of a child's writing desk. The top of the desk was decorated with a small treasure of colorful stones, and two skulls, one human and one almost human. An oil lamp sat between the skulls, lighting all but the farthest corner of the den.

Rough log beams and a spiderweb network of rotting planks held the ceiling up. His attempt to board up the packed dirt walls made the place look like a warped cabin.

Ridgerunner lay against one of those walls, hugging his knees to his chest, breathing in great, wet gasps.

He was in pain, and probably intelligent enough to know what would come next, but he did not try to run or hide.

I pulled the handkerchief from my rifle's muzzle, chambered a round, drew a bead on his sloping forehead.

"Hunter." The word was more a growl than actual speech, but I understood him.

I squeezed the trigger, satisfied as the headless body jerked and fell to the earth.

Behind me, in the part of the den untouched by lamp-light, someone screamed. The scream went on and on, and after several moments it faded to sobs.

When my heart settled, and I was able to move again, I took the lamp and approached that dark corner. I didn't want to know who, or what, might be crouching in the darkness there, but I *needed* to.

It was my sister, Michele, older than her years, haggard, skin leathery and caked with filth. Her hair matted and fanned around her head. She held a baby in her arms. Its body was pink, smooth, but the hair on its small head was long and thick. It watched me approach with dark eyes.

Its father's eyes.

NIGHT OF THE DOG

Dave Lancaster saw the little dog as he took the off-ramp to Midway, Idaho. It stood hunched over something in the ditch, its shoulders tensing and relaxing, its head darting down over something he couldn't see. He slowed from thirty-five to twenty-five just in case the little hairball decided to join the flow of traffic. Not that there was any traffic heading into Midway. Traffic on Highway 90 was sparse as evening edged toward twilight, but *no one* was visiting Midway.

The dog was a pug; flat face, stubby legs, corkscrew tail and bugging eyes, the butt-ugliest dog in the animal kingdom. Dave had never seen a pug that didn't look like it had suffered severe brain damage. He had no idea how such a useless animal had made it this far out of town, and considered, briefly, trying to catch the little monster to take it back, but decided against it. He'd put a lot of work into the Nissan, a souped up gold Maxima Limited SE, black leather interior, and didn't want the little monster crapping on his upholstery.

Dave had passed this little shit-splat town twice a week on his way to the job in Wye, Montana, and home again, and always stopped for a Bacardi and a Spoiler, The Midway Diner's half-pound burger with the works and a plate of fries. Once he got back home he'd be back on salads and Weight Watchers until he left Sunday night, at least until he'd melted a couple inches off his middle. His fiancé said she wanted him fit for the wedding and had taken to slapping his gut in way of a greeting.

The dog looked up at Dave's approach, and he saw what it had been picking at, something small and bloody in the weeds near the white line. It tensed, eyes bugging out, and bared a mouthful of sharp little teeth. It launched at his car with a volley of barely audible yips, then disappeared beneath the bumper.

"Whoa!" Dave stomped the brakes, but too late.

It yelped, then crunched beneath the front driver's side tire. A jet of blood spattered the blacktop in front of the car.

"Shit!" He pounded the dash, checked his rear-view to make sure he was still alone on the off-ramp, then put on his flashers, backed up, and killed his engine. The moment of silence that followed ticked away like the cooling of a still motor.

After a few seconds he sighed and popped the trunk. He found his gloves next to the toolkit, old leather, well-worn and grease-stained. He pulled them on, slammed the trunk closed, and walked around to face the mess.

The crumbling asphalt was decorated with blood and hair, but the dog was gone.

No way it got up and walked away, Dave thought.

He ducked down and peered beneath the car, saw

nothing, and finally found the pug squeezed up inside the wheel well hanging from the tire, its jaws opened well past their breaking point, teeth embedded in the rubber. Determined to kill the Nissan even as it squashed him.

Road pizza.

It was squashed all right, damn near flat. Loops of intestine hung from his rectum, swinging like rubbery turds. One eye dangled from its socket, stared at him from the side of his crushed head. The other eye was gone, the crushed socket oozing a thick mixture of blood and eye-jelly.

Dave turned away, fought to keep his lunch down.

The pug's corpse squeezed out a final, wet doggy fart – its final *Fuck You* to the world.

"Fucking really?" His stomach lurched, then settled again, and he grabbed the dog with gloved, shaking hands, his anticipation for his Friday night Spoiler gone.

He had to pull hard before the dead animal relinquished its hold, the damn thing's teeth were embedded to the gums in rubber. Broken vertebrae crunched in its neck, he was afraid its head would come off, but it finally pulled loose.

Little as he wanted to, he leaned in closer to the flattened dog and read the tag on its collar. No address or phone number, only the animal's name.

Xander.

He grunted and held it out at arm's length.

Stupid fucking name, he thought.

The adrenalin of his scare was wearing off and Dave began to feel the evening's chill. Steam rose from Xander's body. It was hot in his hands, even through his gloves.

"Sayonara, you stupid pancaked fuck."

Dave bent to place the corpse where some city road crew could see it, and saw what Xander had been picking at before joining the bottom of the food chain.

A tiny hand picked clean of flesh, a mangled arm and small torso half-hidden in the tall grass. A scrap of pink cloth lay next to the baby, all that remained of its dressing gown.

Dave turned away and blew his lunch onto the pavement between his feet.

He stood like that for seconds that seemed to stretch out to minutes, waiting for the shock, and his roiling stomach, to settle.

"I did not just see that." He spoke as if trying to reason away a delusion, but he knew what he'd seen.

There was a liquid gurgle from below, and for a moment he thought he was getting ready to puke again. Then he realized the gurgling was not his stomach. He looked at the dog, hanging limp from one fist.

It lifted its head, growled at him. Its dangling eye pulled back toward the empty socket, then popped back into place.

Dave screamed, dropped Xander to the blacktop, stomped on him until the growling ceased, and ran for his car.

The final few miles to Midway passed in what seemed an eye-blink, and Dave blew past the Welcome to Midway billboard and its accompanying 25 MPH sign (We Love Our Children – Please Don't Speed) at 75. He didn't touch his brakes until he saw the town's single stop light a half-block away. It blinked red at Midway's only controlled intersection, and Dave slid sideways through it, stopping in the dead center of town. There were no other cars on the road, no pedestrians. Midway's resident State Patrol car sat in its usual spot across from the Midway Diner, but the trooper that belonged with it was not in evidence.

Dave laid his palm down on his horn, breaking the town's eerie silence, then spun a half circle beneath the blinking light and slid to a stop inches from the State cruiser. He beeped the horn again for good measure as he climbed out, but no one came to investigate.

"Hey!" He slapped the cruiser's hood, then ducked down to peer through the tinted glass into an empty cab. "Anybody!"

Nobody.

A slick smear of blood marred the cruiser's waxed black paint. He'd forgotten to take the gloves off, and that beastly little fuck's blood was smeared all over them. He peeled them off and dropped them to the street, then turned in place, scanning the streets and yards, sidewalks and storefronts.

Midway's single scuzzy bar was lit up and apparently open for business. A neon *Open* sign glowed in the window, and a sandwich board on the sidewalk read *Screw AA – come on in and get drunk with the boys*, but the usual drunken babble and racket of country music was absent.

The town was silent, still. A car idled in front of the antique phone booth next to the small public works shop. The door was open, and a single shoe lay on the blacktop beside it.

"Where the fuck is everyone?"

Dave ran for The Midway Diner.

***

He found them in the diner.

Not everyone from Midway, but enough of them to leave one hell of a mess.

Parts of them were strewn around the floor, tables, and counter. Scraps of torn clothing, shoes, some with the bloody stumps of calves protruding, a John Deere hat with a large bite taken out of the brim. Bones with raged strips of flesh, a gore slicked skull with the top crunched off, hollow but for a few blobs of gristle and brain. Dripping, empty rib cages, all flesh and organs absent. A scrap of scalp with bright orange hair, the almost fluorescent orange of a bad dye-job, was all he could find of the waitress who had served him countless meals on his trips to and from the job.

Every surface was drenched with blood. He looked down and found himself standing in a still-tacky pool of it.

The smell hit him a moment later, the sick coppery scent of blood, the stench of torn bowels, the rich miasma of flesh just beginning to rot. Dave turned for the door, pushing it open with his shoulder as he burst back into the fresh air, and came face to face with perhaps the last living person in Midway.

***

He was a large man, tall, wide, and fat, three hundred pounds of farmer stuffed into old threadbare bib overalls.

His face was bearded, pasty, shining with sweat and speckled with blood. The white shirt beneath the straps of his bibs was dark with age and accumulated filth. His big clunky boots were maroon with dried blood.

He held a large ax in a two-fisted grip in front of himself, almost like a shield.

Dave screamed and stumbled back, almost falling through the doorway back into the abattoir that had once served the finest burgers in northern Idaho.

The man screamed and jumped back a step in tandem with Dave. His massive gut jiggled inside the seam-stretched bibs, and he raised the ax as if to swing.

Dave's hand fell on top of cold steel, and he grabbed it in reflex, dragging it in front of himself. A large steel bowl, speckled with rust and full to the rim with crushed cigarettes, welded to a steel pole set in a concrete base.

Dave lifted and swung it, dumping cigarette buts down his front.

"Stay back!" Dave swung his makeshift club in a clumsy arc. "Stay the fuck back!"

The big man tensed, then lowered his ax.

"No man, you got it wrong," he said, lowering the ax further and raising one empty hand, palm out. "I didn't ..."

Dave swung again, and with all the force he could muster. The concrete block smashed into the offered hand.

The big man howled, dropped his ax, cradled his hand to his chest.

"Shit man, don't do that!"

Dave swung a second time, a slow and clumsy swing that clipped the man's elbow and sent him staggering back a step.

The pole slipped from Dave's sweat-slicked hands and crashed through The Midway Diner's shaded front window.

Dave darted past the big farmer and sprinted toward his waiting car.

Get outa here, he thought. *Jesus fuck I gotta get outa here!*

"*Damnit, wait man!*"

Dave turned to find the big man running after him.

"*You can't leave me here,*" the man shrieked, then, as if reading Dave's thoughts, "*you gotta get me outa here!*"

"*The fuck I do,*" Dave shouted, and slid to a stop in the gravel, thumping into his car. He yanked the door open, slipped behind the wheel, and threw a rooster tail of dust and gravel as the big farmer fumbled at the passenger door handle.

"*Don't leave me!*" The man gave chase, but Dave left him in the dust of Midway's Main Street.

I'm not stopping until I get home, he thought.

He'd phone the state police as soon as he was back in cell range, but there was no way he was ever coming back to this slaughterhouse.

He did stop though, just short of the sign reading *Thanks for visiting friendly Midway. Come back soon.*

The dog, Xander, was trotting down the broken yellow line into town, dragging what remained of the naked, savaged baby in its too-wide mouth.

Dave stomped the brakes without thought, leaning over the dash as Xander stopped and sat in the middle of the road.

For a moment man and dog stared at each other, then Xander stood again, and Dave saw the little dog seemed to have grown to twice its previous size. It gave its head a shake, whipping the dead baby back and forth like an old chew toy. At last the tiny neck tore and the body flew free. Xander advanced at a trot, then a sprint, and leapt up onto the Nissan's hood.

There was no sign of the dog's previous injuries. The broken body had healed, the dangling intestines were back where they belonged, the torn hide was unbroken, and the missing eye was restored. The head had grown even more than the body. Xander was now a living caricature of a pug. A hundred long and pointed teeth cradled the baby's head in a sinister grin.

Xander gave a snort, blowing snot and blood on the windshield, and then crunched the head in its jaws and gulped down the pulp of flesh, brain, and bone.

Get the fuck out of here!

Dave popped the clutch, Xander stumbled but kept his feet, but the car stalled. Dave made a desperate keening whine as he cranked the ignition.

Xander looked up, past Dave to the road behind him, and leapt over the hood.

Dave turned and watched Xander sprint toward the big man in the bib overalls.

The man saw Xander coming, stopped, screamed, turned tail back toward town.

He didn't get far.

Xander, now the size of a large pitbull, leapt at the retreating man's back and bore him down. Dave heard the mingled screams and growls, saw blood and limbs fly, saw an outstretched hand disappear with a snap of Xander's jaws, and his paralysis broke.

Dave laid rubber and left the demon dog to its meal.

He hit the exit at sixty-five and slid through two empty westbound lanes, chasing the setting sun. He checked his cell, cursed at the *No Service* notice, and scanned the empty lanes. He had no hope of finding a state trooper, they were never around when you actually needed one. It would be another half hour to De Borgia, the nearest town, maybe twenty minutes until he entered cell range again if he maintained his current speed.

Fuck current speed, he thought, and stepped down on the gas.

He'd reached the Nissan's top speed, just over one hundred and sixty miles per hour, when he glanced in the rear view and saw a strange shape far behind him, but gaining.

"No," he said, refusing to believe his eyes, but the shape resolved as it closed on him. "No!"

The large shape continued to gain and continued to grow.

And began to bark.

Dave focused on the road ahead again, barely avoiding an old, battered Falcon, swerving to pass and ignoring the impotent bleat of the old car's horn.

Xander barked again, and Dave watched in his rear view as the pug casually bumped the Falcon nose first into the ditch. The old car flipped and rolled, its weak head-lamps highlighting a rag doll form flying from the smashed windshield.

"Fuck me!"

Dave swerved around a small pickup, blew by a short box truck, passed a road sign reminding him that he was almost to De Borgia, checked his phone and almost shouted in relief. Almost ran into the ditch as he dialed, checked the rear view again and found Xander finally beginning to slow a few car lengths back. No sign of the trucks he'd passed.

Xander, the size of a small truck himself now, sprinted on with his tongue lolling through a strangely goofy pug grin, his eyes bright in the Nissan's tail lights and pointing in slightly different directions.

Dave had always thought pugs were fuck-ugly.

"911. What is your emergency?"

Dave almost dropped the phone in his surprise. Had not really expected the call to go through, not with the way his luck was running.

"*There's a giant fucking dog chasing me,*" and realizing how lame he must sound, "*it ate a fucking baby!*"

"What is your name, sir?"

"*I'm on Highway 90 near De Borgia,*" he shouted, "*and this fucking monster is going to eat me!*"

"Sir, what is your ..."

Dave screamed and dropped his cell phone, didn't even have time to yank the wheel as he came up too quickly on an old shitbox Lincoln, and rammed it. A forward snap as he came to a violent stop, the bite of his shoulder and lap harness, the punch of the airbag, and a short nap.

———

Dave awoke no more than a few minutes later by the light of the sunset shining through his cracked windshield. The hood of his Nissan was crumpled, blowing steam. The

Lincoln was stopped half in the ditch. No one stirred from it.

The Nissan was dead, probably forever, but it was not still. It rocked forward and back, down and up, in a rhythmic motion.

He reached for the door handle, then yanked his hand back. A giant paw pressed against the door, pinning it. A single claw had punched through the glass. He turned to the passenger door and saw the same.

Slowly he turned, pushing the deflated airbag out of his way, and saw the rear windshield obscured by the bristly fur of Xander's belly, rubbing and bumping in sync with the rocking of the crashed car.

"Fuck me," Dave said again, almost sobbed, and watched the rear seat's back rest bulge, relax, bulge, relax, bulge, and finally fall away as the giant dog's thrusting penis smashed it down.

Dave screamed again and pulled his head away as Xander's penis shot forward between the front seats.

The car bounced. Above him, Xander panted.

"Sir? Are you okay? Sir, can you answer me?" His cell phone lay on the floor between his feet, but Dave ignored it.

He curled up in the driver's seat as best he could and waited for it to end.

WHO KILLED LITTLE BETTY?

Timmy skipped rope on the sidewalk in front of his house, his pretty blue dress fluttered around scabbed knees, the matching bow in his hair bouncing with each jump.

His house was typical suburbia, same as most of the others on Brown Street, but transformed in its neglect. White paint was faded, filthy and peeling to bare wood. Windows were cracked, and the screen door lay twisted and torn next to the front steps. It festered like a lone boil on the otherwise healthy American street. The white picket fence was once sharp and clean. Now it faced the other houses, yards, and families of Brown Street like the grin of a corpse: old, rotten, and gap-toothed.

The house to the left of his was vacant, peaceful and expectant. The realtors had kept it up well, the paint was fresh and bright, the lawn newly mown and crisp as a Marine's crew cut, but it still wouldn't sell. It had been empty for several months.

It was early afternoon, a day alive with sun and the

chirping of spring birds. School had just let out and Timmy could hear kids coming from a block away. They were laughing. Timmy didn't go to school anymore, his principal had expelled him at the start of the year and he had not gone back. Mostly he spent his days jumping rope on the sidewalk or playing hopscotch. Sometimes he sang while he skipped or hopped, in a voice that was high and girlish. Sometimes when he sang his lips did not move.

Who found Little Betty – lying on the floor,
Colder and bluer than she was be-fore?
Momma and Papa didn't want her no more.
Who killed Little Betty – who killed Little Betty?
Momma and Papa didn't love her no more.
Who killed Little Betty?

The school kids passed him on their way home, gawking as he sang. A few looked uncomfortable. A few pointed at him and laughed. They passed him every day, some of them went out of their way to Brown Street to watch him, if only for a few seconds.

Always from across the street though. They didn't want to get too close to him.

Timmy ignored the laughter, the calls, or didn't hear them at all. He skipped rope until his arms were tired, then he hopscotched in the grid he had drawn for Betty the year before. It was dead too, seasons of wind and rain had scrubbed away the chalk, but he still knew where it was. He saw it just as Little Betty remembered it.

He sang.

Timmy played and sang until the dark and cold told him it was time to go in. His mother didn't call him in. The dark was his mother now, the cold his father. It was the dark that held Little Betty as she slept in her new bed underground; it was the cold that kissed her cheek.

The cold told him to hurry, raising goose bumps on his exposed arms and legs. The wind blew the ruffles and laces of his dress behind him like a sail and buffeted the bow in his hair. He brushed the dress back down over his knees and went inside.

Little dead Betty all covered with bugs . . .

His mother slept on the couch. She had fallen asleep listening to the record player, the phonograph needle coughed and burped along the final grooves in the vinyl as it spun, waiting to be stopped or changed. Timmy lifted the needle, removed his mother's record, and put Betty's favorite on. It was a 45, a dramatization of Hansel and Gretel. The witch had always scared Betty, but it was still her favorite.

Timmy was hungry now; he couldn't remember when he had last fed himself. Before eating he replaced the empty bottle in his mother's arm with a full one from the liquor cabinet. She didn't wake right away, not even to the sound of music as Hansel and Gretel played. She stirred, groaned and frowned, but did not wake until Timmy finished his peanut butter sandwich and began to scream. She woke slowly.

He watched her come full awake, and when her blood-shot eyes settled on him, the screaming stopped. She glared at him for a while, said nothing, just fixed him with a look of pure contempt. He returned her silence with a silence of his own, and a sturdy, probing glare that did not stop at her eyes, but went beyond.

She looked away. She noticed the full bottle sitting in the crook of her arm and twisted the cap off. She drained a quarter of the bottle in one long swallow.

"You little fucking freak." She scowled at him, mouth turned down in an ugly slope. Her lips were cracked, her teeth stained brown-green with nicotine and lack of brushing. She tipped the bottle again, drinking deeply. Some of it spilled down the front of her shirt, and she barely shivered at the sensation. When she looked up again Timmy was still watching her, eyes fixed on some far spot inside her skull.

"What are you still doing here," she asked. "Why don't you go hide under a rock ... or something?" Under her breath she added, "why don't you go die?"

"Who killed Little Betty?"

She rose, almost steady on her feet, and rushed him. Her face twisted in pleasure as she drew back and slapped him hard across the ear.

He fell without a word or whimper. He was small, but the floor was hard and the sound of his fall spoke for him. He didn't try to rise, didn't move at all. Just laid there, staring down the hallway as he had stared at her before, perhaps seeing something that she couldn't see.

"Don't you ever say that name to me. Ever!" She hovered above him, glaring, daring him to stand up, waiting for him to say that name again.

"I asked her," he said, but not to his mother. He stared down the hallway, at a spot on the scratched hardwood floor next to the empty bedroom, Betty's old bedroom. "She won't say."

He sighed.

No sooner than the sigh had drifted out, he responded in a different voice.

"The witch is tricky. Don't let her eat you up too." It was his singing voice. Not musical though, or even sweet. It was like broken glass under feet. "Make her tell."

"Shut up," his mother said, but her voice had no command in it.

"Make her tell," he repeated in the high voice, and then again in his own slightly deeper voice. "I'll make her tell."

Mother was crying now. Silent, angry tears leaked from narrowed eyes.

"When your father comes back I'm going to tell him about the hell you've put me through." She took another drink from the bottle, already a quarter empty. "You'll be so sorry, you little bastard."

"Daddy isn't coming home mummsy," Timmy said. Still he did not rise, only shifted his gaze up to her. "He'll never ever ever come back."

He broke into song again, his jumping rope voice.

"Never-ever- ever-ever- ever-come back." He lay there while his mother stomped away, singing with an oblivious smile on his face. His small head rocked in time to a rhythm only he could hear. "Never- ever- ever-ever ...."

The sounds of Hansel and Gretel came to an abrupt stop. The needle scratched as it slid off the record, then came down again on another. The song was Janis Joplin's *Little Girl Blue*. The needle screeched again, stopped on another song. His mother sang along, off key and slurring. The Hansel and Gretel record flew over his head and skipped down the hallway.

"*No*," the voice of Little Betty screamed from his

mouth. He jumped up and ran into the hallway, falling to his knees when he saw the record lying on the same spot where he had found Little Betty that night. His mother laughed in the living room, then sang again.

The record was scratched but not broken. He thought it would still play, but he cried as he ran shaking fingers along the new scratches. It was Little Betty's favorite story and mother had scratched it. He curled up on that spot on the floor, held the record to his chest, and cried until he slept.

He did not sleep long.

"Jesus H Christ, what the hell's wrong with your kid?" A strange man stood over him, thumbs hooked casually through a braided leather belt, head cocked to the side. Dirty hair fell over the man's bare shoulders. He wore a sweat stained tank top that showed his tattoos, *Ride To Live – Live To Ride* on one shoulder, a marijuana leaf on the other. Timmy knew what marijuana was, it was one of the only things his mother liked more than booze.

"He's not mine," she said. "Just ignore him."

The stranger looked down at Timmy for a few seconds.

"Boy, you best get your head on straight. It's a big, mean world out there and it will eat you alive if go out into it like you are." He smiled at Timmy, not unkindly, and said, "the world doesn't care much for freaks and sissies."

He stepped over Timmy and walked to the bathroom,

and a few minutes later passed without looking down on his way to the party.

Timmy listened to their party from the hallway. When Janis Joplin was finished the stranger put on Steppenwolf. Timmy could smell the skunky, nauseating odor of marijuana smoke as it drifted. Then they fucked. Timmy knew what *fucking* was too. It was another thing his mom liked to do a lot.

Timmy lay there the whole time, cradling his sister's favorite record to his chest, listening to the symphony of grunts, screams, and drumbeats in the living room. He waited silently for the ugly music to end.

Not last night but the night before, Little Betty - Little Betty lying on the floor.

The strange man had left, and his mother slept. Timmy found her on the couch, another empty bottle cradled in her arm. Again, he traded it with a full one from the liquor cabinet. The cabinet was full now. The man with the hair and tattoos had filled it for her. Timmy didn't scream this time. He sat at the edge of the couch and watched her.

"I don't like being dead," said the high voice in his head. "I miss mummsy and daddy. Give her a kiss for me."

He knelt on the floor, tugging the hem of his dress out from under his knees, and kissed her gently on the cheek. Then he whispered the words in her ear.

"Who killed Little Betty?"

She stirred on the couch briefly, frowned in her sleep. Her lips seemed to move, but no sound came out.

"Who killed Little Betty?"

She jerked in her sleep and cried out. The bottle fell and rolled off the couch. Timmy caught it and handed it back to her. He pressed it into her empty hand, and her fingers closed around the neck as if by instinct. She mumbled.

"Who killed Little Betty?"

Her eyes opened, staring dazed into empty air, then at him. There was no violence in them now. That would come again in the morning, as the afterglow of booze and pot worked her head over. For then she was drunk, stoned, and fucked into a tentative peace. "Go away," she said.

"*Who?*" This time it was urgent, demanding.

"Your father," she said. "Now goddammit leave me alone."

"The witch is a liar. Be quick or she'll eat you too."

"I know," Timmy said.

"Make her say it."

"Who killed Little Betty?"

"Go away," mother said, and began to uncap the bottle.

Timmy grabbed it, pulled it from her hand and held it out of reach. She didn't have the will to take it back.

"Give it to me," she said.

"Who killed Little Betty?"

She closed her eyes and drifted.

Timmy walked to the record player, put Little Betty's favorite story back on, turned the volume up. After a few revolutions the needle found one of the new scratches and stuttered.

He knelt down in front of his mother again and slapped her hard across the cheek. Her eyes snapped open. Her hand tried to feel its way up to her stinging cheek but could not. It fluttered uselessly at her side and fell back to the cushions.

"Who killed Little Betty?"

"You did, you little bastard." She glared at him with fuzzy eyes. She sucked phlegm from the back of her throat and spit it in his face.

Timmy paused for a moment, stared at her, silent tears leaking from his confused eyes, his mother's spit sliding down the curve of his nose. "I tried to save her," he said. "I tried."

"You killed her. You broke her." She looked at the bottle in his hands again. He knew she wanted it more than anything else in the world right then, and he wanted her to have it. "It should have been you," she said, then turned her head away from him.

"Open your mouth, mother." He uncapped the bottle and held it closer to her.

She opened her mouth for him, and he poured the dark liquid in as quick as she could swallow it.

He had found his sister on the floor, curled up on the hardwood next to her bedroom door. It was the middle of the night, and he had had to pee. When he found her, that need had gone away, squirted in a warm stream down his legs. Her face was frozen in a cramp of pain, her skin was odd, like the skin of a wax mannequin. The color of her lips had matched the blue nightgown she wore. She had turned her head and looked up at him, confusion almost as strong as the pain in her eyes. Then she stopped.

Timmy had screamed for his mother and father, but neither had come.

He stretched her out on the floor, and not knowing what else to do balled his hands up together, raising them above his head. He slammed them down in the center of Little Betty's chest. That was how they made people breath again on television.

He had done it over and over again, but it had not saved her. He had not saved her.

He stopped when the blood came up from her mouth, spotting her cheeks and the front of her nightgown. He fell to the floor next to her, crying, then looked up and saw their mummsy standing over him. She was not crying.

She stepped around them without a word and walked to the living room to call the ambulance, even though it was too late.

The doctors said Little Betty had died from eating some bad pills, the ones that their father kept hidden in his sock drawer. Even though he hadn't been there that night, they had arrested him and taken him to jail.

Mother said it wasn't the pills that killed Little Betty. When the doctors and the cops were finally gone, and Little Betty with them, mother had sat him down and told him that he had killed her. She told Timmy that he had broken her when he hit her in the chest to make her breath again.

The witch is a liar. Be quick or she'll eat you too.

The bottle was almost empty. He pulled it away from his mother's mouth. Her eyes followed it, pleading.

"Tell me who did it, mummsy." It was the other voice again - broken glass underfoot.

"You know who," she said. She turned her head to the side and retched. A sticky black mess, booze, bile, and food flowed over the side of the couch and onto the floor. It touched the hem of Timmy's dress, staining it like blood.

"Tell me," Timmy said. "Who killed Little Betty?"

"I did."

"You made her eat the bad pills?"

"Yes."

"Why?"

She didn't answer. She closed her eyes.

Timmy righted her head on the couch cushion. Her mouth flopped open, vomit covered teeth grinned at the ceiling. He fed her the rest of the bottle, just as she had fed Little Betty those poisonous pills. He tipped it up inside her mouth, both hands pushing against the bottom, and forced it in as far as it would go.

Her eyes opened again, watery and bulging, rolling in their sockets in a fury of confusion. Her face burned bright red. Blood trickled from her nostrils. She reached up for him, grabbed at his arms to push him away, but had no strength. A scream of panic and pain built up deep in her throat. He could feel it trying to push its way out, wanting to drown out the stuttering music of Betty's favorite story.

Yet, even as she struggled against the invading bottle, she sucked it dry.

He held the bottle steady with one hand and pounded

it further in with the other. Teeth shattered as he used the bottle to push her screams back down. He pounded the bottle again and heard something inside her head crunch.

She glared up at him in her final moment of shock, sucking the bottle as she fought against it, then she stared through him instead of at him, and was still.

Timmy left her like that. He went back to the spot in front of Little Betty's empty room and slept.

Outside all was quiet, peaceful, as the mostly normal neighborhood slept, dreaming mostly pleasant dreams.

HOT SUMMER NIGHT

The crescent moon winked through broken midnight clouds. Its reflection wavered on the black waters of the Lochsa River, then disappeared again, swallowed by the clouds. Trees whispered in the night. Fir, pine, and closer to the river's edge, willows. The warm summer breeze played them like an instrument. Their leaves fluttered and whispered to each other, dancing shapes of black silk against the distant light from a campfire at Sunrise Campground.

An owl landed on the handrail of the narrow walking bridge that crossed the river from the campground to the nature trails on the other side. Its head swiveled smoothly on its neck, its large medallion eyes shining blankly at its sole companion. It hooted at her, then went back to watching the moon. Moments later a piercing light came from the road back to her camp. It fell over the walking bridge, stealing the sanctuary of shadow. Startled, the owl took wing and vanished into the darkness.

The woman, standing midway across the bridge, smiled at the approaching van.

It rolled slowly into a dirt lot near the bridge, and parked. The engine died, the lights winked out, and the van blended into the night so perfectly, she could see only its outline.

The woman was tall, thin, young, and in love ... just not with her husband. She wore her lightest summer clothes for her rendezvous, a faded pink tank top and cut off blue jeans. Straight dark hair hung to the middle of her back in a wild spill. Sweat gleamed on her neck, shoulders, and the uncovered tops of her breasts. She fanned herself as she crossed the bridge. Her bare feet slapped against the wood plank surface of the bridge with each step.

He appeared from the darkness like a phantom, a tall man, muscular with broad shoulders and an easy stride. He wore jeans, a long sleeve button up shirt, and cowboy boots, all black. His dark hair was slicked back on the sides, wavy in front, and shoulder length in back. His eyes were lost in shadow, but his wide smile showed, large white teeth bared, with the stalk of a wild red rose clamped between them. He went onto the walking bridge and met her half way.

She purred at him, plucked the rose from his teeth, and pushed the stem into her cleavage. The roughness of the stem raised goose bumps and a thorn pricked the flesh of her left breast, drawing blood. She hissed in pain but did not mind it. A gust of wind blew the petals across her skin, and she shivered.

The man grabbed her forcefully, crushing her in his arms, and kissed her. The kiss was long and passionate, and when it was over she pulled away slowly, a line of blood dribbling from her lip.

Her lover loved to bite.

"You're such an animal," she said, then lowered her face to inhale the rose's fragrance.

"Grrr." He slipped his large hands under her shirt and began to squeeze her breasts. The thorn dug in further.

She started, then moaned, one hand holding him firmly by the back of his neck while the other caressed, then squeezed the bulge in his crotch.

He began to explore the cleft of her thighs, then to unbutton her cutoffs.

She moaned again but slapped his hand away.

"No. Not out here."

"I thought you liked nature," he whispered to her. "I thought you liked animals." Another button came loose; her shorts began to loosen, then slide over her hips. She wore nothing underneath.

"Not out here," she said more forcefully. "In the van."

He grabbed her by the waist and lifted her easily. She wrapped her arms around his neck, her legs around his waist with vise-like force. Again, they kissed deeply.

"On a hot summer night," he whispered into here ear, "would you offer your throat to the wolf with the red roses?"

"*Yes!*"

She loved that old Meatloaf song, and he knew it.

They kissed, holding each other in a death-grip as he carried her to the van.

The back of the van was converted into a large bed. King-sized, with red satin sheets and pillows, and a black comforter. All of the windows were tinted, and a bead curtain separated the cab. It was the vehicle of an over-sexed man-child, a drugstore Lothario, and she knew it. It was dangerous, meeting like this in her husband's camp-ground, even at night while he slept.

She knew things would end badly between them, but the end was not yet.

He stripped her as she lay sprawled across the red satin. The air conditioning felt good on her naked body. The cool air raised more goose bumps on the smoothness of her skin.

She watched him with a smile as he stripped.

Then he was on top of her and inside of her.

They did not make love. What they did to each other was too rough, too base to be called lovemaking. She slapped him across the face. He growled and slapped her back. She clawed him all over, leaving long angry lines down his back. He bit her, once again drawing blood. She screamed, bucking hard underneath him.

She climaxed, raking his back with her nails again. He climaxed and bit her again. Again, she cried out.

Back at Sunrise Campground, a young girl awoke to the sound of her screams and shivered inside her sleeping bag, thinking she'd heard a monster.

She watched the van drive away from the center of the walking bridge. Despite the late hour, the heat outside was oppressive. She smoked and fanned the heat away with a willow frond she plucked as she walked back to the bridge. She needed to get back to camp soon, before her husband awoke and found her missing, again. She needed to make use of the remaining quiet hours, and just think. She drew the cigarette's cherry down to the butt and flicked it into the river.

She needed another cigarette first.

She leaned heavily against the rail, her eyes closed, her head hanging, enjoying the light spray from the rushing water below. The willow frond slipped from her hand, splashed into the water.

An owl, maybe the same one as before, maybe not, dropped from the trees and perched on the rail. The medallion eyes glowed at her. It hooted once and took flight.

She looked toward the camp.

It was quiet now, but her husband would be up soon, before the dawn as always. He had to open the kitchen, straighten up the vacated cabins, clean and rake the beach, and perform a hundred other chores that he couldn't afford to hire out.

Time to get home, she thought. The day would be hot, again, but she would have to wear something with long sleeves and a turtleneck to hide the bite marks.

She started back across the bridge, and stopped. A dark shape blocked her path. A familiar shape. It held something out to her.

"You forgot your rose," he spoke softly to her.

"Get out of here," she said slowly. "I have to go."

She tried to push past him, but he moved to block her.

"I'll leave after you take your rose." His voice was low, rough, tempting.

She felt the familiar heat down below at the sound of his voice. "Back off," she hissed, simultaneously aroused and revolted. She pushed him aside, knocking the offered rose from his hand.

God, what am I doing, she thought. *This is insane . . . I have to end it.*

It was easy to entertain thoughts of ending it after she'd been satisfied, harder to stay on the safe course after a few days apart.

She was ten paces from the end of the bridge when she felt his hands on her again. There was no foreplay in his touch this time. It was rough, but not arousing. His arm circled her in an iron grip, crushing her to him and pushing the breath from her.

"On a hot summer night," he whispered into her ear, and she realized it was not the voice of her lover.

She struggled inside the confining circle of his arm to face him, whoever he was, to scream for help and wake the entire campground if she had to.

A gloved hand found her throat, closed over it before she could force a scream, lifted her from the planks of the old footbridge.

The face in front of hers was a grinning, pale caricature. Powder white with an electric blue mohawk, black teardrops painted beneath black eyes, a bulbous nose as raw and red as a cherry. His mouth was stretched in a wide grin, and the rose was clamped between his teeth. He giggled at her, a cheerful sound.

There was a quick flash of steel, reflecting the moon as

it teased the night through the broken clouds. She saw the blade, the razor-sharp silver crescent, and opened her mouth in a choked, breathy shriek. Then the pain came, down low, just above her privates. Like a punch in the gut, but much worse. A sound like tearing cloth or something being unzipped, except it was her being unzipped. The pain leapt into her chest, hot at first, then cold.

She felt wetness, her chest, her waist, her legs, and the top of her feet. She heard something land on the old planks of the walking bridge with a wet slap.

She screamed again, weakly.

Another flash of steel, and her scream stopped.

He dropped his blade, plucked the rose from between his teeth, planted the long stem deep in her cleavage.

"On a hot summer night . . ."

LUCIN

My obsession with rock and roll started at fourteen with glam rock groups like Poison and Rat. I wore the T-shirts and group buttons, carried cassette tapes with me everywhere, and even grew my hair long. As my taste for pot eventually led to more insidious poisons, glam rock led me to heavy metal. I listened to Ozzy Osbourne, Iron Maiden, Alice Cooper, Metalica, and the likes, but my favorite was Jarek Poe.

Jarek Poe, the beginning and end of a short-lived trend called psychoactive rock. He was the Timothy Leary of rock and roll. During his five-year recording career, Jarek Poe grew a faithful following. His music, and his message of psychic expansion changed the lives of many young people in the early 80's. It drew them away from the booze, pot, and hard drugs, to what he called *The Divine Fez*, or sometimes *The Piss of God*. *The Divine Fez*, more commonly known as mescaline.

Once his career was over, the radio stations stopped playing his old music. His influence mostly lived on in the form of tribute bands who played his old music for low pay in small clubs. I was the drummer in one of them, we were called The Stoners, and I gotta be honest, we were pretty bad.

What I'm saying is that he wasn't exactly a one hit wonder, but he was forgotten pretty quickly by the mainstream. His lasting legacy consisted of a few diehards, like me.

———

The last song Jarek Poe wrote and recorded was a ballad called *Lucin. Lucin* was written and recorded in the space of an hour in the studio basement of Poe's Arizona home. According to an interview given by his bassist, Poe claimed to be walking through The Spirit World, where the music and lyrics to *Lucin* were dictated by a great spirit. *Lucin* was never rehearsed. They played it once, and when they finished, Jarek left his home and wandered into the desert. He was never seen again.

The following year a body was found in the desert outside of Phoenix, badly decimated by wildlife and time. The head was gone, so they were unable to identify it through dental records, but most assumed it was Poe.

Last year a singer named Tarin Kane released his first album - *Non Omnis Moriar. Non Omnis Moriar*, translated, means *I Shall Never Wholly Die*. The thirteen-track album featured all original material, except for one song, a first time ever, note for note remake of *Lucin*.

———

Most of the Jarek Poe memorabilia I collected during my mescaline clouded youth is gone, burned up in the garage fire that killed the bassist and singer of The Stoners. That fire happened three years after Poe's death, when my band mates and I traded in our mescaline for heroin. Our bassist, Joey, started the fire when he used a propane torch to light a cigarette. I survived because I was locked away in detox at the time. Our guitarist, Alex, was serving three to five for aggravated assault when the fire happened, but he died a year later. He was drunk on whisky made from fermented potato skins when he passed out on the floor of his cell and choked to death on his own vomit.

What a totally rock-n-roll way to die.

I've been clean for a few years now. I work for a magazine now, a music magazine called Metal Parade. Actually, I work in the mailroom of the New York publishing house that owns Metal Parade, but I hope to write for it someday. I do have access to Metal Parade's archives, so the comparative research I did between Jarek Poe and Tarin Kane was simple. They have roughly the same build, the same blue eyes, the same haunted look. The biggest difference was the hair. Poe's was shoulder length and auburn; Kane's was waist length, usually concealing his face, and jet black.

The physical similarities were there, but mostly it was *Lucin*, a song that no one else seemed to remember. I remembered it. It was the reason I decided I had to interview Kane. The press credentials were not hard to fake. I followed the Kane tour through ten cities, three States, before he finally granted me the interview in Boise, Idaho.

I met Tarin Kane in a darkened backstage room after the concert. The rest of the band was elsewhere. He sat alone in a chair at the far end of the room, balancing a crystal sphere on the fingertips of his left hand. He watched the crystal with a relaxed intensity, not staring but not snoozing. He wore his stage clothing, black everything. He could have been a shadow sitting there. I could see his face reflected into the crystal sphere. Even his eyes were black.

In a moment of fear, caused I believe by the sight of his solid black eyes through the crystal, I turned quickly to leave.

"Welcome," he said, stopping me with the single word.

I turned to face him, my unease growing more intense by the second.

"Forgive me, I am being rude," he spoke softly. "I am very easily distracted." He glanced at the crystal again, and with a quick motion of the wrist, made it disappear into the palm of his hand. It was an impressive maneuver. I looked into his eyes again. They were blue, not black, and shot with red, as if he were stoned or simply exhausted. He motioned to a chair sitting across from him, and I sat in it, fumbling through my bag for my mini-recorder. I could not see well in the dim light.

Kane clapped his hands together, a sound like gunfire in the quiet room. I jerked in my chair, dropping my bag to the floor. The lights in the room came on.

"The Clapper," he explained with a grin. "Wonderful gadget."

I found my recorder lying on the floor by my bag. I

bent to reach for it, but it was in Kane's hand before I could finish the movement. When I looked up again he was sitting comfortably in his chair, a good five feet from the fallen leather bag. He was eyeing it with the same fascination he showed the crystal moments before. Of the crystal, there was not a trace.

Realizing, with some embarrassment, that I had not uttered a word of greeting to the man I was there to interview, I cleared my throat and prepared to speak.

Looking up from the recorder, he stopped me with an upheld palm. "No pretenses," he said. "If you are a reporter, then I am Ludwig Van Beethoven."

"Excuse me," I whispered. I had a strong feeling I was about to be thrown out.

"I said, you are not a reporter." Then he smiled and said, "don't worry, we're cool."

"How do you know, did you see it in your crystal ball?" In retrospect I suppose it was a smartass thing to say, but it didn't piss him off. He laughed.

"No," he said at last. "It is pretty, but it does not tell me much." He held the orb up to the light. It glowed brightly, a six pointed star flashed within its depths. The recorder was no longer in his hand. It was in mine. I held it so tightly my fingers turned white.

How did you do that, I wanted to ask, but my throat was too dry for speech.

"Trade secret," he said, as if in reply to my unspoken question. He made the crystal disappear again, then leaned forward and fixed me with an intense stare. "Where would you like to start?"

Before beginning the strange interview, I checked the recorder to be sure it worked. The cassette and batteries were fresh, it was the insides I was worried about. I was afraid the drop may have damaged them. I turned it on, set it on the floor between us, and spoke to it.

"Testing . . . testing."

Without being asked, Kane contributed to my test by reciting from memory, Edgar Allan Poe's, *The Raven*. Very accommodating for a man I had lied to, and I found his choice of authors very curious. When he finished I played it back, and to my surprise the quality of the recording was better than expected. His voice played back clear and loud. I sat back and enjoyed his recitation of *The Raven* again. His voice was a rich, melodic baritone.

I did not rewind to the beginning of the tape before starting our Q and A. I wanted to keep his recitation of *The Raven*. In a space of a few minutes, Kane instilled in me an appreciation of literature that years of public education could not. I left a five second delay after the poem, then began the interview by pushing the Record button on the small recorder and setting it on the floor between our chairs.

I set out to do this interview with a specific list of questions, starting with the basics and ending with a series of more leading questions. I didn't plan on asking him outright if he was Jarek Poe, I wanted the interview to sound legitimate, so I could submit it to Metal Parade. I saw this as more than an opportunity to meet my teenage idol or satisfy an odd curiosity. I saw a career opportunity as well. Tarin Kane was fast becoming one of the biggest names in rock music.

I regretted not writing those questions down for fear

of looking like an amateur, because sitting under the mellow scrutiny of Kane, I could not remember any of them. I improvised.

"Where would *you* like to start?" I asked. "What questions do you wish people would ask, but they never do?"

He smiled and gave his head a small shake.

"Let us start with the reason you are here," he said.

My heart sped up a little at that. I had heard that Kane had a talent for making people squirm. I think he got off on it.

He brushed a tangle of hair from his face. His dark eyes were narrowed at me. I noticed him holding the crystal again, rolling it in his palm like a worry stone.

"Let's talk about music then," he said.

At which point the interviewer became the interviewed, I couldn't say, but Kane took quick control of the conversation. There was no formal Q and A. He talked about music, his and others, his band, how the tour was going, shit like that. He asked me a few questions about myself, which I answered truthfully. When the interview was over he knew more about me than I knew about him. It was clear to me that I would learn nothing about him unless he wanted me to know it.

I only asked him two questions during our interview, the only two questions I felt were worth interrupting his discourse. The only two I thought he might answer honestly. The first was about his recitation of Edgar Allen Poe, which he answered with a five-minute speech on Early American Literature. I recall thinking, *if you chopped*

*his hair and gave him a pair of spectacles he could pass for a
literature professor.*

My second question was about *Lucin*, an obscure song
with no radio play. A single that was never promoted, and
received a total of two weeks on the shelf.

He smiled and leaned forward in his chair.

"At last, someone has asked a question worth answering." He made the crystal, which he had held through the
entire interview, disappear, and rose from his chair. "But
not here, and not with this thing listening."

He bent down, picked up the recorder, and with a
sleight of hand that would put David Copperfield to
shame, made it vanish as well.

Thirty minutes later I found myself on the back of his
Harley Davidson, holding on for dear life and heading
toward the desert outside Boise.

It was a warm June night lit by a bright half-moon and a
clear sky full of stars. He drove East toward Mountain-
home, then south to Bruneau. Bruneau is the mythical
small-town Idaho, a crumbling double lane main street,
gravel side streets, and a business district that consisted of
a combination gas station/grocery store in what appeared
to be a remodeled barn, and two bars. The sign leading
into town said *Warning to Tourists – Don't Laugh at the
Natives*. The sign was riddled with dents and bullet holes.
We didn't stop in Bruneau, but turned down a side road
and drove another ten miles or so to Bruneau Dunes State
Park.

The Bruneau sand dune is the largest moving sand

dune in North America, or maybe the world, I can't remember which. I understand it is quite an attraction in this part of the country, but the twisted path leading to the dune, and the public parking at its base were quiet and empty that night.

Kane ignored the public parking and pulled up to the edge of the dune, kicked the stand down, and killed the Harley's thunder. I was happy to be off the bike, to have control of my movement again. I was not comfortable being so far away from my own transportation, but I was willing to suffer the discomfort for this career making interview. I paced at the edge of the dune, stretching my legs and waiting for Kane to dismount his bike. He didn't move right away. He sat, staring into the sky with his bound hair hanging in a tail down his back.

"The desert has a quiet magic," he said softly. "In the shadows between dunes and under tumbleweeds, between the crystal grains of sand, and in the song of its watchful guardians and the quiet breeze. The whispered breath of God."

He dismounted the bike in a quick, graceful arc.

The sand puffed up by his booted feet did not fall back to Earth, but became tiny dust devils, whirling in separate directions into the night. He looked at me, deep into my weary eyes, with an intensity that frightened me.

"Are you unsure of yourself? Have you come all this way with me not to ask the single question burning so brightly in your mind I can see it printed in your eyes?"

In a motion too quick to register, he moved forward and stood before me. He stooped slightly so his gaze was level with mine. His eyes were ink-black.

"Fortune favors the bold, and so do I. If you wish to go

any farther, ask your question." That said, he turned and walked away, stopping in front of the giant dune, his arms crossed. Waiting.

My fear quickly dissolved into wonder, my trepidation into fascination. My trifle curiosity became something more. Before I wanted only to know who he was, now I needed to know. Who he was. What he was.

He waited.

I swallowed the lump in my throat and asked the question.

"Are you Jarek Poe?"

I felt the tension that had built between us in those last moments, dissolve. I could not see his answering smile, but I felt it.

"Yes," he said, and the last protracted syllable seemed to slither from his lips like a snake. That word seemed more like an affirmation than an answer.

He bent suddenly, scooping up two handfuls of sand, and tossed them into the air. The quiet breeze, the whispered breath of God, whipped them into a whirlwind that engulfed us both. The sand swallowed us in its spinning dance, striking the skin on my arms and face hard enough to sting. I closed my eyes against it, crossed my arms in front of my face in an involuntary defense.

Seconds later, when the whirlwind died away, I lowered my arms and opened my eyes on a different world.

I stood, staring into an endless world of sand. It was still nighttime, but the moon was brighter and the shadows deeper, almost solid. Giant cacti stood like desert sequoias in the distance. A tumbleweed the size of a large boulder rolled past us, even though there was no wind to push it. A bright, bloated moon hung in the sky above them. I thought I saw the outlines of a face on it. The white sand moved and rippled like the water of some great, dry sea.

While I busied myself trying to fight off the cocoon of unreality that had enveloped me, brought on by the inexplicable change of setting, Poe raised his bent arms in the air in what seemed to be an eerie imitation of the distant cacti. He made a crooning, keening sound that made my spine twist and my skin crawl. It was inhuman. The unnatural sound carried and echoed back to us, even though nothing stood in the desert for it to echo off of.

The only break in the rippling expanse of desert was a chasm, maybe a hundred feet wide, and god knew how deep. It waited in the distance, ready to swallow anyone who might venture too close.

Had I the strength, or the presence of mind, I would have run screaming from it. It and the creature that brought me there.

Poe relaxed, dropped his pose, and walked toward me. Watching the sand slash up under his booted feet, I realized for the first time that there was a reasonable explanation for all that I had experienced. I laughed out loud and noticed only loosely that my laughter made no echo.

Poe continued to approach me, smiling the crooked smile that I recognized from many of his interview photos.

"We're stoned, aren't we?" I asked. "You got me high on mescaline, didn't you?" I was convinced he had somehow slipped me his favored drug, how else to explain what I was seeing. I wanted to be angry with him for ending my long sober stretch, but I could not. I even tried frowning at him, but the failed attempt sent me into a fresh burst of laughter.

Still smiling that odd, crooked smile, he shook his head.

"I no longer partake of The Divine Fez," he said. "It was an imperfect avenue to what I sought. There was an abstract pleasure, but I don't need it now."

He produced a cigarette from behind his hair-shrouded ear, it was unfiltered and appeared to be hand rolled. I am positive there had been no cigarette there before. He put it to his lips and drew. There was a faint popping sound as the end of his smoke lit itself. He blew the first drag out and passed it to me.

"You have not had a smoke in over five hours. You used the last of your cash to buy batteries for your recorder."

My feeling of good humor was gone, vanquished by Poe's uncanny display. As I said earlier, I think he got off on it.

"How do you know that?"

"My crystal ball told me," he said with his devil's grin.

Behind him, with the fanfair of thunder rolling through a still valley, a roaring flame appeared. All around us the numerous shadows stood out in contrast to a light that was so bright that they seemed three-dimensional. Stranger yet, these shadows had no source, no solid object to cast them. The aberrations began to move around us, circling us, surrounding us.

They took on form, then color as they drew closer. They were animals. Two wolves, a fox, an eagle, snakes, scorpions, and more. There was even a Saint Bernard and a long-haired domestic cat. They stood around us in a distant circle, watching, but nothing more.

"Brother," Poe said, drawing my attention from the silent group. He pointed to a pair of flat, knee-high rocks that faced each other from opposing sides of the fire.

I obediently took a seat. Poe took the opposing stone seat and leaned in closer to the flames.

"Now the real interview begins," he said.

"Short but sweet," Poe promised. "Ask your questions, and I promise to answer them as truthfully as possible."

My first question was simple. "Have I gone insane?" I asked in a shaking voice I barely recognized as my own.

"No," he stated simply.

I had to swallow several times before asking the next question. Fear of his probable answer had caused my throat to go dry.

"Am I . . . dead?"

He favored me with the crooked, devilish grin again, then alswered. "No, you are not dead, brother."

"Why do you call me brother?" I asked, growing agitated. "I don't have a brother. I'm an only child."

"Because you are my brother," he said, this time without the smile. "Or soon will be."

His cryptic answer defused my anger, if not my confusion.

"Where am I?"

"That I cannot answer," he said. "At least not in terms you would understand.

"Are you a . . ."

"Ghost," he finished for me, "a spirit?"

I nodded.

"Yes," he said. "Would you like to hear how I died?"

"Yes," I said.

———

"The lyrics to the song, you know the one I'm talking about, came to me in a vision. I wrote it and recorded it on the same day. The rest of the band hated it, they thought I had finally lost what mind I had left. They were not into the mescaline, the lifestyle, or the ideas I sang about. It was just a profitable gig to them. I think they went along with it just to shut me up.

"After the session I left them, just wandered off not even sure of where I was going. None of them tried to stop me. I must have wandered for several hours, because by the time I came back to my senses it was nighttime, and I was lost in the desert.

"I tried to find my way back to Phoenix by following my tracks, but the wind had erased them. By the time the moon was on its decline, I was completely lost. I kept walking anyway, singing my new song to pass the time. Listening to my own lyrics, I was beginning to wonder if maybe I had not finally lost my mind.

"When I finished the final verse, my wolf brothers appeared." He nodded toward the pair of wolves sitting side by side to my right, watching with interest.

"They tore me to pieces," he said. "My body was found some time later I believe, but they could not identify it."

"Why did you come back," I asked, not without some

apprehension. I feared I already knew the answer.

"For you, brother."

"I should go now," he said rising from his stone seat. "My brothers and sisters grow impatient."

He circled the fire and began walking toward the distant chasm. The spirit animals joined him, changing once again. They became human.

Many were natives, a few in full ceremonial dress, some in modern clothing. There was also a stout man in a business suit, an acne scarred teenage couple holding hands, and a woman dressed in fifties' clothing. The long-haired cat became a small girl, dressed in Little Mermaid pajamas.

I stood quickly and faced them, but I dared not follow.

"*Why?*" I shouted to him.

He stopped and turned.

"You were chosen, why ... I do not know. Fear not brother, this is not Hell. You are not among the damned."

His following words seemed to me a message from beyond, dictated much the same way as the lyrics of his final song.

"Eternity is a multifaceted gem," he said. "It is your heart that dictates which facet you are destined to occupy."

He turned to leave again but paused.

"One last thing," he said. "*Lucin!*"

His entourage reverted to animal form and disappeared into the night. Poe also changed. Into a bird. A raven.

A low growl erupted from the depths of the fire, and I saw the shape of its source before it pounced. It was a fox.

It hit me hard, drawing blood from my cheek with a swipe of its claws. I spun, swatting at the animal, and fell backward into the flames. They did not burn me though. When I landed it was not on burning sand or hot coals, but on the shabby bed of my Boise hotel room.

I lay there for a long time, exactly how long I don't know. I hadn't dared to rise right away. Not until I was confident I could do so without falling over unconscious.

When I finally did get up, I went straight to the room's small, sterile bathroom. My favorite thing about hotels, the good ones anyhow, is that you never have to clean them yourself. Dirty when you leave, clean when you return. It's like a magic trick.

I inspected the cuts on my face in the bathroom mirror. Four angry red lines starting at the cheekbone and ending at the chin. They were not as deep as I feared, but they had bled quite a bit. The left side of my face was almost completely covered with blood. I wetted a hand towel and carefully blotted it clean. I knew I would have to disinfect the wound, but I had no rubbing alcohol, so I used hot water and soap. It hurt like a motherfucker.

I let the hot water run and stood over the sink with my eyes closed, breathing in the hot steam, clearing my mind.

Trying to anyway.

It was a dream, I remember thinking. *I fell asleep and missed the concert, then clawed myself before awaking. That's all.*

It didn't explain how I'd returned to my hotel room, but one impossibility at a time.

I heard a squeaking sound, like the chattering of a mouse, and opened my eyes. The bathroom was thick with steam. It felt like a sauna. Written on the fogged-up mirror was the night's final argument against the sane and mundane world I no longer fit into.

See you soon brother - J. Poe. On the blood-soaked hand towel, I found a small crystal sphere, the one Poe had played with endlessly.

I checked out and left Boise in the dark of early morning.

———

Two days later, on the way back to New York, I saw a picture of myself on the television at a roadside dinner. It seemed I was sought in connection with the disappearance of rock star Tarin Kane. Because of evidence found in my vacated hotel room, a blood-soaked towel, foul play was suspected.

None of the other patrons, truckers mostly, were paying attention to the broadcast, so I slipped out unnoticed.

———

I am a wanted man now, so I can't go back to New York. I'm driving to Mexico instead. The authorities will never believe my story, or they will use it to prove I'm insane. Even if forensic testing proves the blood on the towel is mine, they will find a way to use it against me.

The last I heard, they found Kane's Harley at the Bruneau Dunes. They are still looking for his body.

I was mugged at a rest area while using the bathroom. The bastard beat me up pretty bad, then stole my wallet. He got my Visa card, but at least he didn't take my car. I managed to get away from the rest area before anyone found me, which was good. I must not be found.

I ran out of gas after crossing the Texas border. I was in the middle of nowhere, so I ditched the car and walked. I followed the highway for about ten miles before I saw the state trooper. The cruiser was approaching fast from the south, lights flashing but silent. I prepared to run, but it passed me without stopping. After that I moved away from the highway, further into the sprawling desert land that reminded me uncannily of the countryside outside Boise.

Lost in the desert. No food, no water, not a chance in hell of making it to Mexico. I still have the crystal that Poe left me. I would rather have a cigarette, a bottle of wine, and the last week of my life to do over again. I think I will find a nice place to sit down instead. I'll watch the crystal ball and wait for the night. Wait for the quiet magic to begin, and for my brothers and sisters to come for me.

THE CASK OF A THOUSAND DILDOS

Perussi Faeculentus Quod Intereo · This Blasphemy Brought To You By Doodie-Fetish Snuff Films LLC

The thousand injuries of McLaughlin I had borne as best I could, but when he replaced the microphone at my short story reading with a vibrating dildo, I vowed revenge. You, who so well know the level of security at the World Horror Convention, would not have heard me give utterance to a threat. *At length*, and by *at length* I mean early the next morning, I would be avenged. This is understood by now, I'm sure. But how to accomplish this without being caught? I must not just punish, but for the sake of this homage, punish with impunity. A wrong is unredressed when its redresser gets passed along the New York penal system like a pack of unfiltered Winstons.

Understand, I gave McLaughlin no reason to suspect me. I continued, after having him inscribe the dildo, *One Wobbly Wang To Another,* to me, to smile in his face, and he never suspected that my smile was at the thought of where I was going to shove that *Wobbly Wang*.

He had a weak point, this Clown Prince of Horror. Though in most cases a man who would point and giggle at The Reaper himself, cracking wise about Death's boney ass and unfashionable robes, he did have one soft spot in his whoopee-cushion of a heart.

Albino Pigmy Bukkake.

Few native midwesterners have the true Albino Pigmy Bukkake spirit. For the most part their enthusiasm is better adapted toward sheep hazing and incest, making cheap home videos that sell for a few dollars a copy on eBay. In his other passions McLaughlin was, like his midwestern countrymen, a hack, but in the matter of white Pigmy cum-baths, he was sincere. In this respect we could not have differed more, I preferred porn stars with a healthy tan.

It was near dawn on the second night of the convention when I accosted McLaughlin outside the third story men's bathroom, having just relieved himself of an excess quantity of absinthe in an attempt to make room for more of the same. The man wore a Motley Crue T-shirt, with tight fitting striped pants, and sitting crookedly on his head, a jester's cap with grinning skull-shaped bells.

I was dressed as The Doctor. Early Matt Smith, before the plumb colored overcoat and tophat.

So pleased was I to find him, that I thought I would never be done wringing his hand.

"Ouch," he said, massaging his thoroughly wrung hand. "Easy does it, Doctor Poo."

I grinned, tipping slightly on unsteady feet and adjusting my bow tie. In truth, I hadn't had a drop to drink, but I was wary of the old adage *Never trust a sober man at a horror convention ... especially if he's dressed as The Doctor*, and thought it wise to feign intoxication.

McLaughlin flinched away as I patted his back. "You are well met, my good man," I said.

"Why are you talking like that?" he asked, watching me as if I were a dog he suspected was about to hump his leg.

"No reason," I said, widening my fools grin. "It's just that I've made a most amazing discovery, and since I wasn't able to find you, I was seeking Shane Ryan Staley. He is the only man I know whose appreciation of obscure porn surpasses your own."

"Porn?" McLaughlin said, and with the utterance of that one word, his entire demeanor transformed from one of bleary-eyed suspicion to one of barely contained excitement. I feared, for a moment, that he would begin to hump *my* leg.

"Indeed," I said. "Not just garden variety porn either. Albino Pigmy Bukkake!"

His jaw dropped, and a fine line of drool ran into his goatee. "You're shitting me!"

"I shit you not," I said, then adopting a look of concern, added, "but I see you're indisposed at the moment. You need sleep, or a butt-load of coffee. I'm afraid you're in no condition …"

"It's nothing," he said. "I write drunker than this!"

"My concern is only for your well-being. Perhaps I should find Shane." I pointed over his shoulder at a drunken crowd at the far end of the corridor. "I think I see him now."

"Bullshit!" he ejaculated. "Oh, sorry about that. Did I get any on you?"

"Not to worry," I said, wiping my sleeve against the wall to scrub away McLaughlin's premature enthusiasm. "You appear to be warmed up and ready to go."

He nodded, glassy-eyed, and allowed himself to be led away.

"We should make haste. The show starts soon."

"Bukkake," he said under his breath.

"And this is no mere recording," I said, spotting my room number at the end of the hall and dragging him ever quicker toward it.

"Bukkake."

"This is a live shooting, being filmed on location in a dark and drippy set …"

"*Bukkake*," he marveled.

"… And the director needs extras for today's shoot."

"Me! Me!" he shouted, waving his arms like an over excited Catholic schoolboy with a nun fetish. "I'll do it!"

It was by an odd and improbable series of circumstances that I came by the location of which I spoke, a series of bleary-eyed wrong turns I shan't bore you with. It is enough to say that while searching for the toilet in my hotel room the first night of the convention, I found a passage leading from inside the closet of my third-floor room directly into New York's subterranean sewer system.

The previous night I had failed to tip housekeeping, knowing it was enough to ensure, one and all, their absence from my room that night.

McLaughlin followed me willingly enough into my room, not commenting when I hung the *Do Not Disturb* sign out, but he balked when I opened the closet door and motioned him inside.

"You jest! What is this?"

"The show," I said. "It starts soon. We must hurry."

Still, he hesitated.

I shrugged and closed the door. "Perhaps Shane is still around here somewhere."

McLaughlin spat at the mention of Shane's name.

"Staley's interest is mere pretension! He is an ignoramus! He wouldn't know good bukkake from a common circle jerk!" With that, he threw open the closet door and strode boldly inside.

Retrieving my sonic screwdriver flashlight from my tweed coat's inner pocket, I shut the door behind us and led the way.

We walked for a time in silence. The only sounds were that of distant, dripping water and the rapid breathing of my randy companion. He followed me along twists and turns through the underground labyrinth. Several times we doubled back, circled, passed points I had marked well only minutes before. I knew where I was, but my companion was thoroughly lost.

"What is that smell?" he asked at length.

"We're close now," I said, and pulled two baseball caps from my inner pocket. I put one on and handed the other to him.

He read the logo aloud. "Doodie-Fetish?"

"The production company," I said.

He looked at the hat again, his fingers tracing a Latin phrase *perussi faeculentus quod intereo* below the logo. "What is this moto?"

"Do you know Latin?" I asked.

"Of course I do!" He cleared his throat and lifted his chin importantly. "E Pluribus Unum."

"Ah," I said.

"Caveat emptor."

"Impressive," I said.

"Dominus Vobiscum."

"Bravo!"

"Doobe doobe doo wap!"

"Wow!" I said. "Good looking and well educated."

"Buffoon," he said with a derisive snort. "That one wasn't even Latin." He removed his jester's cap and put the Doodie-Fetish hat on, then replaced his belled cap over the top of it, pulling it snug.

I noticed a steadiness in his movements, and a general clearing of the speech that implied impending sobriety. Fortunately, I had anticipated this. I halted him, and pulled a bottle of absinthe from my inner pocket.

"Surely, an occasion such as this deserves a toast."

"Then a toast to you, sir," he said. "And to the pigmies."

"I thumbed the cork loose and handed it to McLaughlin, who tipped the bottle back and drank."

"Do you have to narrate out loud?" he said. "It's annoying."

"Sorry."

He drank again, then, with a wicked grin, wedged the bottle between his legs like a crystalline penis and made jack-off gestures, spilling absinthe down the front of his striped pants.

I looked at him, but said nothing.

He repeated the gesture, a grotesque one, then glared at me and drank again. "You're not in the Order then?"

"The Order?"

"The Porn Lover's Guild."

"Yes, yes," I said. "I am."

"You? Get outa' here!"

"Yes."

"Give me a sign."

I pulled the signed vibrator from the improbably deep inner pocket of my tweed coat and switched it on. Its buzz filled the empty corridors like the drone of horny bees.

"Bah!" He waved a dismissive hand at me. "Come on, to the show."

"To the show," I agreed.

At last we reached the place, a narrow dead end corridor closed to the main artery of the maze by a rusted steel door. I pulled the door open and shone my sonic screwdriver inside.

Before us, pointed at the unseen far wall, was a tripod and camera, a shrouded object that could have been a .50 cal machine gun, or a robot, and beside that a cask.

"What's that's for?"

"Props," I said. "Inside. The starlets will want to meet you."

I pointed the flashlight's beam at the end of the corridor. Two small, pale figures sat against the wall.

McLaughlin rushed inside, eager to meet the stars.

So complete was his inebriation that he spoke with them for a full minute before realizing they were nothing more than half-inflated blow-up dolls. By the time McLaughlin caught wise, I had shackled him to the wall between them. He strained against the shackles around his ankles and neck to no avail.

"What is this?" he demanded.

"Notice the cables," I said, pointing in turn to the

cables clamped to the chain on his neck shackle, and the one on an ankle chain.

He followed them with his eyes. Both were fastened securely to the stone wall behind him and ran to a series of car batteries arranged in the corner to his right. The negative cable intersected a small silver box next to the batteries.

Acme Remotes.

I ignored his demands for freedom and turned on the stage light behind the camera, then aimed the camera at him and pushed *record*.

The image in the camera's viewfinder was exquisite!

Stunned into the briefest of silences, McLaughlin spoke again. "What is the meaning of this?"

I unfolded a canvas director's chair. A small hand-held remote with a single red button lay in the seat. I picked up the remote, sat, and waited.

He pulled against his chains, giving the bells on his cap a violent ring.

"*I demand …*"

I pushed the button.

"*Ahhh! Fuck,*" he said.

I pushed the red button again and grinned while he did a low voltage jitterbug.

"*Help,*" he screamed.

"*Help,*" I echoed.

"*Somebody,*" he shouted.

"*Anybody,*" I added.

McLaughlin fell silent and glared at me. "If this is about that vibrator thing then you have got to lighten the fuck up!"

"Listen," I said, raising a shushing finger to my lips and turning my ear toward the door.

The *squish-slap*, *squish-slap* of approaching feet echoed in the corridors beyond.

"Ha!" He laughed aloud. "Someone heard me! You are in so much trouble when I get out of these. I'm gonna' kick your ass! I'm going to tell everyone you're a closet Harry Potter fan! I'm going to post bad reviews of your books on Amazon!"

I said nothing.

The sound of feet slapping the crap-crusted stone floor grew louder, closer. Then they entered.

There were a dozen of them, short and skinny, with white, hairless bodies and wangs like mutant cucumbers.

The smile fell from McLaughlin's face.

The Albino Pigmies had arrived.

They gathered around him in a semicircle, dicks in hand, leaving enough of a gap up front for the camera to get a good shot. These guys were real pros. They knew what they were doing.

"*God in Heaven! No!*"

"Action," I shouted.

It was the most god-awful thing I have ever witnessed, but I did watch. Every few minutes I would give the red button a poke, and amid the sounds of squealing, grunting Pigmies, and McLaughlin's shouts and gargles of protest, there would be a low electric buzz and scream of pain.

At last, the Pigmies stamina was spent, and they lay in a panting semicircle around him, blistered cucumber dicks flopping grotesquely against bony thighs. The smell of fear and electrified Pigmy spunk challenged, but did not overpower, the signature sewer scent.

After a rest, the little men marshaled their strength and helped each other to their feet.

"That's a wrap, boys," I said. "Good work."

"Everybody has to be good at something," the lead Pigmy said as he led his fellows from the room.

McLaughlin and I were alone again.

"What's wrong, my friend? Not still mad about the little Pigmy joke, are you?"

McLaughlin wiped handfuls of jizz from his face, then looked away.

"The whole screaming for help thing didn't work out like you'd hoped, did it?"

Nothing from my pouty companion.

No worries. Phase two was about to begin. He'd be singing again soon enough.

I yanked the shroud from the object beside the camera, and his pout became a look of dark speculation.

Acme Power Pitcher 2000.

"What is that?"

It was my turn to give the silent treatment. It was a dumb question anyway. It was perfectly obvious what it was. There was even a big sticker with the name on it.

I raised the cask's lid and pulled out the first *prop*.

A huge neon-green dildo.

"You have got to be kidding?"

I was not.

I turned the pitching machine on, the energetic *whirr* of spinning wheels within the contraption drowning out the distant *drip-drip-drip* of leaking pipes, and yelled, "Scene two ... action!"

I dropped the dildo into the ball chute at the back of the Power Pitcher, and it flew from the front like a green alien rocket, pounding head first into McLaughlin's chest.

The impact bounced him against the wall, forcing a pained squeal from him. I thought I heard the crack of a snapping rib, but that may have just been wishful thinking. I reached into the casket again, where nine-hundred and ninety-nine more dildos of varying size and design awaited their turn at the Clown Prince. The one I withdrew was short, thick, red, with spikes circling the misshapen head. I dropped it in and watched it fly.

McLaughlin tugged at his shackles, but to no effect. The red dildo struck the side of his head, jarring it violently to the side. He sagged against the wall, semi-conscious and moaning.

I adjusted the Power Pitcher aim and dropped the next dildo into the chute.

It nailed him in the groin, smashing his sweet meats against the stone behind him.

His eyes snapped open, and he howled.

This was even more fun than I had imagined it would be!

I reached into the casket and withdrew another. Three down, nine-hundred and ninety-seven to go.

───────

Time passed, how much I could not tell.

McLaughlin hung from his shackles, unconscious, pummeled beyond recognition by the shock-and-awe assault of rubber man-missiles. His shirt was torn, his arms lumpy and bruised. Blood ran from his nose, mouth, and a cut on his forehead where swelling had split the skin. His left eye was gone. In its place, dangling from the socket like a turd that just won't drop, was a bright yellow dildo streaked and spotted with blood.

He might have been dead, except for the regular wheezing breaths he pulled in.

I wanted him awake for the coup de grâce.

I pushed the red button.

His body tensed with the buzzing, but he did not wake.

I pushed it again.

He bucked briefly. His eyes opened, then fell closed again.

I pushed the button a third time.

"McLaughlin!"

Nothing. Just the wheeze of his breathing.

He did not die but would not wake.

I resigned myself and prepared phase three.

I raised the camera's tripod to its highest setting and fixed McLaughlin in the viewfinder again, then checked the cable feeds to the recorder outside the room. Slowly, I approached him. Cautiously, as if he were a sleeping animal which might awake and bite me. He did not move. Above his head was a broken pipe, and a handwheel operated valve. I opened it, and a trickle of brackish water ran onto McLaughlin's head, streaking his face.

A hand grabbed my arm. Finger bones broken in an attempt to shield himself from the thousand dildos popped and clicked.

I jumped back, heart pounding, a cold sweat breaking my brow.

McLaughlin lay as he had, eyes closed and slumped against the wall.

I left him there, took my sonic screwdriver flashlight and went outside into the main corridor, shutting the door behind me. It did not take long to seal the cracks between door, floor, and wall.

The main valve to the broken pipe above McLaughlin's head was corroded and stiff, long in disuse, but it turned.

I put an ear to the door and listened for a scream amid the liquid rush as raw sewage filled the room. Wanting to hear that last scream more than I had wanted anything in my life.

It did not come.

I left him there.

For half a year, no mortal has opened that door.

McLaughlin is famous now, a star in his very own video. You can buy it for three dollars a copy on eBay, courtesy of Doodie-Fetish Snuff Films LLC.

Perussi faeculeutus quad intereo.

Eat shit and die.

GO GIRLS RULE!

"I used to be a star," Penny said, not knowing why she had. It was just random chatter, nonsense that had escaped her lips in the afterglow of okay sex. She sat naked on the edge of her messed, narrow bed, stared out the open window at the glowing New York night. There was a hole in the skyline where the twin towers used to be, like the broken smile of an old, battered woman. She shook a cigarette from the open pack on her nightstand, a Camel, one of his, and listened to the nightlife four stories below as she lit it and smoked. "A long time ago. Me and my sisters, we were all stars."

"You still are." Johnny sat up behind her, stroked her neck and ran his fingers through her long tangle of dark hair. Johnny wasn't his real name, it was just what she called him. What she called them all. She didn't know his real name. Didn't want to.

She shivered at his touch. "That feels nice." She smiled, took another drag.

"A star," he whispered in her ear. His hands slid away

from her neck, down her back, around to her small breasts. He kissed the back of her neck and she shuddered.

He's trying to seduce me, she thought. *Trying to talk me into a freebie.*

He was one of the nice ones. She might just let him. But then his hands were gone, and she felt the bed shift as he rolled away from her.

Someone shouted from the street below, the voice clear through her open window. Someone else honked a horn. She took a few more drags of the Camel and tamped it out half smoked. She sat in silence while Johnny dressed.

She wondered how her sisters were.

She checked the clock on her nightstand, a quarter to one in the morning. Good, she hadn't missed her show.

When she looked up again Johnny was standing in front of her, smiling.

She smiled too, bitterly.

"You don't believe me, do you? You think I'm making it up." Not that it mattered, he was only another Johnny. She would live, or die, regardless of what he thought of her.

"I believe you," he said. "I know."

He leaned toward her, and she braced herself.

Here it comes, she thought. *He's going to have another go with me whether I want it or not.*

It wasn't the first time this had happened. Wouldn't be the last.

But he only kissed her, a quick, light kiss on her forehead.

"Go Girls Rule," he said, and left her. He dropped a fold of bills on her cluttered vanity and said, "goodbye, Penny."

Penny watched the door for a while, unsure if she wanted him to come back. He knew her! He remembered her name from the show, the one her friends called her, even though most of them did not know about her few years of childhood fame.

He did not come back.

She walked to her vanity and looked at the cash. The crinkled edge of the top bill said one hundred. There might be four, maybe five bills in the fold, more than her standard fare. Maybe it was because he had recognized her, maybe sex with Penny the Go Girl had fulfilled some longstanding fantasy. She left the money where it was. She wasn't a whore until she picked up the money, so she left it where it was for the time being. There was a business card next to the cash. She picked the card up instead.

Jim Stoddard, it said. *Talent Scout and Agent.*

Written below the name and designation in black ink, perhaps while she sat naked and smoked his cigarette, a personal note.

You are still a star, Penny. Find your sisters and call me. We'll show the world that you are still a star.

She shook another smoke from the pack he left and smoked while she dressed. She was finished working for the night, so she dressed casually, a pair of cutoffs and a white tank top. She closed the curtains, shutting the outside world away as best as she could, and turned the TV on.

The American Oldies Channel, all oldies, all the time, if you counted *Three's Company* and *Gilligan's Island* as oldies, that is. It was a few minutes to one in the morning when she turned it on, and the intro music for *The Go*

Girls, supplemented with flashy still shots like a Best Of slide show, began.

Here we come again, to save the world,
Jenny, Penny, Kat - We're the Go Girls.
Fighting bad guys, all around the world,
Meanies have no chance against those super girls.
Go Girls rule!

The last line of *The Go Girls* theme song was Kat's, the sweetheart of the show.

She was younger than Jenny and Penny by two years, and small for her age. Blond hair and dazzling blue eyes set her apart from her sisters, sisters by adoption, not blood. She was Shirley Temple in superhero tights. She also had a good deal more talent than her sisters, a fact that was plain to anybody who watched the show regularly.

At seven years old she'd had a bright future, assuming drugs, booze, or plain old famous girl crazy didn't end it for her.

Jenny and Penny, whose name was Margot before the show, but Jenny, Margot, and Kat didn't have much of a ring to it, were sisters. Jenny and Penny were identical twins with raven hair, dark eyes, and pretty faces. Jenny was the brains of the team, the leader. Penny was always second string until the action started, but she was usually the one who faced down the baddies at the end of each episode.

Kat was the heart of the Go Girls.

She was also the most fragile of the three, in character and in fact, and after three years of syndication Beaumont "Bo-Bo" Johnson, their adoptive father and the show's producer, finally broke her.

Penny started a pot of coffee during the first commercial break, and it was ready when the second break arrived. The break came leaving Jenny and Kat at the mercy of the evil Mr. Meanie, a trap for Penny, who would surely come to their rescue. It was standard Go Girls fare, in the tradition of *Batman* or *The Green Hornet*, but *Batman* had never been that adorable and spunky in his cape and tights.

"Good episode, but not my best performance," she said to the lonely apartment. "Meanie was in top form that day though."

She smiled, thinking of the crusty but kind old method actor who had played Meanie, Edom Bilks.

Penny's smile faded. She poured coffee, toasted and buttered an English muffin, and made it back to her seat before the end of break. When the break was over she watched her younger self, decked out in pink tights, sweeping black cape, and a black mask with a bow and kitten ears, sneak past a dozen numb-nuts cronies. Her special Go Girls power was a fine-tuned precognition, which warned her whenever danger was near and helped her avoid it. She was the psychic Go Girl, uncatchable.

For reasons never explained, Mr. Meanie fell outside of Penny's powers of prediction. Jenny's power of mind control had never worked on him either. They had to rely on brains and good old American wit to beat Meanie, and even though they always won he usually escaped at the end of each episode.

The patented Go Girls method of defeating Mr. Meanie always looked like something Rube Goldberg might have devised after a couple hits of really good acid.

Watching her younger self on the tube, Penny blushed. She'd never considered how trashy their old Go Girl costumes were. Skin tight and padded in all the right places to make their young bodies appear more developed than they were. It was not overt, only subtle swells on the hips, butt, and where her breasts would come in another few years. She remembered how difficult those costumes were to get into, Bo-Bo with his hands under the skintight fabric taking forever to get those pads in place.

She drifted off before the finale and dreamed she was with Kat.

They were high up somewhere, the top of a tall building. It could have been New York or LA, there was no defining landscape to tell her which. The building was a prop, she realized, not real. It was one hundred stories of leaning paper mache. It stood in the middle of their old studio, and they were so high up that the people on the studio floor looked like grains of sand on white paper.

Kat's mouth stretched wide, face flushed in a scream that dropped dead, silent, in the air between them. She screamed, but Penny could not hear her words.

"What?" Penny tried to reach for her little sister, but the distance between them seemed to swell. Kat wore her old Go Girls costume again, was stuffed into it. No need for the supplemental padding now, Kat was all grown up and had her own curves to fill it out. Penny noted with a little jealousy that Kat was still the prettiest of them.

Kat shouted, and again there were no words. One of the chief symptoms of Kat's madness these past years had been silence. Even when she was aware and responsive, her silence endured. Though her lips moved, there was no sound. What Penny could not hear from Kat's lips, she read on them.

Help me, Kat's lips said. Then, *he's coming*. She scratched at her left arm with the long fingernails of her right hand, tearing through fabric stretched past its endurance. It ripped easily. What Penny, at first, mistook for sloppy wet fingernail polish turned out to be blood.

"Who's coming," Penny yelled.

Somewhere below one of the grains of sand called out, "*Action!*"

"Is it Meanie?" But Penny knew it wasn't. Edom Bilks had died shortly after their final episode, and he was never really their enemy to begin with, just an old actor trying to squeeze a few more paychecks out of his declining career.

Kat turned her eyes away from Penny, grimaced, backed away a step, as if tracking something or someone Penny couldn't see. She mouthed the word *no*, took another step back, closer to the edge. Then she turned and faced the drop before her, arms spread like wings, as if to fly. Flying was one of Kat's super powers, her other was levitation. She could lift things with her mind, small things mostly, and use them to pummel the villain of the day. Her flying skills were less than reliable. More often than not, when she tried to fly, she crashed.

"No!" Penny screamed, and ran to stop her sister, but she could not close the distance between them. It swelled, and the world around them stretched in and out like the throbbing of an unseen organ.

Kat turned back to Penny one last time, arms still outstretched, the left arm dripping blood.

Go Girls Rule, she mouthed, and leapt over the edge of the leaning paper mache tower, froze for a few moments in the air before she fell.

Penny woke just before noon the next morning to the ringing of her phone.

"What's shaking, Sis?" It was Jenny.

Penny was surprised to hear from her, Jenny might stay out of touch for months at a time, then suddenly drop back into Penny's life as if they'd never been separated, then run back to LA again without a word. She was nervous, too, because she never knew what sort of trouble her sister might be in when she did call.

"What are you into now?" She said without thinking and felt bad once it was out.

There was a pause, short but heavy with tension. Penny heard the tapping of long fingernails against the receiver on the other end of the line, a ragged intake of breath. "Don't be a bitch, Penny."

"Sorry," Penny said, but now she wasn't. In the past few years there had been tension between the two of them, and every time Penny spoke to her California doppelganger she felt on the verge of exploding. She suspected Jenny felt the same way, but that she was better at hiding it. "How are you?"

"I'm fine."

A first, Penny thought, and then cursed herself. *She's right, you are being a bitch.*

"Come to LA," Jenny said. "I miss you. I know sometimes we don't get along so well, but you're my sister." There was another pause, Jenny waiting for an answer.

There was none. Penny was thinking about the business card sitting on the vanity next to her bounty.

"Come to LA," Jenny said again.

Don't do it, she thought. *We're going to be at each other's fucking throats.*

She did it anyway.

"No," Penny said. "You come to New York."

She cleaned her little fourth floor apartment until the scent of ammonia and pine made her want to puke. She decided enough time had passed, so she counted the money on her dresser. Six hundred dollars. A nice guy and a good tipper.

There would be no Johnny that night thanks to Jim Stoddard's generosity, maybe never again if his offer of renewed stardom was for real. It had been a long time since she'd allowed herself to feel this kind of hope. The unfamiliar emotion filled her with anxiety, a buzz purer than anything she'd ever known since her druggie days.

Jenny had agreed to come to New York. She would catch a flight that very day.

Expect me around ten tonight, if I can catch an early flight. If not, I'll call back and let you know.

Jenny had not called back, so she would be somewhere over the Nevada desert by then, Penny guessed.

It was time to go visit Kat.

Her subway ride to Queens passed quickly, thinking about the one sister that lived close enough that she could visit any time she wanted, but never did. It had been months since she'd seen Kat.

Preoccupied with thoughts of her damaged sister, she almost missed her stop and had to run to make it out the door to the platform. Back on the surface she waved down a cab and fifteen minutes later she was at the front gate of the State institution that had been Kat's home the past decade.

Inside, the receptionist asked Penny her business.

"I'm here to see Kat Johnson."

Eyes lifted suspiciously over the top of gold-wire rim bifocals. She was new, new enough at least that Penny couldn't remember her. "You another one of those *True Story* folks, cause if so you can turn around and show yourself out."

"No, I'm her sister. Penny Johnson."

The receptionist's eyes, eyes so dark they were almost black, stayed on her, and the thin eyebrows above them lifted.

Right, that look said, *and I'm Elton John's bastard half-sister.*

Penny dug into her purse, withdrew her pocketbook and flipped it open to her ID.

The receptionist's eyes widened for just a moment, then she nodded toward a small, empty sitting room.

"Be just a moment," she said. Then, almost embarrassed, "my girls loved your old show. They never missed it."

Penny smiled, thanked her, and made her way to the nearest seat.

She waited no more than five minutes, reading a two year out of date *TV Guide*. She noted The American Oldies Channel timeslot for *The Go Girls* was one in the morning, even two years ago, before she had started watching it again.

On one hand, it was nice to know they were forever you through the power of syndication. On the other, it sucked that they would never see a dime in residuals. Bo-Bo had screwed them there, too.

In another moment of insight, a sequel to her observation of the suggestiveness of their old costumes, she wondered how many five to ten-year-old girls were awake at one in the morning to watch it. She shook her head, tossed the *TV Guide* back on the table.

Maybe *The Go Girls* had finally reached its real target audience, lonely middle-aged men who prefer prepubescent girls in racy costumes to the big and scary world of adult women. Men like Jim Stoddard, who was probably old enough to buy beer when she was still squeezing into her trashy little costume. Apparently, he remembered her fondly.

"Ms. Johnson," said a small, prissy voice. Penny turned

and faced a short man in a gray suit. He had a desk-jockey slouch and small, wandering eyes.

"Yes." She rose, held out a hand to him. "And you are?" She let the question hang.

"Doctor Avery," he said, but did not take her hand. He looked at it instead with mild alarm and stepped back a pace.

"Can I see my sister now?"

"Your sister left a few weeks ago, Ms. Johnson. We don't know where she is now."

All it took was that one second of fear, just that little flash of time and Penny the Whore became Penny the Bitch. Whamo-chango, just like on the phone with Jenny that morning.

"What the hell do you mean, you don't know?" She advanced on him a step, and had to force her hand, now a fist, to her side.

"Please calm down, Ms. Johnson." His eyes made a quick search of the waiting room and lobby and seeing no one besides the receptionist, turned back to Penny. "Your sister's committal status was upgraded to voluntary several months ago. She stayed because she didn't think she was ready to go."

"She's your patient for almost ten years and you didn't bother to ask where she was going?" Penny dropped back into her chair, turned away from the doctor. "Jesus Christ! Do you know anything?"

"She received a letter the day before she left," he said. "I remember it because it's the only personal mail she's received since she's been here. Besides you, the only people who seem to remember her are the tabloid reporters."

"Who was it from?"

"Bo-Bo," he said. "No last name on the envelope. Just Bo-Bo. It was hand delivered to us. No postmark. Just *To my little Kitty Kat, Love forever, From Bo-Bo*."

Penny wandered a bit, digesting what that smarmy little prick Avery had told her.

As much as she wanted to blame Dr. Avery, she could not. He knew about Beaumont Johnson, no doubt. He had undoubtedly heard the stories about Beaumont, how he had molested Kat in the director's trailer one day after shooting, the same way he molested Penny and Jenny in their shared trailer. Even if he did not know those things, he would have known that Beaumont could not have written to her. But few people outside of the biz knew Beaumont by his nickname.

Still, he should have called her, let her know. Kat had been gone for two weeks, and even though it had been months since she'd come to visit, the son-of-a-bitch could have at least called Penny to let her know.

Jenny came through the terminal at LaGuardia, just after ten as predicted, and Penny met her there. It had been months since they'd seen each other, but Penny knew her the moment she parted from the crowd. It was the same face Penny saw, and sometimes shied away from, every day in her own mirror.

Jenny saw her and froze for a moment, then ran full out parting the crowd as she screamed, "*Penny! Penny!*"

She was laughing and crying at the same time.

They met halfway and didn't so much collide, as explode into each other's arms.

They embraced, cried, laughed. Alone in the sea of people, together again.

"Kat's gone," Penny said finally, breaking the glee.

Jenny's smile faltered, searching her sister's face for the lie or the punch line of some sick joke. "What do you mean?"

Penny led her through the crowd, outside, found an empty bench and told her the story from the meeting with Jim Stoddard to her trip to the hospital and the letter Kat had received.

"No," Jenny shouted. Then again, "No, it can't be him!"

Heads turned, and Penny hushed her.

Jenny shook her head.

"It can't be him, Penny. You know it can't." Then in a whisper, "He's dead, Penny. We killed him."

"Yes," Penny said. "I know."

It was fifteen years ago, after shooting the very last episode of *The Go Girls*. A to be continued episode that never aired.

The murder of Beaumont Johnson was not standard Go Girls fare, not the laughable Rube Goldberg on acid scenario. It was quick, graceless, and bloody. The two little girls, pretty twins who looked like miniature funhouse monsters in their gore splattered costumes, each with a bloody knife in hand. Bo-Bo lay dead where he had slept. There were almost fifty holes in him where the knives had gone in. His neck, his face, his chest, his crotch.

Kat was slouched in the arms of the chair where Bo-Bo had put her after he had finished, naked, bruised, bleeding. Unseeing. Unhearing. This was the roll she would play on and off for the next several years. A vegetable.

"It can't be him." Jenny fell against her sister's shoulder and began to cry. "You know it can't be."

"I know," Penny said again, and she was crying now too. "It isn't him. Bo-Bo can't come back."

But there was a lingering doubt in the part of her mind that remained flash frozen on the moment fifteen years ago. She'd been standing over her adoptive father with the knife still in hand. Countless minutes had passed since the quivering of his hands and lips had ceased when Bo-Bo's head had rolled toward her and the corner of his mouth twitched once, just a little twitch, barely perceptible. His remaining eye had opened to her.

The studio, Penny later realized had had its huge, slimy hand in covering up the nightmare. They'd ushered Jenny and Penny through the court system and out the other side and put Kat away for safe-keeping.

―――――――

Penny and Jenny searched the city for three days before they found Kat. They started with the homeless shelters, and then moved on to the hospitals. The morgues would come next, they knew, if they hadn't found her elsewhere. The hospitals were tough, administration and staff were less than helpful, but they finally found her registered as Jane Doe in Beth Israel Medical Center's critical care unit.

After getting a positive ID on her Jane Doe, the night shift nurse left them to watch over their sister while she slept.

Kat was still pretty, even battered as she was from her fall. The pale shadow of death had passed over her, then fled. She had not fallen from some impossibly tall studio constructed monstrosity as Penny had dreamt, but from the top of a condemned tenement building in Newark. The fall should have killed her but did not. A third-party account, related to them by Nurse O'Rourke, was that she had actually glided most of the way down, that the free fall had started less that twenty feet from the ground.

"Crazy things people see," O'Rourke had said, then grinned a little. "She's one lucky lady to still be around."

"Do you think she'll wake up?" Jenny didn't look at Penny when she asked this, just continued to stare at Kat. She hadn't taken her eyes off Kat since their arrival.

"Yes, she'll wake up," Penny said without hesitation. Her answer surprised her, she'd been asking herself the same question as she watched Kat. Now she knew that Kat would wake up, the same way she knew that Jim Stoddard was at that moment standing outside her apartment door, gearing himself up to knock and ask the million-dollar question. Could they get the Go Girls back together again?

A touch of the old Go Girl magic perhaps.

Precognition, indeed.

She opened her purse, searched for a moment, and

pulled Jim Stoddard's card out. There was a cell phone number. She would call him after Kat woke up.

Jenny closed her eyes, rubbed at her temples.

"You okay, Sis?"

"Yeah, I'll live." She opened her eyes and turned to Penny. "I've been clean for almost six months, but I still want it. Some days are harder than others."

Penny nodded but said nothing. She understood what Jenny was going through. She understood all too well.

Jenny rose, stretched, began to pace the small room.

"Wake up, Kat. Open your eyes and let us know you're going to make it." She sat on the edge of Kat's bed and gripped her hand.

Deep lesions marked Kat's left arm, meaty rips that had festered with infection. The self-inflicted cuts, the message from Penny's dream that proved their darkest suspicions.

Bo-Bo is back.

If Bo-Bo had come back for Kat, then he had come back for them all. They were together again, and just maybe they had a future together. Together they had always been good. As before, they would stand together and together they would win. This time they would win.

"Wake up, Kat," Jenny said again. She still gripped Kat's hand, and her other hand brushed a few stray locks away from the sleeping woman's face. She stared at Kat's unresponsive face for several moments without blinking, as if willing her to open her eyes. "Wake up, Sis."

Kat opened her eyes. She looked up at Jenny, then over at Penny. She smiled.

"Go Girls Rule."

SISTER

They found us in the trash bin behind a Circle K in Spokane. No one knows who put us there. We were sisters … twins. I still have scars on my neck where the rats tried to eat me. I lived. Sister didn't.

No one knows that I know this. The Hearts don't even know about it. They think my father died in a police action overseas and my mother in a hit and run accident. That's what they told me anyway.

I was a few hours old when the Circle K clerk found me in the trash. I was nine months old when the Hearts adopted me.

I shouldn't know these things, but I do.

Sister told me.

She tells me a lot of things.

She says I stole her body. Maybe I did, I don't remember. She says she does. Sister remembers everything.

Mamma is a hooker on 83rd and Frey -
We saw her standing there the other day -
She's the one to see if you want to ball -
Her business card says, for a good time call...

She gave the number, the one she said was our real mother's, and laughed. The sound of her laughter unnerves me because it sounded so much like me. There was a time I could just tell her to go away and she would, eventually. About the time I turned thirteen, she became a permanent voice in my head.

She does things like this when she wants to ruin my concentration or wear me down emotionally. Usually it's just a song from the radio that I don't like, brainless chatter, or some hurtful bit of trivia.

I tried to ignore her, and when that didn't work I fought back with the *Dead Babies* song. That usually shuts her up for a while.

I don't like that song. My *brother*, Max, the Heart's real kid, was a metal head. The first time I heard that song coming through the wall between our rooms it made me sick. It also drove Sister out of my head for a while, so I searched for the lyrics to it online and memorized them. I don't use them unless I have to. It drives Sister crazy. She hates being reminded of what she is. She comes back mad though, and she always gets even.

She's a vindictive little bitch.

I closed my eyes and ran through the first chorus of *Dead Babies* in my head. She screamed, threw a fit between my ears. It felt like little feet kicking the inside of my head. It was a frustrated scream, a tantrum scream, and she was gone.

I finished the essay and walked it up to Mr. Warner's desk. I told him I didn't feel well and asked if I could go to the bathroom. I wanted to be away from the other students when Sister came back.

The halls were empty. I passed the double doors of the gymnasium, and then I was gone for a while. The next thing I remember is standing naked in front of the girl's room mirror, my face painted up like a harlot-clown with drying menstrual blood.

Written above my breasts in streaked red letters was the word *Bitch*.

"Oh my God!" Ms. Fox, the phys ed teacher, stood in the doorway. Her hands fumbled their way toward her mouth, covered it. I thought she would faint, or be sick, or both.

Instead, I fainted.

———

She cleaned me up and dressed me, and when she was sure I could walk without passing out again, she led me out by the arm to her office. I begged her not to say anything, but she wouldn't acknowledge me once we were outside the bathroom. She wouldn't even look at my face.

I was so goddamned embarrassed.

Sister had never gone this far before. I didn't know that she could. Usually when she wanted to get even she made me blurt things out or put images or ideas in my head that I couldn't block, things that made me sick. That was the first time I *remember* her getting physical. I wondered if it had ever happened before, what she may have made me do without any memory.

All the way to the office she snickered inside my head. She played back the image of me standing in front of the mirror, dipping with my index fingers down below where I was bleeding and painting my face and chest. It was a wide screen horror movie inside my mind.

"You fucking bitch!" I didn't realize I'd said it aloud until Ms. Fox's grip tightened. She quickened her pace, almost dragging me.

"I didn't mean you," I tried to explain, but gave up. What could I tell her?

The secretary looked more than a little confused when she dragged me in and shoved me onto the bench. "Keep an eye on her."

Ms. Fox didn't go into the principal's office. She went to see the school counselor. She was in there for a long time. The bell rang, and the halls filled up with students on their way to lunch. Pimply, snickering faces slowed as they passed the office to stare at me.

Sister laughed with them.

At last the door opened and Ms. Fox passed me without slowing. The counselor called me in and directed me to the seat across from his desk. He seemed unsure of what to do next.

"What in the world were you doing?"

"I don't know," I said. "I'm feeling sick."

He wrote in his notebook, tore the sheet out and pushed it across his desk toward me. A two-day vacation. Yeah, that was going to go over well at home.

"Can you make it home?"

"Yes."

"Ms. Fox won't tell anybody about ... you know," he

said, blushing furiously, "but I will have to let your mother know."

He shooed me out, and I walked home.

———————

I sat at the vanity in my room running a brush through my hair. I stared into my eyes, reflected, somehow discolored by the light of the lamp. I ignored Sister's taunts by focusing on my pupils.

Ran the brush through my hair and tried to make my head empty.

The brush turned in my hand, rolled my hair like spaghetti on a fork, and Sister pulled the brush with all the strength I had.

I bit my lips to hold the scream in. I started to cry, but I was also smiling, a cruel smile full of Sister's sharp feelings.

It's my body. You can't shut me out.

You're dead, go away.

Not dead, she said. *Just waiting my turn.*

The new shade of my eyes wasn't a trick of the light. It was only a little different than my usual shade, but it was still different.

I crawled into bed, pulled the sheets over my head, and slept the afternoon into oblivion.

———————

"You are in so much trouble." Max stood at the foot of my bed, pleased as hell to be the bearer of bad news. "Dad wants you downstairs."

Mother Heart was conveniently absent. She always flaked out when things went bad.

I found him waiting in his study.

"Your history teacher called," Father Heart said. He didn't like me, this was something I knew from my earliest recollections. He didn't want a daughter. He had a son, and when Mother Heart's uterus collapsed after giving life to Max, I don't think he could have been happier. This is conjecture, but I'd bet money that it's true.

Mother Heart wanted a daughter. Bringing me home was her idea. He was never shy about reminding me of this.

I took a deep breath and braced myself, then sat down at the table across from Father Heart. "What's wrong?"

"What's wrong?" he says, not to me, but to the room at large. Maybe he had an invisible friend. Smarmy bastard.

"What's wrong?" he asked again, and shook his head. He produced a cigar from the inside pocket of his suit vest, lit it with a gold-plated Zippo.

"What did I do?"

"What did you do? You mean aside from that freaky shit you pulled in the bathroom in front of your PE teacher?" He leaned across the table toward me, blew smoke in my face. His thin lips pulled into a twitchy smile when I coughed. "Mr. Warner read your *essay.*"

He sat back in his chair and glowered at me, as if that should have explained it.

I didn't know what I was supposed to say, so I said nothing. I could feel Max behind me. It was like spider legs on the back of my neck.

Did you know that Max comes into our room at night and

watches us while you sleep? Sister seemed determined to get on every last nerve.

Seconds passed. Father Heart watched me. I found a water spot on his desk and focused on it.

"How long has this been going on?" he asked.

How long has what been going on? I wanted to ask but didn't quite dare.

"I'll be damned," he said, shaking his head. Talking to the air again, or his invisible friend. "Our little slut is at a loss for words."

I felt sick. I closed my eyes, tried to shut Father Heart's face out.

What did you do?

Sister did not answer. She was gone, or content just to sit back and watch.

What did you do?

"Get your ass back upstairs," Father Heart said. "I don't want to look at you."

That was fine with me. I didn't want to look at him either.

Mrs. Heart came home later that night, stumbled up the stairs and into my room. She was drunk. When I tried to talk to her she held up a hand and shook her head.

"Don't," she said. "I don't want to hear it."

She'd been crying, but not for me I thought. She'd been defending her need to adopt me from the beginning, and now I was indefensible. I still didn't know what I was supposed to have done to Mr. Warner, my history teacher. What hurt the most was that Mother Heart wouldn't even talk to me about it. Like her husband, she had already written me off as bad.

"How could you do it?" she asked. "Offering your body for a good grade?"

Then she left without giving me a chance to defend myself.

She wants to send you away, Sister said, and laughed inside my head.

I had a dream that night. There was a faceless someone in my bed, I almost knew who it was. He was on top of me, pulling my nightshirt up past my waist, past my stomach and breasts. His hands were all over me. I didn't like it, but I didn't fight it. His hands were rough, clumsy.

The dream felt so real, even down to the pain when he entered me. Whatever the Hearts thought of me, I had been a virgin.

I pulled his face close to me. I tried to make out his features in the darkness. I almost knew who it was, and it scared me.

He buried his face against my neck and quickened his pace. Rough and clumsy, and then the end came. He stiffened against me, pushed harder. It felt like he was trying to push himself out through my back.

When I woke up it was Max who I saw looking down at me. He was sweaty, out of breath, his smile full of disbelief and gratification.

We were not in my bed. We were in his. I ... Sister had gone to him.

He rolled off me and wiped a mop of greasy hair from his face.

I sat up and pulled my nightshirt down. There was blood on the sheets, between my legs. My period again, or maybe my virginity soaking into his sheets.

I did not want to cry. I got out of his bed and walked to the door.

"Wanna do it again tomorrow night?" he asked.

No!

"Yes," I heard myself say as I left his room.

I couldn't sleep after that. Sister was in the back of my head, smug and sated for a time, pleased with herself. Waiting in the deep of my mind. Waiting for me to look away so she could take control again. I sat and stared in my vanity mirror, waiting for her smile, and the slightly different shade of her eyes.

"Get out of my body."

My body, she said.

"It was never yours. You died."

Did I?

"Shut up in there!" Father Heart shouted. "If I have to tell you again, I'm bringing the belt!"

Sister smiled.

Bring the belt old man. Punish me.

Don't you dare!

It happened again the next night. I woke up in Max's bed.

He was asleep, still lying on top of me. After that I stopped sleeping. Things didn't go back to normal, but that made it harder for Sister to get control. I couldn't concentrate in school and my friends avoided me, but I didn't care. There was no more menstrual blood finger painting in the girl's room, no more waking up with Max on top of me, still inside me and panting like an old, sick man.

The first night Max came to my door at midnight and got mad when I wouldn't let him in. The next day he pouted, and the next night he tried again. I let him in and told him if he didn't leave me alone I'd scream rape. He left me alone after that.

I was surprised at how long I held out without sleep. I've learned something about the power of the human will. Sister taught me that. Her will was strong, getting stronger with each small victory. I had to be strong too.

She grew restless sitting cut off in the back of my head, allowed only the occasional potshot.

The next week the school counselor called me back to his office. My teachers were worried about me, and so was he. He wanted to know what was wrong. It was during that meeting that she broke through again.

———

"We just want to help you," he said. "We're not going to get you in trouble."

"There's nothing wrong," I said. I tried to sound amused, barely interested. If I admitted to anything being wrong, he would keep at me until I admitted everything. Good intentions or not, it would end with me in a rubber room, my blood pumping with antipsychotics and sedatives.

"You look exhausted. When was the last time you slept?"

"I'm sleeping fine," I said. "I just got out of Mr. Denny's Government class. You'd be exhausted too."

His notebook came out again and he made notes. Then he watched me, waiting for me to spill my guts.

"Lunch is almost over. I'm hungry. What do you want from me?"

"The truth," he said. "You're not a very good liar."

"You wouldn't believe it," I said, and knew it was a mistake as soon as the words came out.

"Try me," he said.

"I have a better idea," Sister said through me, and before I could stop her she slid my skirt up to my waist and spread my legs for him.

He stopped in mid-concern and stared at me with his mouth wide open. For a second I thought he would take up Sister's offer. Then he ran for his office door.

"I'm calling your parents," he said.

If there's one thing I've learned about Sister, it's that she doesn't like rejection. She doesn't like to be balked.

"Fag," she screamed, and jumped from the couch. She took a swing at him as he passed the couch, her fist, my fist, landed on his jaw, just under his ear, and he fell against the wall.

The next thing I remember was the secretary and the principal pinning me to the floor, threatening to call the police if I didn't calm down. The principal had scratches on his neck and face. I saw them and thought about the old rat scars on my neck. That memory startled Sister into submission, and I got control again.

"I'm sorry," I said, and started to cry. I saw the counselor through the open door. He sat at the bad kid bench with the school nurse hovering over him. A bruise swelled beneath his eye, and his lip was split and puffy. Blood ran down his chin. He looked at me, wiped the blood away with an absent swipe of his shirtsleeve, then looked away.

"Call her parents," the principal said, and the secretary relaxed her grip on my wrist. When I didn't try to fight she released it and left the room.

"Go sit down," the principal said. He stood and backed away a few steps.

I went to the couch. He stood in the doorway. He didn't take his eyes off me until Mother Heart arrived half an hour later.

The Hearts fought that afternoon, about me. When it was over Mother Heart packed an overnight bag and left. I stayed in my room. Max didn't bother me at all that afternoon.

I was as exhausted as I'd ever been in my life. I turned on the clock radio and fine-tuned until my favorite station came in.

I fought sleep and ignored Sister's relentless taunting.

Father Heart came in without knocking a few hours after his wife left. He looked at me but talked to the air.

"What am I going to do with you? Expelled," he added, unnecessarily. "Fucking expelled!"

He sighed extravagantly, put his hands on his hips.

"What am I going to do with you?"

"Bring your belt and we'll talk about it," Sister said. I saw her reflection in the vanity mirror behind him, her off-color eyes.

He said nothing to this, stood silent for a moment, then left, closing the door behind him.

I knew he would come back.

Do you give up yet? Sister asked.

No.

You will.

I sang the *Dead Babies* song in my head.

Stop it!

Do you give up yet? I asked.

No answer.

They left me alone for the rest of the night. Father Heart waited until Max was asleep before he came back. I heard his footsteps, light as he could make them, coming down the hall toward my room.

I sang the *Dead Babies* song in my head. I needed to stay in control.

Sister screamed, then retreated.

He cracked the door open and peered in. He looked uncertain.

I said nothing, was neither inviting nor forbidding. Just watched and waited.

At last, he entered. He came to my bed in slow steps. His traditional scowl was gone, his eyes were wide, blood-shot, his face flushed. He'd been dipping into Mother

Heart's private stock. He didn't drink often, so it wouldn't take much, just enough to build up his courage.

He stopped at the side of my bed, sat down. His hands moved toward me, hovered over my blanket. They shook.

"What is wrong with you?" he asked again, but this time it sounded like a sincere question.

"What are you waiting for?" I asked.

He gripped the sheet with unsteady hands and pulled it off. He didn't notice the claw hammer, pilfered from his own shop, that I held at my side until I swung it. It made a crunching sound against the side of his skull. One swing put him to sleep, but I didn't stop at one swing. I hit him until I was sure he wouldn't wake up and come for me again.

Then I went to Max's room and did the same to him.

There was a lot of blood. The smell of it brought Sister back. I took a shower, hot as I could stand it, and scrubbed until my skin was raw. The blood came off my skin, but the charnel house smell stayed with me. I was afraid to go back to my room, so I went downstairs to the breakfast bar between the kitchen and dining room wrapped in a towel.

Mamma is a hooker on 83rd and Frey -
We saw her standing there the other day -
She's the one to see if you want to ball -
Her business card says, for a good time call...

"What is her number?" I asked.

I felt her smile with my lips. She gave the number, and I called our mother.

I was afraid she would be asleep, but she picked up on the second ring.

"What?" she said. A tone of annoyance. Had I interrupted something? Her voice was a cigarette-roughened facsimile of Sisters. A voice that could coax with a whisper or cut with a word.

"Mother," Sister said. She wanted to say more but didn't know what. I don't think she had planned beyond hearing her voice. She was scared.

A pause, then, "I don't know who you are or what you want, but you've got the wrong woman. I'm nobody's mother."

Then she hung up.

For the first time ever, I heard Sister cry.

I broke our one-ended connection, waited for the dial tone, and dialed 911.

———

Sister is free now, but that freedom is tainted by a new kind of bondage. We spend most of our time locked in a single room, and much of that strapped to our bed. She does have several hours a week with the staff psychiatrist, and she especially enjoys the male nurse's aide that comes in a few times every night to check on us.

Sometimes all that freedom gets to be too much for Sister, and they have to sedate her. When she's drugged I come back. You'll know it's me when you hear the singing.

MOTHER OF KITTIES

Dave Thomas thought he would probably enjoy CatCon more if it wasn't for all the fucking people. He loved cats, cats were great because they mostly left you alone, but cat people were just so … weird, and peopley. Except for Phoebe, who was also weird, but in all the right ways. Phoebe was also the reason that Dave was fighting his way through a press of strangers, making his slow way to the restroom of the Pasadena Convention Center in California, instead of catching the Summer Slaughter Tour in Grand Rapids.

He was wearing his Soreption concert T-shirt in honor of the show he was missing, and drawing strange looks from an assortment of blue-hairs and uptight fur-mamas littering the hallway. He had to piss, and badly. If he couldn't bust through the crowd between him and the bathroom he was likely to piss right down his leg.

A skinny guy with stringy black hair, a wisp of mustache, and a Grumpy Cat T-shirt watched Dave's approach with a sneer.

"The fuck you looking at?"

The skinny guy jumped like Dave had reached out and goosed him, then turned away and moved on, opening a path through the crowd past the men's room door.

Dave smiled, feeling a little better about the day, and shouldered his way through the shrinking gap in the crowd before it could close again.

He heard the screams while he was washing his hands. The first one was isolated, out of place in the low hum of conversation beyond the restroom door. He ignored it as he shook the water from his hands, then thumped the button on the hot air hand drier with his elbow. No matter how clean they looked, public restrooms were disgusting places. Pressing the flush on a public toilet made his skin want to crawl right off his body, but that couldn't be helped. Anything he could avoid touching with his hands, he did.

The general din in the hallway increased, he could hear it over the racket of forced hot air, and he wondered what was going on out there. Probably a Colonel Meow sighting in the hallway. He dreaded the probability of having to push his way through an even larger crowd to get back to Phoebe.

Then the forced air died, and he realized that the noise beyond the door no longer qualified as a low hum, or even a din. It was a cacophony. Raised voices, shouts, trampling feet, and screams. Screams of pain. Screams of terror.

His mind conjured up a hundred dreadful possibilities

as he ran to the door: fire, flood, a crazy asshole with a gun and some political or religious agenda, a Kim Kardashian sighting in the lobby, or maybe the zombie apocalypse.

He was reaching for the door when it swung open and slammed him into the wall. A dozen or more men and women pushed past him and crammed themselves in the stalls, hiding from ... he didn't know what.

"Don't go out there, man," someone shouted as he reached out to catch the closing door. *"They've gone crazy. Fucking crazy, man!"*

"Who's gone crazy?" Dave paused on his way out, waiting for a bit of clarification. "What the hell's going on?"

"Shut the goddamn door!" A woman in the far stall screamed at him. *"You're going to let them in!"*

For a second, Dave teetered on the brink of retreat. He considered letting the door close, maybe propping the trashcan under the handle to bar it before forcing himself into one of those tight little stalls.

Phoebe's out there.

He was out into the hallway and running the way he'd come before he realized he meant to go.

At first he was running against a strong current of panicked, screaming bodies, elbowing and shoving people aside.

"Phoebe!"

He scanned faces even as he pushed past them but didn't see her.

A burly man in checkered golf pants and an oversized paisley shirt grabbed him by an arm and swung him around.

"Are you insane?" Dave felt the knuckles of the man's long, meaty fingers crackle as they squeezed his arm. "You're running the wrong way!"

Dave wrenched his arm from the man's grip and shoved him aside.

"I gotta find Phoebe!"

The man regarded Dave for a shocked moment, then backed away from him.

"Fuck you then. Go get yourself torn up." That said, he turned tail and sprinted with the ebbing flow of cat lovers toward the convention center lobby.

Dave's cell phone buzzed in his pocket. He realized that it had been in there, forgotten and buzzing against his leg as he panicked and ignored what might be Phoebe's last frantic call to him. He dug for it and tugged it out, leaving the inside out pocket dangling against his leg.

It was Phoebe, but she wasn't calling. She was texting.

There were a half-dozen new texts.

Hurry up sweetie!

And...

Morris is here! OMG!

The third was a picture of a fat, orange tabby stretched out in what looked like a silk-lined cat bed. The current incarnation of 9 Lives cat food mascot, Morris the Cat. A white plastic food dish with his name printed across the side sat ignored next to him.

A loud scream brought Dave's attention back to the mostly empty path ahead. For the first time he saw the blood streaking the walls and dotting the carpeted floor. An enormously fat man burst through the open door of

Exhibit Hall B, where a select few famous felines were displayed for their adoring public.

Dave had been warned in advance that there would be no touching of the famous cats. You could look all you wanted, take a picture if their handlers allowed it, but you couldn't interact with them in any way. Actual meet and greets would be available later, in more private settings, and for a fee.

The screaming fat man's face was carved up and bleeding badly, and when he turned toward the sound of Dave's shocked shout, Dave saw that one of his eyes was gone. The man tripped over his own tangled feet and hit the floor hard.

Dave was moving again, rushing to help the man up, when the cats pounced.

First two, then four, then half a dozen, they leapt onto the prone man, hissing and wailing, digging with their claws, biting his shoulders, the back of his neck, the top of his head. A Maine Coon the size of a dog and with a lion-like mane of gray hair tore a chunk out of his throat, and a surprising fan of blood sprayed Dave, drenching him from the knees down.

Dave screamed, and the cats turned to regard him.

He waited for them to attack, grateful that he'd already emptied his bladder.

They looked at him, then past him, and rushed toward fading screams and shouts of the fleeing cat fanciers. The Maine Coon brushed against his leg and purred for a second before catching up with the rest.

The fat man gurgled briefly, then died.

Dave's phone vibrated in his hand.

He scrolled past two more pictures of famous cats, one

of them was indeed Colonel Meow, and read the last two texts.

Where are you honey, I need you!

And ...

I love you, baby.

"Phoebe." It was little more than a whisper. He didn't have the breath for anything stronger.

The phone buzzed, and a new picture appeared.

A sea of cats, more cats than could have possibly been in attendance, even at the largest of CatCons. There were pampered celeb-cats, well-groomed but more-or-less average attendee's cats, big cats, small cats, old and young, and dirty, matted, mangy strays who seemed to have somehow gotten past security.

All of them facing Dave through the picture Phoebe had just sent. Closing in on her.

"Phoebe!"

He leapt over the fat man's outstretched legs and ran through the open door into Exhibit Hall B.

———

There were perhaps twenty Celebrity Cat booths set up throughout the spacious hall, and all of them destroyed in the chaos. Tables were overturned, backdrops trampled into the ground, promotional posters of the convention's most famous feline attendees torn and scattered, and their human handlers either dead or fled.

There were bodies everywhere.

Some of them were still moving, moaning, screaming, so, Dave supposed, they weren't technically bodies yet, but the remaining felines were busy correcting that. The cats chewed on wrists and throats. One tiny kitten was half-hidden in an unconscious woman's hiked up skirt, chewing into her thigh. A second later the woman's femoral artery let go with a gush, and the kitten climbed onto her chest, mewing in triumph.

Another text alert sounded out, and every cat not currently occupied with turning a human into a corpse turned to him.

"*Shit.*" Dave's voice was little more than a whisper, but the cats meowed at him, as in to say *Yes indeed, human. Shit.*

He backed up a step, turned back to the hallway, and found his path blocked.

Another text alert, and the cats, now surrounding him on all sides except one, meowed again.

Dave had the absurd notion that they were telling him to check his damn phone.

What they didn't do was attack him.

Dave checked his damn phone.

The first of the new texts said *Ballroom*.

The second said *Hurry up, honey. There isn't much time.*

Dave moved the only direction the gathering cats would allow, forward, deeper into the abattoir that was Exhibit Hall B. The faster he moved, the faster they followed. He was running by the time he saw the opening in the partition wall between Hall B and Hall A, sprinting by the time he passed through it into the empty and previously blocked off Exhibit Hall A.

Not empty anymore.

Every cat in the city seemed to have converged on CatCon, and they were all gathering in the unused Exhibit Hall A. They filled it wall to wall, parting for Dave when he rushed in blindly, closing behind him when he skidded to a stop.

They writhed, mewed, yowled, and squawked, then rushed at him in a wave.

A wave of cats, Dave thought as he felt himself sliding smoothly out of consciousness. *Too bad no one else is alive to video this. No one is ever going to believe me.*

Then the wave crested, then fell over him.

Oh, right. I won't be alive to tell anyone either.

Sharp, nipping pain brought Dave back to an unreal reality.

His first surprise was realizing he was still alive to wake up. His second was realizing that he was moving, and rather quickly, but not under his own power. The cats were conveying him across the empty convention hall like fans at a rock concert. Dave was crowd surfing across Pasadena Convention Center's Exhibit Hall A on a mewling tide of cats.

There was another nip, drawing blood from a fingertip.

"Ow!"

There was another, gentler nip, then what might have been a dozen rough tongues licking the injured finger.

The wave beneath him, moving him ever quicker, ever higher above the floor, was purring now.

Then Dave was standing upright, not under his own power, but supported by hundreds of cats. He tried to pull free of them but was caught fast by claws and teeth sunk into his clothing.

The wall at the end of the exhibit hall was nearing, and Dave realized that he was about to smash face-first into it.

He clenched his eyes shut, but couldn't squelch the scream of anticipated pain.

The pain didn't come.

There was a crumping, crumbling sound, the sound of a wrecking-ball knocking down a wall, and a dusting of splintered and broken pressboard in his hair, on his face.

Then Phoebe's voice.

"There you are, honey! What took you so long?"

Dave Thomas opened his eyes and beheld the love of his life, the reason he was knee-deep in gore and neck-deep in psycho killer cats instead of a mosh pit, rocking out to the best in modern metal.

Phoebe was reclined on a throne of living cats. She swayed gently from side to side as they moved, trading places beneath and behind her as part of her throne, then darting back out onto the floor as others took their place.

The giant Maine Coon was in her lap purring so loudly Dave could feel it vibrating the air between them.

Phoebe waved, grinning ear to ear, showing teeth that looked quite a bit pointier than Dave remembered them being earlier in the day.

"Uhh...?" Dave said.

Dave crowd surfed the cats right up to the foot of Phoebe's living, purring throne, and then they set him down before her and parted to give him room.

He wobbled on his feet for a moment, thought his knees were going to unlock and drop him where he stood. He kept his feet with a great effort of will, and tried to formulate a question more intelligent than *Uhhh...?*

"What in the hell is going on, Phoebe?"

"Did you know I was a cat goddess?" Phoebe sounded both surprised and delighted. "I didn't!"

"No," Dave said. "I didn't know that."

Somehow, he wasn't as surprised as he should have been.

Phoebe nodded down toward the massive cat reclined in her lap.

"This is Titus. He's my familiar!" She giggled. "I didn't know I had one of those either."

"Hi, Titus." Dave gave Titus a little wave.

Titus regarded Dave in perfect silence for a moment, as if appraising a competitor for his mistress's affection, then gave a low, amiable yowl.

"He says he's come to elevate me to my rightful place in the universe and lead all of feline-kind to supremacy over humans." She sounded dubious, but Phoebe had always been pretty openminded, and she did love cats, so Dave thought she was prepared to accept Titus at his word on at least a provisional basis. "Titus says that humankind is a failed race destined to bring total devastation to the Earth and all of its creatures."

Dave let that sink in for a moment, and decided Titus made a good point

"He's not wrong," Dave said.

Titus seemed almost to smile at him.

"I told them no way was I going to become the dark goddess of cats and harbinger for the destruction of mankind unless they let you come with," Phoebe said. "Titus said I could keep you."

"So, will that make me a god?"

"Naw," Phoebe said. "More like a pet."

Yes, her teeth were definitely pointier than they had

been that morning. Her eyes much greener too, and the pupils more like dark slits than regular old round pupils. Also, she seemed to have grown a tail.

The ballroom had gone silent. All the purring, licking, and feline fidgeting ceased. All eyes were on him. Waiting.

"So," Phoebe said. "What do you say?"

"Sure," Dave said. "Why the hell not."

THE CHRISTMAS CORPSE

Seattle PD Detective Flynn was aggravated going on angry, and Lisa Compton understood his frustration, even sympathized, but that didn't make his attitude with her easier to take. She was frustrated too. Horrified, traumatized, frazzled, and frustrated. She'd taken her children, Janet, Jake Junior, and Janet's friend Chloe to Northgate Mall to see Santa and do some Christmas shopping while her husband wasn't tagging along. It was hard enough shopping for the man, he bought anything he wanted throughout the year, but she hardly ever got out of the house on weekends without him. He was entertaining his mother that Saturday, giving Lisa a golden half-day to find his present without him staring over her shoulder.

Witnessing a multiple murder was an unexpected hiccup in her plan for the day.

She looked across the crowded food court where another uniformed detective was entertaining her kids, then back down the nearly empty mall to where a half-dozen patrol and forensics officers took pictures, made notes, and looked confused. She could just see the red-coated corpse laying at the foot of Santa's throne, tangled in the red ropes used to control the flow of kids waiting to meet the big man. She couldn't see the worst of the mess from her seat at the other end of the mall, but she didn't need to. She'd been in the middle of it. She was sure she'd see it clearly again that night when she finally managed to sleep.

The man they'd handcuffed was nowhere to be seen now. He was either locked in the back of one of the responding cruisers, or already at the station.

The mall rent-a-cop had arrived too late, found him covered in blood and holding the knife, and had held him at gunpoint until the real cops arrived. Neither the rent-a-cop or the responding officers had listened to her, or any of the other hundred witnesses.

They had arrested the wrong man.

"Mrs. Compton," Detective Flynn said. "Are you positive this is the statement you wish to give?"

"It's what happened," she said.

He riffled through his notebook, skimming the pages rather than rereading them in their entirety, then closed the book and dropped it on the table between them.

"A clown?"

"Yes," she said. "A clown."

He glanced around the room and she followed his gaze to the other detectives currently interviewing witnesses.

He sighed.

"I'm going to walk over to the subway." He hooked a thumb back over his shoulder toward a couple of teens in green caps looking mildly freaked, standing behind the Subway counter, waiting for somebody to tell them to go home, or order a sandwich. The shops nearest the crime scene were closed for the rest of the day, but the food court was still open, though no one seemed to have much of an appetite. "Gonna get a cup of coffee, take a short break. When I come back we'll go over it one more time. Maybe you'll remember something while I'm gone."

Or forget something, his tone said.

She said nothing, only watched him until he sighed again and left her alone to reconsider her official statement.

There was nothing to reconsider. Lisa knew what she saw.

She picked up his notebook and flipped it open, rifling the pages until she found the beginning of her statement, then she read what he'd written.

Janet and Chloe enjoyed the noise and chaos of the mall in the Christmas season, but Jake, a year younger and without a friend on this trip to boost his confidence, was on the ragged edge of a nervous tantrum. Too much noise, too much activity, usually put him on edge. Janet's tendency to ignore or tease him when she was with her friends only made it worse. They'd bickered in the car on the way over, Chloe looking uncomfortable seated between them in the back of the van, and now Jake wasn't talking. Lisa didn't like it when he went silent and broody. It reminded her too much of his father.

She clutched his hand, almost dragging him along as the girls ran ahead of them through the crowd to the northwest entrance.

"Get back here, Janet!" Lisa shouted at the girls, saw Chloe slow and begin to turn her way for just a second, and then follow Janet inside.

Lisa sighed, then sped up.

"Come on, Jake, before she gets lost."

She saw a brief, twitching smile appear and vanish on Jake's face, probably at the prospect of losing his sister in the mall, but he walked faster, pausing for a moment when he saw how packed the short hallway beyond the entrance was. Inside, he pressed himself so close to her that he was in danger of getting underfoot.

She found the girls at the window of Just Cozy.

"Mom, they have Christmas leggings." Janet pointed at a headless, armless tween-sized mannequin dressed in festive, skintight green and red. "Can I get some?"

"I'll think about it," Lisa said, though she had no plans to buy Janet leggings of any kind. She didn't get the point of them. Skintight and whisper thin, you might as well go out into the cold naked. Worse, she thought, they made girls who wore them look like little streetwalkers. She'd observed too many grown men ogling little girls in belly-shirts and leggings to be comfortable dressing her own daughter in them. "Let's get in line before it gets too long."

Santa wasn't scheduled to arrive for another half-hour, but already the line stretched from Santa's throne halfway down the mall's main corridor to Nordstroms. She wanted to get in line before it went all the way to the food court.

They were nearly to the end of the line when Jake stopped dead and yanked on Lisa's hand.

"Jake, what...?" The words died in her mouth when she

saw his face. He pointed at a small alcove by Sky Jewelers, a short hall to the restrooms, and the man standing there.

Lisa's heart seemed to stop for just a moment, then raced in her chest. She felt her muscles tighten, her limbs go rigid as adrenaline dumped into her system, felt an urge to turn and run, and knew her sudden paralysis was the only reason she didn't. The man, dressed in a clown's colorful motley, his face painted a sinister parody of good cheer waved at Lisa and Jake, then winked. He danced an uncoordinated jig as they stood and stared.

Lisa had never liked or disliked clowns until the recent plague of aggressively sinister clowns sighted and filmed threatening and stalking people around the country. Now they unnerved her, and this one, standing barely twenty feet away and dancing for her, terrified her.

Jake's opinion of them was far more definitive. He'd hated and feared them since one visited his class a few years back.

"Come on Mom, hurry up!" Janet shouted back to her in irritation as another large group joined the line.

Janet looked back at the alcove and found it empty. The man, whoever he was, was gone now, probably back into the men's room. He'd played his little prank, startled a few people, and decided to change into normal clothes before his little prank pissed off someone who didn't scare as easily as she did.

"Mom!"

"I'm coming," Lisa shouted back, drawing frowns from an old couple passing her going the other direction.

She checked the alcove one last time as she passed it. It was still empty. The clown was gone.

They waited for fifteen minutes before Janet and Chloe convinced her to let them go to Forever 21. Janet had no more than twenty dollars of pocket money, and she didn't think Chloe could have much more than that, so she supposed they couldn't do too much damage. They returned a half hour later, when the line had finally started to move. The young couple standing behind them with their pudgy, wailing toddler groused about people cutting the line, but shut up when Lisa turned to regard them.

A few minutes later the young mother left the line herself, and Lisa watched her drag her screeching progeny into the alcove by Sky Jewelers.

She resisted the urge to call the woman back, remembering the clown that had teased her and Jake before vanishing into one of the restrooms, but held her tongue.

Jake seemed to have forgotten all about their earlier scare, and was actually smiling now, stepping out of line and jumping in place to catch a view of the jolly fat man.

"Don't be a spaz," Janet said.

Lisa sighed and waited for the bickering to start again, but Jake ignored his sister, then cheered when Santa stood up for a moment to stretch.

A small group left Santa's staging area, a throne wide enough to accommodate the big man and three or four children, surrounded by stacked faux gifts with a Santa's Workshop backdrop and managed by a pair of suspiciously tall elves. Another small group moved in to take their place, and the line moved forward again.

They were nearly there, only a few families between

them and, Lisa had to admit, a convincingly jolly Santa, when the man behind them screamed.

"Is this yours?"

It was the clown again, standing beside the young man and holding out the toddler who had been blatting behind them not too long ago. Lisa remembered the child's mother taking him to the bathroom, her brief spasm of shock and her suppressed desire to call the woman back. The woman was absent, and a wet splash of blood across the clown's colorful blouse and the toddler's white bibs suggested she wouldn't be rejoining them.

The clown held the child out, awake but silent, passive, and pressed him into his father's arms.

The young father screamed again, clutched his child and backed away until his butt hit the wall.

Laughing, the clown pulled a long, bloody blade from under his belt and held it up.

More screams, the line to see Santa broke apart and scattered. Janet and Chloe were already halfway to the food court, but Jake seemed rooted to the ground next to his mother.

The clown made a half-hearted jab at them with the knife as he walked past, screamed with laughter as Jake flinched back and tripped over his own feet, then made his way to Santa's Workshop.

One of the elves tripped and tangled himself in the red ropes and chrome stanchions trying to get away. The other picked up a large, decorative candy cane and held it like a baseball bat, ready to swing as the killer clown closed in. Santa himself seemed unable to rise from his throne. He stared at approaching death with wide eyes and a gaping mouth.

"Ho, ho, ho!" The clown screamed as he crossed the threshold into Santa's Workshop.

The elf with the candy cane, a young woman, Lisa saw, only a teenager, took her swing. The giant candy cane broke over the clown's face, smashing his bulbous nose flat across his cheek. Blood sprayed, but the clown seemed not to care. One more stride took him to her, and he planted the knife in her gut, lifting her off the ground by the hilt, over his head, casting her back over his shoulder.

"Don't go anywhere," he said to Santa, pointing the knife in his direction.

"Ahhhhhh!" Santa said. "Hnnnngh! Hrrrgh ... ahhhhhhh!"

Laughing, the clown started kicking and stomping the other elf, still on the floor and tangled in red rope.

A man from the crowd closed in from behind and grabbed the clown around the middle, pinning his arms to his side. He was short but widely built, and Lisa could see corded muscles bulge beneath a tight-fitting shirt.

"Someone call 911! Someone call 9-fucking-11!" The man screamed as he struggled to pull the clown away from his bleeding victim.

The thing that happened next was a problem, not for Lisa, who was there and knew what she'd seen, but for Detective Flynn, who thought she'd lost her goddamn mind. The clown's head spun around until it faced the man holding him, and suddenly, like a good special effect in a horror movie, the clown's back became his front. The clown, taller by a head than the man holding him, bent over, his face darting downward, and bit the man's nose off.

The man let go and ran away screaming, blood flowing from the new hole in his face.

The clown spit his nose out, cackled mad laughter, and went back to work on the groaning elf.

Santa had found his guts and his feet. He charged, bellowing, at the clown.

Lisa finally regained her senses, then her voice.

"Run!" She shoved Jake behind her, heard him hit the ground with a cry. "Run!"

The clown looked up at her, directly into her eyes, and grinned. His grin was inhumanly wide. His teeth little white arrowheads of bone, like shark's teeth.

Santa hit him from the side, knocked him to the floor, and began to punch.

The clown only laughed, then rammed his long blade up into the underside of Santa's jowly chin. Rammed it all the way to the hilt, then a little beyond. Blood gushed down over the clown's hand and ran in smaller streams from beneath Santa's cap. The clown stood, lifting Santa's twitching body up by the handle of the long blade stuck in his head. Lifted him as if he weighed no more than a large rag doll.

Without realizing she'd meant to do anything but run away, Lisa found herself picking up a broken chrome stanchion, lifting the wide, weighted end above her head like a club. She brought it down on the clown's head. Brought it down with a scream of horror and rage.

The clown stumbled but kept his feet. He cast Santa aside, knife and all, and focused on her.

"Would you like a balloon animal, little girl?" He patted the crotch of his baggy clown coveralls, and a moment later something inside them inflated and bulged against the cloth like a long balloon. "I'm quite good with it."

Lisa backed away, then her feet tangled in more of the damn rope, and she fell backward.

She saw the clown's clutching hand reach for her and miss as she tumbled backward, and for a moment she knew only pain and panic as the impact blasted the air from her lungs. When her breath returned, and her vision cleared, the clown stood above her, bent almost double at the waist, his face inching closer to hers. His mouth was open, pointed teeth bared, blood running from his split scalp over his face. He wiped it away, and she saw that the white pancake makeup didn't run or smear, as if it were not makeup at all, but his real skin.

"Or maybe I'll just eat you."

Lisa screamed, and though she didn't realize it until later, wet her pants a little.

Then the clown grunted and paused his sharp downward lean. His mouth closed, and he looked down to consider the length of sharp steel that protruded from his chest. No more than an inch or so, Lisa saw, but when he stood upright again and turned toward his newest attacker, she saw the blade he'd used on Santa now plunged to the hilt in the center of his back.

The clown took one stumbling step toward the man who had saved Lisa, fell to his knees, then pitched forward onto the floor next to Santa.

The man bent and quickly yanked the knife free, held it ready in case the clown got up again.

But the clown was gone. Nothing left but a smear of blood where he'd landed.

———

Detective Flynn returned with his coffee and regarded Lisa. The notebook was back where he'd left it.

"Anything you'd like to add?"

Lisa shook her head. She was tired and wanted to go home. Wanted a long, hot bath and a change of clothes. Wanted to begin the long and probably futile process of trying to forget this day ever happened.

"We're sticking with the clown story then?"

"You have my statement," she said, and a thought occurred to her. Something she would have thought of much sooner if she'd been in a better frame of mind. "You can't tell me this mall doesn't have video surveillance. You probably have the whole thing on film from a half-dozen angles."

Probably just as many cell phone videos too, she thought, but didn't say. She'd be surprised if this wasn't already uploaded to the Internet.

Detective Flynn nodded.

"There are, and we have a detective reviewing them now, but we still have a problem."

"And what's that?"

"No goddamn clown," he said.

Lisa grinned a little at that, but there was very little humor in it.

"He was my problem when he was here and stabbing people," she said. "He's *your* problem now."

Detective Flynn conceded her point with silence, gathering up his notebook and coffee.

"Are you finished? Can I go now?"

"You can go now," he said. "Expect to hear from me again."

"I'm sure I will," Lisa said, and left him.

She had her own shit to handle before retiring to a long, hot bath. Jake and Janet were going to be nervous wrecks, and she'd have to tell Chloe's mother what had happened. The parking lot was bound to be a riot of reporters and looky-loos, and if she didn't get on the road quickly she was going to hit rush hour traffic.

And she hadn't even managed to get her husband's Christmas present.

DANGEROUS TOYS

Janelle Johnson was nearing the end of her two weeks off of work, sleeping by day and watching the same city block every night from dusk until dawn. She'd been propositioned and catcalled countless times, mugged once, and groped twice in the first week before finally arming herself with both a can of pepper spray and a knife. The night after the second groping, one of the men returned, this time not content for a copped feel. He'd snuck up on her blind side while she stood beside her rented Toyota Camry, smoking a cigarette, slapped a hand over her mouth before she could call out, and dragged her into the alley she'd been watching so closely.

He'd slammed her face first against the brick wall, bloodying her nose, scraping up her forehead, splitting her lip, and began yanking her pants down past her hips. While he was occupied with her pants, she fumbled one of her new purchases free of her coat pocket. The knife was not a switch blade, but was spring assisted, long, and probably illegal. She'd triggered the blade and stabbed out blindly, felt the blade strike flesh twice before the man screamed and forgot about getting her pants off. He'd stumbled off, weeping openly and loudly, clutching his gut while she pulled her pants back up and wiped blood from her face with a shaking hand.

She'd waited, crouched in the alley for her shakes to subside, the tears of fear and rage to dry in her eyes, maybe for the man to return with a knife of his own. He did not return, the cops did not show up looking for her, and eventually the weight of another fear, her fear of the thing she'd been waiting for all of those nights, forced her back to the safety of her car. She meant to find the … thing, and she meant to confront it, but she did not relish the idea of it sneaking up on her unseen.

She did not abandon her watch. She would not abandon her watch. If her two weeks off work passed without her finding what she was looking for, then she'd juggle her day job and her night watch until exhaustion forced her to abandon one or the other. If she had to make the choice, she would choose the watch.

The clown had been sighted in this neighborhood, in that alley, too many times to believe it wouldn't be back. The video that had prompted her to take up this nightly watch in a city two hours' drive from her home was the clown menacing a member of a local white supremacist gang called Bulldog Skinz. The banger, not much more than a kid with a lot of bad ink, had come calling the clown out, had come looking for trouble while a friend recorded from close to the spot where she parked most nights.

The clown had come, and the video had ended with

the tall, motley figure dragging the screaming, bleeding young man into the mouth of the alley by his foot.

His friend had run away, and apparently the clown had not chased him down because he had survived to put the video on YouTube.

This was near the height of the clown craze, cell phone and surveillance videos from around the country capturing creepy clowns menacing motorists and pedestrians. A few had been arrested and unmasked as garden variety troublemakers, a few had been run off or beaten up by their intended victims, and most simply faded back into the night after scaring the shit out of people.

A lot of the clowns turned out to be harmless pranksters.

A lot of them were not.

The one she was waiting for, the clown with the hearts on his cheeks, was not harmless.

She called him Grobiano Villis after a clown that reportedly died in the Riplinger Circus fire in Mystic, Connecticut in the summer of 1932. He wore the same clothes and face paint, including the red hearts on his cheeks, as the long dead performer. The same startled shock of fine green hair surrounded his head in a wild nimbus. Grobiano Villis was a lecherous, low brow act. He smoked giant novelty cigars, a foot long and big around as a man's wrist, drank from a giant clay jug with the classic XXX signifying pure alcohol moonshine, leered and groped women performing in the ring, and chased other performers around the big top, other clowns and roustabouts whose only purpose in the act was to be on the receiving end of his pantomime violence. He was a clownish parody of violence and vice, a favorite during his time with the Riplinger Circus.

She knew about the infamous Riplinger Circus clown because of her daughter's doll. She hated the thing. Leave it to her ex to give something as sinister as a stuffed Grobiano Villis doll to a child, but Kristen loved the grotesque thing and would not be parted from it.

Chris had pled ignorance, of course. The clown doll was just something they'd found in a secondhand shop, but the Riplinger Circus fire was one of the most famous catastrophes in American history, and Grobiano Villis was one of its most famous victims.

Her Grobiano Villis was not a part of any act that she knew of, and his violence was not pantomime. The banger he'd dragged into the darkness of the alley was now a missing person. Unofficial because no one cared enough to report him as such to the police, but the rumors surrounding the video were that no one from his gang knew where he was now.

There was a slight rise in Spokane's unsolved homicides and disappearances, most around the River Park area, and the only link between those crimes and the clown was her own suspicion, but the sightings were well documented. He'd been spotted in and around Riverfront Park dozens of times in the past few months, most notably and spectacularly in the alley between the Banner Bank and Mobius buildings on Post Street.

But not since she'd started watching it.

If he was around, he wasn't letting Janelle see him.

There was a tap on the passenger side window, and Janelle had to bite down on her lips to keep from screaming out. She turned, expecting to see the man she'd knifed the previous week come back armed and ready for revenge, expecting a cop to shoo her off, or maybe arrest her for stabbing the bastard who had tried to rape her, expecting the clown.

It was none of them.

It was an old man in an oversized and dirty pea coat and wool cap. His face was mostly hidden behind a wild tangle of grey beard, and stringy locks of greasy grey hair swung in front of him as he bent down and stared in at her.

He didn't act like a crazy, didn't sneer, shout at, flash, or otherwise accost her. Only waited patiently. When she made no move to answer his tap at her window, he made a cranking gesture with his left hand and held up a square object to the window with his right.

It was a jack-in-the-box, and an old one. An antique with chipped maroon paint and tarnished brass edging, unlike any she had ever seen. The only thing that distinguished it from a jewelry or lock box was the crank on its side.

The old man made the cranking gesture with his free hand again, and she hit the switch to roll it down, but only far enough so they could speak. His smell, cigarettes, sweat, and brandy, invaded the cab of her car.

"Hey lady." He gave a little wave. "I'm supposed to give you this."

He bumped the box against her window.

"Who's it from?" She asked, but thought she already knew.

"Du-know his name," the old man said. "He said you'd know."

"Was it a clown?" She couldn't forego a glance around them, down the alley, but they had the street to themselves. "Was he dressed like a clown?"

"Naw," the old guy said. "Just some guy."

He paused for a moment, as if trying to recall something important.

"He had tattoos." He pointed to his right cheek, then his left. "Hearts … and his mouth was too big, but weren't nothing funny about him."

Janelle put her right hand in her coat pocket and grasped the can of pepper spray, then pressed the passenger side window switch with her left. The descending window let more of the man's aroma in, and she thought she smelled piss in the unpleasant bouquet.

"Put it on the seat."

He moved to comply, then seemed to think better of it and withdrew the hand holding the maroon box.

"Sure is pretty, ain't it?" His eyes narrowed beneath the grey bushes of his eyebrows. His mouth opened inside of his out of control beard in a wide smile. "And old, too. Bet I could pawn a pretty thing like this for about …"

Janelle sighed, and reached for her purse with her left hand. Her right stayed in her pocket, holding the pepper spray.

"How about fifty?"

His smile widened.

"Lady, that's just about what I was thinking."

Janelle knew how much she carried and where she kept it, and was able to fish a single fifty out without removing her eyes from the old man. She had to lean closer to the passenger door than she was comfortable with to drop it on the empty seat, but the man kept his distance until she was back in her own seat.

He snatched up the fifty in a flash, and for a long moment seemed on the verge of taking off with his money and the antique. Then he glanced back in the direction of Riverfront Park, only a few blocks from where he and Janelle transacted this peculiar deal, and the smile fell from his face. Janelle thought he shivered a little inside his tent of a coat.

He deposited the box on her passenger seat as swiftly as he'd picked up the fifty, then backed away.

"Thanks," Janelle said.

He nodded, his long hair bobbing around his face.

"I'd be careful of that guy if I were you, lady." There was a moment of silence. He took another step away from her rented car. "That guy ain't right."

He turned and left before she could reply, and she watched him until he vanished down the next side-street, moving away from the park, before daring to pick up the antique toy.

The lacquered maroon paint was dull and felt greasy beneath her fingers. She turned it to inspect each side, not sure what she was looking for, only knowing she wasn't feeling brave enough to turn the crank on it just yet. There were no manufacturers marks, no sales stickers, no child's name painted or written on it. She looked at the bottom, then gave it a gentle shake. Nothing inside moved. She wondered if it was empty, it was certainly light enough. She wrapped it with a knuckle, frowned. It didn't sound hollow. It was like knocking on a solid piece of wood.

She looked around again.

Post Street was still deserted. She supposed someone could be watching her from the darkness beyond the mouth of the alley, but the only way to know was to get out and look.

She didn't want to explore the darkness of the alley. What she wanted was to set the box down and have a smoke.

Instead of getting out to smoke, she placed the box in her lap, gripped the handle of the crank in a loose, tentative fist, and began turning it.

The song it played was a rondo, a simple, repeating melody, like the final movement of Beethoven's sixth symphony or Fur Elise, with occasional off kilter notes that she found somehow unnerving. It was a song designed to give goosebumps.

It was the kind of ear worm that sticks in your head long after it's finished playing, and Janelle had an idea this rondo would be the soundtrack of nightmares to come.

The last note fell dead with the metallic *sproink* sound of a bent or damaged reed.

The lid popped open with enough force to jerk the box in her lap. It struck the steering wheel, and her rental's horn sounded off in the silent, still city night.

She jumped at the sound, then screamed when this particular box's Jack popped out. It was the head, torso, and arms of a stuffed clown. Stained red and white silk, pale face, red hearts on the cheeks. The bulbous red nose and flyaway green hair. The too-long arms unfolded and fell forward into her lap, and the head rocked back and forth, as if in silent laughter.

Janelle cursed and began stuffing the overlarge clown

back into his box, trying to hold it in and push it down as she closed the lid.

"I'm not so easy to put back in the box once you've let me out." The voice came from directly behind her, so close she could feel the speaker's breath on the back of her neck. It was light, playful, full of insane hilarity.

Run, she told herself. *Get out and run*!

Her body would not obey the command. Her insides went cold, and it seemed that even her heart had frozen still in her chest. Then it banged back to life, hammering as she lunged forward, trying to get away from those puffs of hot breath on the back of her neck. She reached for the door handle and felt herself yanked back against her seat by two strong hands. They held her by her shoulders, and she felt long fingers tapping her chest, just beneath her throat.

"You wanted to find me, and so you have." The tapping fingers stilled, the hands holding her shoulders slid toward her throat, then gripped it loosely. She'd felt the strength of those hands on her shoulders and didn't like the thought of them tightening on her throat, so she willed herself to be still, not to panic, to give him no reason to restrain her again. "If you came to play games with me then just say so. I like to play games."

His left hand closed around her throat, the fingernails so long and sharp that she felt a slow trickle of blood track down the hollow of her throat as one nicked the skin below her larynx. His right hand crept down and cupped one of her breasts, then slid over and raked her side as it traced its way back up to her shoulder. She heard the thin cloth of her blouse tear beneath his tracing nails, winced as another one nicked her skin and let out another trickle of blood.

"I know lots of games."

Speak, she commanded herself, but found her throat locked. She couldn't breathe, let alone speak.

"But I don't always play nice."

Janelle tried to talk past the lump of fear in her throat, managed a weak wheezing sound.

"You're starting to bore me, woman." His previously playful tone was gone. The hand on her shoulder began to squeeze. The hand gripping her throat slid up to grip her jaw. "You wouldn't like me when I'm bored. Tell me why you're here!"

"I'm looking for my daughter," she said, ejecting the words like vomit. Now that they were out, she found she could breathe again. She breathed in deeply, trying to settle herself, and partly succeeding. He might drag her screaming into the dark alley for some final, unthinkable game, might just cut her throat with those impossibly sharp fingernails and leave her to bleed out in this squalid little rental car, but he was here, and she had waited for him to return for a reason. "She disappeared three years ago on summer break with her father in Provo. She was walking to a friend's house, and they stopped at a 7-Eleven. Her friend went in to use the bathroom, and when she came out, Kristen was gone!"

Now that she had begun, the words would not stop. She realized that the restraining hands were gone now. Her fear of the monster in the back seat was also gone, replaced by a mother's fury.

"The last time anyone saw her, she was talking to a clown! A lot of kids wouldn't have, but Kristen liked clowns because of this fucking doll she had. He had hearts on his cheeks and green hair, just like her doll ... *and just like you!*"

She was screaming by the time she finished. A part of her was shocked by her bravery in the face of the horror, but most of her was ashamed of her previous cowardice. She reached into her pocket and removed the first item her fingers closed around. The can of pepper spray. When she looked up into the rear-view mirror she found the corpse-white face of Grobiano Villis smiling at her. The green hair, the bulbous, ruby nose and black eyes. The hearts on his cheeks, and lips that were both too full and too wide, almost ear to ear. The old homeless man had been right. His mouth *was* too big.

He pulled a cigar, one of the comically oversized ones, from inside his coat. The coat was silk, or maybe satin, red and white, old and dirty. He sucked on the prop cigar, and the end burst into momentary flame, the flash blinding her for a moment. When her eyes adjusted back to the darkness, he was puffing out plumes of smoke as thick as steam from a train's smokestack. It smelled terrible.

"She always said you would come looking for her," the clown said. He seemed to have cast away his mock-jolly persona. His black eyes seemed to stare straight into her through the rear-view mirror. "But she didn't think it would take you so long."

Griping the pepper spray canister tightly, she turned in her seat to face him.

"What have you done with her," Janelle said, her voice breaking on the last word. She steeled herself against the worst, and most likely answer. Her vague plan to confront and punish the kidnapping monster seemed foolish now that she was staring him in the face, but she decided she would at least leave her mark on him before this night's game was over.

"Why, nothing at all." He grinned around the ridiculous cigar. "I didn't kill her. I didn't hurt her."

He plucked the cigar from his overlarge mouth and blew a cloud of smoke into her face, momentarily blinding her. She waved it away, coughing, and when she could see into the back seat again, it was empty.

"I didn't even take her," the clown said, and Janelle turned to find him sitting in the front passenger seat with the open jack-in-the-box sitting in his lap. He tucked the lit cigar back inside his jacket. "In fact, she was the one who took me."

Janelle pulled her pepper spray and fired it in his face.

She held the trigger down while he screamed and flailed, covering his face with his hands. She saw the white makeup running down his arms, onto his silky coat and the shirt beneath. The spray weakened, then died, and the clown screamed and flailed about in the passenger seat.

Janelle coughed, gagged, was suddenly viewing the clown's spectacular performance through a film of tears. She fumbled the keys out of the ignition and went for the door handle again, panicking as the spray began to burn her eyes and lungs. The door flew open and she flopped out onto the street.

The clown followed her, still cradling his face, flopping onto the vacated driver's seat, then through the open door and onto the street beside her. The box landed with a clatter beside him, the stuffed clown inside flopping all the way out again.

She kicked at him, shoved herself away from him, almost found her feet, fell down again, clumsy in her panic and pain.

His theatric thrashing and screaming stopped and he dropped his hands from his face.

"*Peekaboo!*" He began to laugh, a strong, full-throated laughter that filled the night, echoed down the empty street. "*I see you!*"

Beneath the white makeup her pepper spray had washed away was more makeup. His skin was still the same flat white, his eyes the same oil black, the red of his nose and cheeks undiminished. He rolled onto his back and kicked his legs in the air, pounded the pavement with his fists, rocked with the force of his laughter.

She tried for her feet again and found them, wiped at her eyes with the sleeves of her shirt to clear them, and found him standing, facing her.

His laughter died down. He held the open box in the crook of his left arm, reached out to her with his right.

Janelle turned and ran, screaming.

She ran straight into the darkness of the alley between the Banner Bank and Mobius buildings, realizing too late that she had left the light of Post Street behind only when darkness enfolded her. She ran for what felt like minutes but didn't come out on the other side and onto Lincoln Street.

The clown's mad, echoing laughter chased her down the narrowing brick throat of the alley until all vestige of light from the street behind her was gone, and there was only darkness.

"Hi, Mom."

Kristen Johnson had been an angelic baby, a trying toddler, and an angry, difficult child. Janelle and Chris's divorce did not improve her demeanor. She was five when they separated, Chris moving into an apartment with the woman he'd been seeing on the side, Janelle remaining in the family home until she realized she could no longer afford it without Chris's help.

Before Janelle and Kristen left their house in Provo, Utah for a more affordable apartment, and a better paying job, in her hometown of Clarkston, Washington, Kristen raged about having to stay weekends with her father and his girlfriend in their apartment. After the move, she raged about having to live with Janelle in such a small, backward town. Chris made the eleven-hour drive at least once a month to spend the weekend with her, but it wasn't her father she missed, it was her friends in Provo, her old house in Provo, her old life.

She spent summers with her father and his new wife Rebecca, not the girlfriend he'd left Janelle for, in his new and bigger house in Provo, and Janelle thought the only reason she came back every year was to get away from her hated stepmother. From what Chris said on the few occasions they discussed their daughter, Rebecca disliked Kristen as much as Kristen hated Rebecca.

School was not a problem for Kristen. She was smart and studious. She impressed, and sometimes mystified her teachers, by how quickly she learned new subjects, and sometimes how much she already understood about subjects she had never studied before. Her only problem in school was the other children, or rather she was theirs.

The school had sent Janelle a half-dozen notes and called her as many times about Kristen's bullying of other children. Her alleged victims never complained, would not speak a word against her, but the teachers had witnessed troubling conversations and treatment that eventually prompted Janelle to get her daughter into therapy. The sessions left Kristen angry and sullen, sometimes she wouldn't talk to Janelle for days afterward. Her therapist's eventual diagnosis of *conduct disorder with callous and unemotional traits* confirmed Janell's worst fears.

Kristen had always been standoffish, her affection very much conditional, and she was very good at manipulating her peers to get what she wanted from them. When she spoke to Kristen's school counselor, he agreed with her therapist.

"She's very charismatic, very likable, but her charm is just a good affectation," he'd said. Janelle had had to bite her lips against a reflective rebuttal.

You don't know what you're talking about, she'd almost said. *You don't know her at all!*

Perhaps he'd seen something of it in her expression. He smiled, an expression of sympathy that only increased her unease.

"Her condition isn't as dire as you might think. Most children with antisocial tendencies *learn* to socialize. They learn social boundaries."

What he's saying is that they learn to fake it, she thought.

She didn't quite dare to say it out loud though. She was afraid of the answer he might give.

Kristen's behavior at school did improve. The calls and letters stopped, and Janelle checked in with the school counselor at least once a week to be sure that Kristen was

keeping to *socially acceptable behavior*. He was not opti-
mistic. While Kristen was no longer getting into trouble,
several of her friends, kids who had never been in trouble
before, were. Bullying, cheating, skipping classes, and at
least one girl had been caught shoplifting. All behaviors
new to the offending children.

He thought Kristen was learning to manipulate them
into behaviors that got them in trouble, and quietly
enjoying the fallout.

Janelle had not been able to bite back her reply that
time. She'd told the man to go fuck himself, and then been
invited to leave his office.

Kristen's therapist was more hopeful.

"She's learning to live within expected boundaries. She
may not understand those boundaries, or like them …"

The rest of it went over Janelle's head. What the
woman was telling her was that Kristen *was* learning to
fake a conscious she didn't actually possess.

Kristen's apparent good behavior held though. She
was as aloof as ever, but she stayed out of trouble.

Then a girl who had been her friend for at least two
years, a girl who had stayed over at Janelle's too many
times to count, a sweet girl with a quick smile, was
arrested and sent to a juvenile detention center for a near
fatal beating of a younger student while walking home
from school with Kristen.

Kristen had not joined in on the beating, but she had
not interfered with it either. She had only stood and
watched as her friend first punched, then kicked, then
stomped the younger girl. Stood and watched as the child
screamed and tried to crawl away, as a woman rushed
from a nearby home to stop the beating and a passing

motorist tackled and restrained her friend until the police arrived. She watched as her friend was taken away in screaming hysterics and an ambulance arrived to take her young victim to the emergency room.

A neighbor woman who witnessed the beating and the aftermath called Janelle at work after Kristen finally left the scene, and Janelle went home early to meet her daughter, her stomach suddenly full of lead and ice. Her daughter had seemed unaffected by the assault, didn't seem to care that the police had taken her best friend away, would not answer any questions that she asked about why her friend would do such a terrible thing. When the police came to question her, she answered their questions with alternating silent shrugs of her shoulders, or with *I don't know*, and *I don't remember*.

Janelle had been happy to send Kristen off to her father when school ended a month later, after extracting a promise from her ex to continue Kristen's therapy, and she had dreaded the end of summer, when her troubling daughter would return.

But Kristen never did return.

She had met a clown outside of a 7-Eleven instead, and vanished.

"Kristen?" Janelle could hardly believe her ears, assumed she was hearing things that simply weren't there, but could not help her hopeful reply. "Is that you, baby?"

There was a long silence, long enough for Janelle to decide she'd imagined her daughter's voice calling out in the darkness. When Kristen did finally reply, it was so unexpected that it startled a scream out of Janelle.

"Where is Hearts?" She didn't sound concerned or alarmed, only curious. "Is he with you?"

"She means me, lady," the clown said from next to her, and Janelle screamed again when his hand closed around her arm.

The moment he took hold of her, the total darkness surrounding her lightened. She could see the narrow brick corridor, no longer just an alley, but a valley of brick and pavement. In the distance ahead of them, a low and cheerful music began to play: calliope music, the hollow boom of drums, clashing cymbals, and laughter.

Janelle punched at the clown with her free fist, tried to tug her captured arm from his grip. He seemed not to feel her assault, or at least not to care.

"You could spend an eternity lost in the dark if you don't know where you're going." His tone told her clearly that it was nothing to him either way. It was laced with a kind of dark hilarity, the same twisted humor that seemed to be his default mood. "You'd probably be better off if you let me lead you where we're going."

He released her arm, and the darkness fell back over her. The cheerful music and laughter faded to silence.

"It's up to you, lady, but don't waste my time. I have a show to get to."

Janelle reached out in the darkness, grabbing blindly until she found a waiting arm. The endless corridor returned, and the music with it.

"Mom?" Kristen again, her voice not just challenging the swelling circus sounds, but burying them. Her voice seemed to come from behind them, and in front of them.

Beneath, above, all around. Janelle searched but could not see her.

"I would answer her," the clown said. "Your daughter is not famed for her patience."

"I'm here, baby," she said, wondering if she had fallen asleep on her nightly watch, was maybe dreaming this strange reunion, or if the clown had killed her already and this was her dying mind's final, cruel joke on her. "The clown is with me."

"His name is Hearts," Kristen said. "He's my friend. He's my tulpa."

"I don't know what you mean, baby. Where are you?"

"If you don't know what I mean, then you won't understand where I am," Kristen said, and laughed. Kristen had never been a joyful child, Janelle couldn't remember the last time she'd heard her daughter laugh, and the sound of it now raised gooseflesh up and down her body. "Just let Hearts bring you. He won't hurt you unless I tell him to."

Hearts stepped forward, and Janelle held onto his sleeve. She was wondering how far down this endless limbo of an alley they had to go when the alley dissipated and blew away like fog in the wind. She was standing next to Hearts in an open flap of hanging canvas, in a narrow path between the packed bleachers of a circus big top.

I'm standing in clown alley of the Riplinger Circus, Janelle thought. There was no wonder, no horror, no emotional component to this realization, only the reality of it. *I am standing with Grobiano Villis, who my daughter calls Hearts, and he is about to perform.*

The only question outstanding in her mind was whether or not this was the show where the Riplinger

Circus big top was fated to burn down and her terrifying host fated to die.

Janelle looked up to see acrobatics tumbling through the air, swinging and leaping from elevated swings and platforms. On the main floor, a man in extravagant tails and top hat played a calliope while a capuchin monkey in similar dress danced around him banging cymbals. Tumblers and trained animals, a large but scrawny ram with an impressive curl of horns, a mastiff in a red vest, and an elderly looking lion among them, cavorted around the center ring.

"Your daughter is waiting for you." Hearts pointed up into the bleachers on the other end of the enormous tent, and despite the distance and density of the crowd around her, Janelle saw her daughter.

Hearts peeled her clutching fingers from his arm, pulled his giant, and somehow still lit cigar from inside his coat, and planted it in his mouth. As he walked away from her, other clowns seemed to materialize all round her. Most ignored her as they followed Hearts out onto the floor, but a few regarded her in passing. Most seemed barely interested, but a few gave her knowing leers. When clown alley was deserted except for her, Janelle made her way to the bleachers, up to the topmost isle, and threaded her way through the cheering, laughing spectators to her lost, and now found, daughter.

Kristen seemed not to have aged a day in the three years since she'd vanished. Her clothes were different, a perfect example of 1930s attire. Janelle's modern clothing had drawn a few curious glances from the spectators she passed, but most seemed to take her strange dress in stride. They were at a circus after all, and she was hardly the strangest dressed woman in the tent. Some of them had mistaken her for a Riplinger employee and made barely heard enquiries as she passed.

If Kristen saw her coming, she didn't let on. She continued to watch the show, the only child in attendance without a smile or expression of wonder on her small face. She didn't look at Janelle until she was standing in front of her.

"Move outa the way, woman!" The man seated on the bleacher next to Kristen shouted to be heard over the cacophony. "I can't see through you!"

Kristen looked from her mother to the man shouting up at her, then wafted an open hand through the air at him, as if waving away a bug or drifting smoke. He faded and disappeared in the time it took Kristen to lower her hand. She patted the now empty seat, a gesture of invitation that Janelle accepted, trying not to think about what happened to the man who had been there only a moment earlier.

No one seemed to have noticed the man's strange vanishment.

"I missed you more than I thought I would," Kristen said. She was watching the show again. "Not Dad though. I could tell he didn't like having me around. I made his new wife nervous."

She had never once heard Kristen call her step-mother by name. She was only ever *his new wife* in Janelle's hearing. She had always wondered what Kristen called Rebecca to her face, but never quite dared to ask Chris.

She didn't trust herself to keep a straight face while asking, or not to laugh at his answer. Things had been tense enough between them without her creating new resentments.

Though every instinct she felt cried out against it, Janelle reached out for Kristen and pulled her closer on their shared bench. Kristen tensed beneath Janelle's touch, but didn't resist when Janelle put her arms around her and enfolded her in a near crushing embrace. Kristen did not return it, but she accepted it, and that was all Janelle needed.

She wept into her daughter's hair, her sobs unheard in the noise and excitement of the circus. After a while, Kristen wiggled and pushed out of the embrace, and Janelle sat up and composed herself.

Kristen went back to watching the circus. Hearts, or Grobiano Villis as he was known in this time and place, chased the other clowns, bopping them on the head with his big prop mallet, wolf-whistling at a trio of nearly naked dancing women, chasing and groping an equally scantily clad beauty who was juggling wooden pins while circling the center stage on a unicycle. When she finally took a painful looking tumble to the ground, one of her flying pins hitting her in the face, he stood over her, pointing and laughing so loudly he overtook the music.

This scene seemed to amuse Kristen more than anything else they had watched so far. Her bland, blank expression became a slight grin.

"I thought you were dead," Janelle said. "I thought that lunatic clown kidnapped you and killed you."

"I know," Kristen said. Janelle heard no regret, no

remorse in her voice. "That's what you were supposed to think."

"Why did you leave?" Janelle fought to hold back the angry hysterics that threatened to burst out now that she had already vented her healthier feelings. "Where have you been hiding for three years?"

"I was bored," Kristen said. "My life was stupid, and my friends were all boring, so I made new friends." She pointed down at the rampaging Grobiano Villis, Hearts, and his retinue. "We go anywhere or anywhen I want. We play with people."

Kristen turned her face from the spectacle below and smiled at Janelle.

"We have fun."

Below them, the ringmaster was acknowledging Grobiano Villis and exhorting the crowd above into ever louder applause as he sent the clowns away.

Kristen stood without preamble and grasped Janelle's hand …

And they were standing outside of big tent, amid a small city of smaller tents where the Riplinger troupe slept and lived when they weren't entertaining the depression era masses.

Janelle turned to take in the new surroundings.

"The best part of the show is over, and it was too noisy to talk in there." Kristen began to walk, and Janelle followed, unnerved by some strange role reversal that had put her preteen daughter in control of their equally strange encounter.

She reached out, grabbed her daughter by the shoulders, and turned her around.

"Tell me what the hell is going on here."

She felt herself thrown back, a leaf in the wind, and landed hard on her back several feet away.

"You shouldn't talk to me like that, Mom. I don't like it, and neither would Hearts." After regarding her for an endless moment with cool, appraising eyes, Kristen walked to her and offered a hand.

Janelle took the offered hand and let her daughter help her back to her feet.

"I'm glad you came, Mom. It was nice to see you, but you should go now before you make me mad again."

"No," Janelle said. "We're both going. I have to take you home."

Kristen gave her head a tiny shake, then closed her eyes. Her smooth brow furrowed, as if in concentration, and rural Connecticut faded around them.

They were in an open, misty vista. No ground, no sky, what might have been a million points of darkness in the hazy white firmament, like dark stars. A house stood in the center of the emptiness, anchored to nothing at all. The old house she once shared with Chris and Kristen in Provo, before Chris stepped out on her and tore their family apart.

Kristen raised her hands up, an evocative gesture, like a magician playing at conjuring. What she conjured was a street, a picket fence that their old house never had, and a trio of tall trees. She couldn't tell what kind, their old house never had trees in the front yard. She thought they might be some fantasy hybrid between willow and sequoia. Plank and rope walkways connected the right and left trees to a tree house in the top boughs of the center, high above the roof of the little house.

Kristen had created the home she missed, and improved upon it, making it better than the real thing.

"This is my home now," Kristen said. She floated away from Janelle, high into the false sky of this made up place and onto one of the plank bridges. "I don't want you here. I don't need you here. I have my friends."

She waved her hands again, a theatric gesture Janelle thought was for her. She thought it was Kristen's way of saying *I did that ... it was me*!

Clowns filled the conjured pavement and yard, stepped from the treehouse and onto the wooden bridges between the fantasy trees, burst from the front door of their old home.

"They're not real, baby! Whatever they are, wherever they come from, they're not real!" There was a shocked, collective gasp as every painted face turned her way and recoiled against her words. A few of the painted night-mares scowled at her, stuck out their tongues and blew raspberries. A few extended middle fingers in silent protest. Most simply stood speechless in the face of such blasphemy. "Just because you imagine them, doesn't mean they're real!"

Kristen was unmoved.

"You're wrong, Mother." She drew Janelle up into the air with a gesture and left her hanging high above the imaginary, but all too real blacktop of this unreal place. "Because I imagine them, they *are* real."

She flung Janelle from her new home with the twitch of a finger.

"You can come and visit again if you want, but not right away. My friends and I are going out to play and we won't be home for a while."

Janelle flailed and turned, weightless in the strange void her daughter had brought her to, and saw one of those dark, distant points coming to meet her.

She threw her arms up in front of her face, slammed her eyes shut, and screamed as the darkness came to swallow her.

———

Janelle awoke laying on the ground and opened her eyes on darkness.

"Kristen? Where are you?"

"She's gone to play," Hearts the clown said. "I think you're going to regret challenging her."

"Where are we?" Janelle reached out toward the sound of his voice. "What do you mean, challenging her?"

"Open your hand, lady," Hearts said, and when she did he slapped something into her open palm. "You don't have enough imagination to do this on your own. You need something material to anchor you."

As he spoke, her vision returned.

"We are when we started. Back in clown alley." He laughed at this. She wondered how long he'd waited to crack that particular groaner. "And you challenged her when you told her that her imaginary friends weren't real."

They were back in the seemingly endless brick and pavement canyon where Hearts had caught her after chasing her down that alley in Spokane, where she had been blind until he'd taken hold of her and led her on.

She looked at the thing in her hand.

"Just because she imagined me doesn't mean I'm not

real." He made a small bow in her direction, extending a hand toward her, as if asking for a dance. A long-stemmed red rose popped from the cuff of his jacket. He held it out to her tweezed between two fingers, and she saw a drop of blood clinging to a thorn.

"Real enough to feel, real enough to bleed." He displayed the bloody palm of the hand that held the rose, the pale flesh torn by the thorn. "Real as roses, and real as rings."

She looked down at the object in her open hand again. A very old pewter ring, shiny with years of handling, but not as worn as it should be considering how old it must be. The flat face of the ring was dominated by the stylized RC of the Riplinger Circus.

"If you won't take the rose, at least put the ring on."

She did and was grateful to see the fuzzy outlines of clown alley sharpen a little.

"What happened to her?" Janelle said. "How did she …."

Janelle didn't know how to finish, so let the question go only half asked.

"She ran away," Hearts the clown said, and grinned. "She just happens to be better at running away than most."

"And you took her to that … place?"

"I told you already, I didn't take her anywhere. She took me. I am her imaginary friend. I am her tulpa." He held out his bleeding hand, the rose was gone now, and the antique jack-in-the-box reappeared on it. "She is an angry child with the power of a god, but lucky for you she still has a soft spot for mommy."

His declaration stunned her to silence.

"Go home now," Hearts said. "It's time to play and

you're beginning to bore me. If you want to visit your daughter again, find a dark place. Alleys, closets, cellars, any of those will do. Put on the ring and step through. She'll know you've come."

He pushed the closed jack-in-the-box at her. She reached out and took it.

"What am I supposed to do with this?"

Hearts shrugged.

"Give it to someone you don't like, leave it on a street corner, give it to that old bum to pawn. I don't give much of a shit where it ends up. She has sent hundreds of her dangerous toys out into the world, and they always find the right people eventually."

He grinned again, and his too wide mouth opened to reveal long long rows of pointed teeth.

"Just don't open it again yourself unless you want to dance with Hearts."

She took a step back from him, stumbled and fell backward ...

And landed hard in the dim light of a Port Street street lamp. She rose, turned, found herself alone. Her car door was still open, the dome light still shining. Her keys were on the pavement beneath the open driver door, where she'd dropped them in her panic to get away from Hearts.

I can't have been gone long then, she thought. *Not in this city, and especially not in this neighborhood. Someone in this neighborhood walks past a car with the door open and the keys out for everyone to see, it's almost a civic duty to steal it.*

She ran back to her rental before someone could come along and do just that, slipping the ring from her finger and shoving it deep into her pants pocket as she slid in behind the wheel. She drove it back to her hotel with the windows down in the diminishing stink of pepper spray, drove slowly through a haze of tears.

It's the pepper spray, she told herself, and maybe it was.

She realized as she was pulling into the parking lot of Hotel 6 that she had dropped Hearts the clown's dangerous toy in the mouth of the alley when she'd stumbled and fallen out of it. She decided it didn't much matter.

Someone would pick it up, maybe this very night, and if they didn't open it, someone else would.

Janelle returned to Clarkston early and spent her last few vacation days locked in her house. She refused to be parted from the Riplinger Circus ring but didn't dare to put it on. It hung around her neck from a scrap of lace she'd torn from an old nightgown. She wept for her daughter, not dead as she'd feared, but badly broken and fearfully powerful.

What kind of mother could have created such a monster?

She returned to work, then to life, and she thought about putting the ring back on every day. She thought of returning to clown alley, of seeing her baby again, of seeing her imaginary friends. They were the real dangerous toys, not the trinkets they were disseminating far and wide. Her imaginary friends. Her killer tulpas.

One day her curiosity got the better of her, and she searched eBay for antique jack-in-the-boxes. She found the twin of the one she'd left abandoned in a Spokane, Washington alley. Then she found another. She also found more pewter rings like the one that hung from her neck,

Riplinger souvenir canes with ivory heads, some clowns, some animals. She found authentic Riplinger top hats, letter openers, and game tokens. She found a very old cast iron clown bust piggy bank. Put the coin in its open hand and press the lever on its back, its eyes roll back comically as it swallows the coin. Just the kind of thing a young kid would love. It had a pointy hat instead of green hair, but it did have red hearts painted on its cheeks.

Janelle dipped into her old bottle of Diazepam, untouched for years, that night. She slept deeply, dreamed badly, and awoke in terror.

Weeks passed, but the urge to put her ring on and go to her daughter did not diminish. Weeks passed, and the clown craze that seemed to have died down a little since the previous summer escalated again. More research revealed that these clown attacks were not a new thing, had in fact been going on through the entirety of recorded history. This new *clown apocalypse*, as people were calling it, was only a modern resurgence of a historical trend. She wondered if these historical clown attacks had happened before her daughter's disappearance, and decided it didn't really matter.

There were pranksters and copycats, of course, but there were also murders and disappearances. There were more phone videos, more security footage, the most well know from a mall in Seattle, where a clown killed a mall Santa, his elves, and a few bystanders before one of them put a knife in his back. The clown's body had vanished, but there was video evidence and a hundred witnesses to his attack.

Janelle recognized many of the painted faces in those videos from her too brief encounter with Kristen.

Hearts the clown was in one of them, not in Spokane anymore, but in Provo again.

Her ex-husband's new wife, the abominable Rebecca, disappeared, and everyone assumed she'd gotten fed up with her husband and just left. Their relationship had been rocky since Kristen vanished, and she *was* much younger than him. Chris didn't believe she had just walked out on him though, and neither did the police. They came to his home a week after he reported Rebeca missing, armed with a search warrant and cadaver-sniffing dogs.

They found parts of her, but only a few.

Chris insisted he was innocent, but no one believed him.

No one except Janelle, and she wasn't talking.

No one would believe her if she did.

Janelle also studied the Riplinger Circus fire. She bought books and collected a mountain of research material, from old newspaper reports to the Mystic, Connecticut fire marshal's report. She found what she was looking for, even if she hadn't realized at the time that she was looking for it, in a special edition of The Mystic Free Press, a long defunct weekly paper that had never been committed to microfiche or digital archives.

She found an old copy on eBay.

She didn't go right away.

She made copies of the relevant pages, wrote a long letter of explanation to Chris, who was still awaiting trial for murder in Provo, changed her mind, tore the letter up and burned the scraps.

In the end her accompanying note was short and explained everything that needed explaining.

xxxii   BRIAN KNIGHT

She dropped it in the public mail drop box on a Friday night in early January, slept the night through with some help from her old Diazepam prescription, and rose late on Saturday afternoon to go visit her daughter.

Janelle cut the lace rope the old pewter ring her hung from and slipped it over a finger, opened her closet door, and returned to clown alley.

She knew where she wanted to go this time and didn't need Hearts's help to get there, but he was there to meet her when she arrived. Hearts and Kristen stood in Riplinger Circus's clown alley, hand in hand.

It was still summer in 1932 Mystic, Connecticut, so she'd only worn a light jacket for the trip, but she was already sweating inside of it.

Kristen smiled and waved, just like a real little girl who was happy to see her mom.

"Hi baby."

"Hi Mom."

Kristen dropped Hearts's hand, and he gave Janelle a short bow before leaving them in clown alley to join his troupe inside the big top.

"Wanna watch the show with me?" Kristen held out a hand to her, and Janelle took it.

"Yes, but can we watch it from the floor?" She spotted a burning oil lamp hanging from a wooden post outside the performers back entrance, and knew it was the one she would use. "Those bleachers are too crowded, and I don't really fit in with the locals."

She stopped before they passed into the tent, bent, and

held her arms open. Kristen paused for only a moment before stepping into them, not wanting the comfort of her mother's arms, not needing it, but willing to give that comfort to the mother who she still had a soft spot for.

Then they entered the big top, hand in hand.

Janelle's free left hand crept into the pocket of her light jacket and closed around the long, folding knife she'd once used to stab an attempted rapist.

It was almost time. Before she did what she had come to do, she would watch the show with her girl.

Chris Johnson's murder case went to trial in May, six months after investigators unearthed parts of his missing wife buried in the crawl space under their house, and four months after the disappearance of his ex-wife.

The well-publicized disappearance of Janelle Johnson wasn't the strangest feature of the case, but it may have been one of the deciding factors. The number of missing women in his life, one of which he was never a suspect for and another who vanished after he was already locked away, became a source of speculation among the pundits. Some suggested it could have been Janelle Johnson who killed Rebecca, and then tried to frame Chris for the murder. As ridiculous as the theory was, it attracted a lot of attention, and when Chris Johnson's defense put it forward as a more reasonable explanation than his client killing his wife keeping a few of her parts around to incriminate himself with when he was inevitably investigated, he created enough reasonable doubt among the jury to set his client free.

The final, bizarre grace note came after the acquittal, when a leaked document held in reserve by his defense but never put forward in court, made the news.

Janelle Johnson's final correspondence with her ex-husband, or anybody else as far as he knew, arrived months before his trial, only a day or two before co-workers reported her missing. It was three photocopied pages from a very old newspaper, a special edition of The Mystic Free Press commemorating the lives lost in the tragic Riplinger Circus fire. Alongside the known dead was a number of unidentified dead.

The first page was a list of deceased Riplinger performers, and Janelle had circled a single name.

Grobiano Villis.

Below this name she had written a single word.

Hearts.

The second page was a black and white copy of The Riplinger flier, showing the faces and names of their more prominent performers. Janelle had circled the grinning face of a clown, pale face, extravagant flyaway hair, hearts on his cheeks. It looked very much like the doll Kristen had fallen in love with one day while out looking around one of Provo's more interesting antique malls.

The third page was dedicated to the unknown, a list of victim's descriptions, personal effects, and anything else that might help identify them. There were photographs of a few victims not too badly burned to identify visually. Janelle did not have to circle the picture she'd meant for him to see. He knew her face as soon as he saw it.

The picture's caption read: *Unclaimed female child age nine to eleven, found in the arms of a woman, possibly her mother.*

Written below in his ex-wife's familiar, messy scrawl was her final message to him

I found her.

ABOUT BRIAN KNIGHT

Brian Knight lives in Washington State with his wife and the voices in his head. He has published over a dozen novels, novellas, and collections in the horror, fantasy, and crime genres.

Subscribe to Brian Knight's Knightmares newsletter for news, updates, and free fiction at www.brian-knight.com.

BIBLIOGRAPHY

The Final Girl, previously published as *The Last Girl* in Deadlights #1.

I Am the Coyote, I Am the Snake, previously published in Dark Discoveries #8 and Sisters.

Campbell's Pond, previously published in Horror Library, Volume 4.

Dakota, previously published in Insidious Reflections #7 and Sisters.

A Night in the Blues, previously published in Sisters.

Number 2, previously published in At the Foothills of Frenzy.

Deathbed, previously published in Cemetery Dance #64.

Toys in the Attic, previously published in Flesh & Blood #14 and Sisters.

Ridgerunner, previously published in Northwest Horrors.

Night of the Dog, previously published in Darkfuse #6.

Who Killed Little Betty?, previously published in Flesh & Blood #13.

Hot Summer Night, previously unpublished.

Lucin, previously published in Redsine #2.

The Cask of a Thousand Dildos, previously published in At the Foothills of Frenzy.

Go Girls Rule!, previously published in City Slab Magazine #2 and Sisters.

Sister, previously published in Sisters.

Mother of Kittens, previously published on Brian-Knight.com.

The Christmas Corpse, previously published on The Gall in the Blue Mask.

Dangerous Toys, previously unpublished.